TWO WRONGS MAKE A MARRIAGE

Christine Merrill

MILLS
BOON®

First published in Great Britain 2012
by Mills & Boon, an imprint of Harlequin (UK) Limited.
Large Print edition 2013
Harlequin (UK) Limited, Eton House, 18-24 Paradise Road,
Richmond, Surrey TW9 1SR

© Christine Merrill 2012

ISBN: 978 0 263 23251 6

Harlequin (UK) policy is to use papers that are natural, renewable and recyclable products and made from wood grown in sustainable forests. The logging and manufacturing process conform to the legal environmental regulations of the country of origin.

Printed and bound in Great Britain
by CPI Antony Rowe, Chippenham, Wiltshire

Christine Merrill lives on a farm in Wisconsin, USA, with her husband, two sons and too many pets—all of whom would like her to get off the computer so they can check their e-mail. She has worked by turns in theatre costuming, where she was paid to play with period ballgowns, and as a librarian, where she spent the day surrounded by books. Writing historical romance combines her love of good stories and fancy dress with her ability to stare out of the window and make stuff up.

Previous novels by Christine Merrill:

THE INCONVENIENT DUCHESS
AN UNLADYLIKE OFFER
A WICKED LIAISON
MISS WINTHORPE'S ELOPEMENT
THE MISTLETOE WAGER
  (part of *A Yuletide Invitation*)
DANGEROUS LORD, INNOCENT GOVERNESS
PAYING THE VIRGIN'S PRICE*
TAKEN BY THE WICKED RAKE*
MASTER OF PENLOWEN
  (part of *Halloween Temptations*)
LADY FOLBROKE'S DELICIOUS DECEPTION†
LADY DRUSILLA'S ROAD TO RUIN†
LADY PRISCILLA'S SHAMEFUL SECRET†
A REGENCY CHRISTMAS CAROL
  (part of *One Snowy Regency Christmas*)

And in Mills & Boon® Historical *Undone!* eBooks:

SEDUCING A STRANGER
TAMING HER GYPSY LOVER*
VIRGIN UNWRAPPED

*Regency Silk & Scandal mini-series
†Ladies in Disgrace trilogy

To Ray-Ray, Betty, Les, Judy,
Jana, and Rose. *Encore.*

Chapter One

Kidnapped! Dishonoured! Forced to marry one's abductor to avoid the scandal!

It was almost too perfect. Jack Briggs could hardly contain his glee, though this was not the moment to reveal it. The plans he'd set in motion at the beginning of the London Season were coming together, suddenly, unexpectedly, and in a way almost too perfect for words. He would have a rich and well-born wife and he'd have her months ahead of schedule.

Miss Cynthia Banester was not the woman he'd expected to catch. There had been no time to lay the groundwork for a less inauspicious campaign for her hand. But she was gentle born, wealthy and more than middling pretty. Jack might go so far as to call her beautiful, for the ginger hair and full figure were very much to his personal taste. She was certainly desirable.

But more importantly, she was everything that the Earl of Spayne had requested Jack bring to his family by marrying. Of course, Jack had expected to present his choice to the peer for approval before making an offer. This impromptu abduction had changed everything. Now that weapons had been drawn, there could be no turning back. He would have her, whether the earl liked her or not.

The girl smiled at him in a hopeful, rather worried way, as though her own happiness depended on his co-operation, and edged between him and the doorway of the gazebo they shared. 'I am sorry, Lord Kenton, but I cannot permit you to leave. If you attempt it, I will be forced to shoot you.'

Jack watched the barrel of the little pistol she held moving in twitching figure eights as she tried to keep it steady. If the gun fired, by accident or with intent, Miss Banester would become the second most beautiful woman to have shot him. But if she did not control her aim, it could prove more damaging than a hurried leap from a courtesan's boudoir window. At such close range, there was a very real chance she might hit something he wished to keep whole.

He kept his hands raised, put on his best smile and worked his magic upon her. 'I would not dream of leaving, my dear. Did I not come willingly to this spot when you requested me to follow you away from the other guests?'

'That was because you expected some dalliance with me,' she said, giving a wise nod. Her assessment was accurate, but delivered with a coldness that surprised him. 'You thought me foolish enough to leave a crowded ballroom to go walking in a dark garden with a man who is nearly a stranger to me.' She tightened her grip on the pistol and for a moment, it stilled, before the muzzle drooped alarmingly in the direction of his manhood.

'I might have suspected some such thing,' Jack admitted. 'You can hardly blame me for it. In most instances, that is precisely what your sudden interest in a tête-à-tête would mean. But I can see that is not the case. Perhaps, if you were to lay down your weapon, you might accept my parole. I am sure we could discuss your reasons for this meeting without the threat of violence. If I have done something to upset you, I would be only too happy to apologise.' At length, and with as much physicality as their inevitable discovery would permit.

He smiled in anticipation. The folly she'd lured him to was still within earshot of the house. One overloud shriek of delight and they would be found out. Her reputation would be ruined. And he would offer nobly, albeit with proper resignation, for her lovely white hand. If he could just coax her out of her pistol, the end of hostility would mean the beginning of seduction. Stitching together the tatters of her innocence for a church wedding would be far preferable to mending a hole in his coat or body.

She stared back at him, large green eyes narrowed in scepticism. 'If I give up the gun, what would I have to protect me from your advances?'

Absolutely nothing. She blinked at him, as though she had heard his thoughts, and her mouth puckered, ready to be kissed. The moonlight glinted in her copper curls and gave a faint luminosity to her already magnificent bosom, making him wonder at the rest of the body hiding beneath her ladylike muslin gown. Such lush curves brought to mind an earthy sensuality not present in the eligible innocents he'd been courting. Though her friends might shorten Cynthia to Thea, Jack thought some variation on Cyn would be more appropriate. She was sinfully tempting and everything he desired in a bedmate. It might be quite pleasant to lose his freedom to her.

He lowered his hands a fraction, turning them palms up in supplication. 'Is it really necessary to keep me at a distance? You must understand that, if I remain as you wish, your honour will be compromised. When we are discovered, as we well might be, I shall be forced to marry you.'

She nodded vigorously. Curls and bosom bounced in response. 'That was precisely what I hoped,' she said.

That was most unexpected, but it certainly saved him time in wooing. 'Your methods for seeking my offer are rather unorthodox,' he said, lowering his hands a little farther. 'I will not hold them against you should we marry. I am not opposed to the institution itself and willing to entertain the proposition that there be a union between us. But I will not allow the woman I marry to bring a pistol into the bedroom.'

'Perfectly understandable,' she agreed. But she showed no sign of relinquishing her weapon.

'Surely, if you are intent on having me, it will do no harm to become better acquainted before that time.' He smiled again, his mouth watering at the thought of her excessively kissable lips.

'I have no objection to knowing you better,' she agreed. 'But I am sure that it can be done across this distance.' She took a tighter grip on the pistol.

'Are you sure?' He adjusted his posture to make best use of the available light and felt the moon outline his profile as he stretched a hand toward her. It was vain of him to strike such a pose, but he'd heard ladies sighing over it, often enough. And until the gun was back in her reticule, he needed all the good will he could muster. 'There would be no risk to our sitting side by side, admiring the roses through the lattice.' He took a deep breath. 'The air is like perfume and the moonlight tints the blossoms with silver.'

'I am sure they will be just as lovely after we are wed,' she responded.

'Which we most certainly will be,' he assured her. 'You have my word of that. Nothing will happen that you do not thoroughly enjoy.' They would both enjoy it, if he was not mistaken.

'It would not be proper.'

'A kiss or two between a couple on the day of their betrothal is not amiss.'

The gun did not move. 'You may kiss me once. When my parents have discovered us and can witness it.'

Damn. He had found in the past that many young ladies were curious about such things and eager to take advantage, or be taken advantage of, once they knew there was no risk of discovery. This one seemed to court disaster, as long as it was disaster delayed.

'Once we are married, I will expect you to kiss me far more than once,' he reminded her. 'And do other things as well.' He raised an eyebrow to imply wicked, but unnamed, behaviours, wondering how much she knew of them. If she was angling after some gallant union, with him sleeping above the sheet and her beneath, she was sorely mistaken.

'You are speaking of performing the marital act,' she said in a prim way that was all the more erotic for its frankness.

'I do like performing,' he admitted quite truthfully. *Regular shows and matinees.*

'I have no objection to that,' she said.

'That is good to know,' he said, imagining her creamy-white skin flushed pink after an acting lesson.

'But not tonight,' she said. 'I must be married first.'

'We,' he reminded her. 'I will be marrying as well. And, if I may ask, why have you chosen me for your groom? Not that I object, overly. I intended to marry this Season and had not fixed my affections elsewhere. But we hardly know each other.'

'It has been difficult to attract your attention,' she said, blinking at him again.

Which was another odd thing. He had always favoured buxom redheads. She was that in spades. If she'd made any effort at all to catch his eye, he was sure he'd have responded. With all the talk of getting her to bed, he was responding now, in an involuntary and physical way.

Then he glanced at her gun, which was still pointed at his middle, and felt the tightness in his breeches easing. 'You have my full attention tonight. If I did not notice you before?' He shrugged. 'At Almack's and the like, young ladies seem to make an effort to be underfoot and in the way. Did you express an interest in making a match with me?'

She bit her lip. 'Until recently, I did not realise how urgent it was that I marry…you.' There was a strange pause, as though she had only just remembered to be enamoured of him, specifically. 'You are the catch of the Season, Lord Kenton. And I am shy in gatherings and did not know how to gain your favour, other than this. As they say, "We should be woo'd and were not made to woo".'

'Shakespeare?' Jack's heart beat iambic pentameter in time with her words. There was no quicker way to gain his attention than quoting the Bard. But she could not know him as well as that, or she'd never have lured him out in the garden. 'And you say it is urgent that you find a husband?'

'Oh, yes.' She nodded again vigorously.

He stared down at her jiggling chest and had to force his mind back to the primary reason that a young lady might have for an urgent marriage. If there was a child in less than nine months, he must hope that it looked more like its mother than its father.

Spayne should have considered this and been more specific before sending Jack on this mission. He had requested a rich daughter-in-law. But he must have known that marriages resulted in babies. Considering his own past, Jack had no right to quibble about legitimacy. If Spayne was so desperate for an heir to act as he had, would it really matter if the child was Jack's or someone else's?

Then the moonlight cast a particularly bright beam through the lattice of the gazebo and he saw the dusting of freckles on her white shoulders, like cinnamon and sugar on a blancmange. Spayne's possible objections could be damned along with the earl himself. A man had needs and the luscious body of Miss Cynthia Banester was suited so perfectly to Jack's that she might have been heaven sent.

He threw his hands in the air in a gesture of helplessness. 'Far be it from me to stand in the way of a lady who knows her own mind. You are from a respectable family. You seem intent on having me.' And he'd have her as well. Though she was damned prickly on the subject tonight, if she was the victim of a previous fall from grace he need have no scruples about the rather unusual nature of his side of their union. A little deception was a good thing, when shared equally between partners. 'I am yours. Since you will not let me have a kiss, let us seal the bargain.' He dropped a hand and thrust it out to her for a shake.

She gave him a sidelong glance, as though searching for the trick, and cautiously offered her left, elegantly gloved hand.

'The right,' he said firmly. 'Else it shall not be official.'

She stared at him, then at the little pistol she held, and then back to him before cautiously setting it down on the bench beside her and offering her right hand.

He seized it and dropped to a seat on the bench behind him, pulling her forwards into his lap, pinioning her wrists between them so that she could not retrieve her weapon. She was a pleasant weight against him. His member, which had flagged at the sight of the gun barrel, sprang to life again.

'Unhand me this instant,' she said, giving a wiggle that was quite delicious.

'In a bit,' he agreed. 'When I am sure you will not just take up arms against me and once we have established that I am the aggressor and not the victim. If you mean us to be discovered, it would do my pride an injury to have the world thinking you had trapped me into marriage at gunpoint.' He wrapped an arm about her waist, drawing her farther forwards until she was very near to straddling him. The kicking of her slippered feet against his legs accentuated the rocking, creating a friction that inflamed his imagination as well as his body.

'It is better that they think I am to blame, taking advantage of an innocent girl. I shall admit that I was overcome by your beauty and acted in haste to secure you. When your father demands an immediate marriage, I will agree.'

'You would really do that for me?' She ceased struggling, her body settling against his in relief.

Her sudden gratitude made him feel almost heroic for wanting to ravish her. He was doing her a service. 'Of course, my pet,' he said. 'But we must do our best to sell the story, so that all might believe it. I am the swain, overcome by desire. And you are the hapless maiden, caught in my clutches.'

'I am,' she said sceptically.

'Of course,' he reminded her. 'See, I am clutching you.' He brought his hands to her bottom and squeezed it, adjusting her in his lap.

'Oh, dear.' The contact between them was intimate. If she had any understanding of anatomy, it would explain why Cyn Banester was finally nonplussed.

He raised a hand to her face and drew one finger down her cheek, tangling with a red curl. 'Now I will take the kiss you offered. When I am through with you, you shall scream and bring the house down upon us, so that I might plead convincingly for your hand.' Those wide green eyes were blinking at him again, more expectant than frightened.

It made him feel strangely dizzy, probably from a loss of blood to the brain. When she looked at him like that, he could not seem to think clearly, even though it would be better to take such a major step with a clear head. He was sure there were things he was missing in all this. Probably some vitally important reason to postpone the decision until morning. But with one last look at her lips, he threw his reservations aside, closed the last inches between them, let the full breasts crush against his vest front and pressed his lips against hers.

Until recently, Jack had had little experience with true ladies of any kind. One could hardly count bored wives and randy widows as genteel. They'd been seeking a bit of adventure and he'd been happy to provide it. But he had never kissed the sort of young lady he was kissing now. She was of limited experience, cautious, unworldly, but with all the grace, innocence and sweetness of a Juliet. So he did his best to be a worthy Romeo, demonstrating all the ardour of first love, but with just a bit more confidence than that doomed lad would have managed. If this first kiss had to last him until the wedding night, then it must be memorable.

Her mouth opened in surprise like the first bud of May, and as he delved into it he felt the growing, urgent heat in his loins. It was a heat that must go unanswered tonight, he reminded himself. But that did not mean he should not give her reason to be eager for more.

He must have succeeded. When he pulled away from her, he felt her mouth trying to find his again, even as he kissed his way down her throat. 'Your lips, like cherries,' he whispered. 'And breasts as white as...' No matter how much he wanted to taste them, it could not be wise to use two food references in a row. 'As white as matched doves.' He could almost hear the groans and the thunder of boots as the gallery hammered on the kicking board to express their disgust at his hyperbole. He was but a hackneyed mummer with no right to improvise. But the words seemed to work on Cyn, for the sigh she offered was of contentment and not protest. He stared down at her body. 'Do I dare to touch them? I cannot. And yet I must.' He placed a hand beneath her breasts and pressed up as he lowered his face to them, covering the exposed skin with kisses, while leaving the best of them tantalisingly hidden.

In response, the little minx rose up on her knees, pressed her body to his and her chest to his lips, her fingers tangling eagerly in his hair until he held her, one hand splayed over the globe of her breast and another over the globe of her hip. She was a perfect armful, and his common sense struggled with his withered conscience to find a reason not to hoist up her skirt and take the evening to its logical conclusion.

Not tonight. He had but to wait a bit and he could have all he wanted of her, gorging himself on the sweetness until he was sick of it. In a few months, Lord Kenton would be experiencing a tragic death and the girl would be a wealthy widow. Then Jack would be free of his wife and richer for the experience. Before he had to visit the 'undiscovered country' he would have ample time to investigate as yet uncharted places on the lovely Cyn. It was hard to imagine that he was to be paid for becoming lord and master to such a tasty bit of pastry. But if some man must make the sacrifice, then why not him?

He sighed in contentment and buried his face more deeply between her ample breasts. Then he remembered that before it went further, they must be discovered here. He sighed an *au revoir* into her cleavage and gave her a vicious pinch upon the bottom, making her shriek.

'Cynthia!' As if on cue, her mother burst into the folly to find the girl, dressed but dishevelled, in the arms of the eligible Lord Kenton.

'Mother!' After a moment of dazed confusion, Cyn remembered her role and threw a hand theatrically across her brow. It was overdone. Given time, he could teach her to play the compromised innocent more convincingly. For now, it would have to do.

The sad display had the desired effect. Her mother rushed forwards to take the disgraced girl in hand. 'How dare you, sir.'

Jack raised his hands again, as he had done when the girl held the gun upon him. 'Alas, I could not help myself, Lady Banester. A surfeit of wine and moonlight, a waltz. And the supreme loveliness, the charm, the fresh perfection of your daughter... I was undone.' Jack could see the crowd gathering in the doorway, preventing an exit which he'd not have sought in any case.

He dropped to a knee. It was the one farthest from the entrance so that the majority of the people gathered could see his profile as he placed a hand over his heart. 'I will do the honourable thing, of course. And with pleasure. I do not regret my precipitous action, if it encourages this sweet girl to a proper union which will make me the happiest of men.'

He bowed his head, as though conquered. 'Say you will accept me, Miss Banester. Take my hand, my heart, my everything. I lay them at your feet.'

Out of the corner of his eye, he thought he saw a spark of suspicion in the cat-green eyes of his lady love. If she hadn't have been so pretty, he'd have been annoyed at the criticism of his acting. He was in full form tonight and the rest of the audience was in the palm of his hand. He could hear sighs of envy coming from the girls crowded in the doorway. They'd have accepted his proposal in a heartbeat. Now that it was made, his intended was looking at him as though she was no longer quite sure she wanted him.

But it was far too late for a change of heart. Her mother had seen the whole thing and clapped hands enthusiastically across a matronly version of the bosom that her daughter had inherited, tossing her dark-red curls as she looked heavenwards. 'Thank you, Lord Kenton, for protecting my little girl.'

'What the devil?' Unlike his statuesque and lovely wife, the diminutive Sir William Banester needed to push his way through the crowd for a better view. 'Kenton, you ass. Get up off the floor. If you want her, you can have her, of course. But you could have asked in the parlour, like a normal gentleman. Now enough of this nonsense. We can settle it in the morning. Thea, come away.'

'Yes, Papa.' His betrothed did her best to look both contrite and happy, but cast one last glance back at him, as though still a little surprised that her plan had succeeded.

He could hardly blame her. He was surprised as well. 'Until the morning, my love,' Jack said, holding out a hand in a farewell gesture. There would be time to sort out the details, he was sure. 'I will visit properly, if your parents will receive me. We have much to discuss.' He gave Lady Banester a look worthy of any hopeful Romeo.

'Of course, Lord Kenton. We would be honoured.' She offered a sweeping curtsy so imbued with grace that Jack nearly stammered the truth: he was the one honoured to be received by such a lady and to be marrying her equally beautiful daughter.

Then he remembered himself. He was not the humble Jack Briggs, itinerant actor. He was Lord

Kenton and he was the catch of the Season. The Banesters should be happy to have him. And he was happy as well, for tonight he would write to the earl and announce the impending and successful completion of his scheme.

Chapter Two

Trying to catch the best light in the shop window, Cynthia Banester flourished the two pieces of lace she held, admiring their drape and softness, but unable to decide between them. Vieux Flandre was beautiful, but expensive, and a bit heavy for the face of a girl with nothing to hide. In comparison, the Brussels seemed almost too simple for such a special event. 'Which is better?' she asked, holding the two veils up to her mother for approval.

'Take them both,' Lady Banester answered without a second thought.

'I am only marrying once and therefore have no need of a second veil.'

'But if you should change your mind later...'

'About Kenton or the veil?'

'Either, dear. It is always wise to have an understudy waiting in the wings.'

Thea sighed. It had been foolish of her even to request her mother's input, for she should have guessed what the answer was likely to be. Father had often joked that he would not trust her to choose the lesser of two evils, should the devil decide to open a shop on Bond Street. 'Mother,' Thea said gently, 'I must make a selection. We no longer have the money for unnecessary extravagances.'

'Perhaps we do not, but Kenton does. Once you are married, you have but to send him the bills. He is a viscount, after all. He will take care of everything.'

Thea winced. That had been her plan from the first. And it was all going much too well. It had been three weeks since she had waylaid the poor man, plucking him out of the card room at Lady Folbroke's ball with promises of a moonlight stroll in the garden and an urgent need for private conversation. He had gone, like a lamb to the slaughter, and they were engaged before midnight. Since then, he had made regular visits to her home, each one properly chaperoned to prevent the ardour he had displayed when they were alone. He had danced with her when they met at balls, escorted her to musicales and behaved like a complete gentleman on each outing.

The church had been reserved, the banns read, the invitations sent and the menu chosen for the wedding breakfast. Had she written the script for a perfect engagement, she could not have done better.

And Kenton had offered no objections to the lack of intimacy, nor shown any sign of waking to the realities of his situation. Why was he not bothered by the fact that she had tricked him? That she had drawn her little pistol and waylaid him like a highwayman stopping a coach? She deserved outrage or ostracism in response. She had feared a total failure, if Kenton measured the worth of her family connections as she did lace veils. A sensible man should have been more eager to take a bullet than her hand.

Her mother tapped her hand with an ivory fan, then replaced it on the haberdasher's counter. 'You are thinking about him again, aren't you?'

'No, Mama.'

Her mother smiled knowingly. 'Of course you are. When you try to conceal your feelings, my darling, you are as transparent as glass. But you have no need to hide these. It is only natural to think of such things, when one is young and in love...'

'Do not put too fine a point on it, Mother,' Thea said firmly. 'You know my reasons for seeking him out and they have nothing to do with love.'

Her mother cast a sidelong glance in her direction. 'Judging by his speech to us when we discovered you, you've charmed him. He was most fulsome in his praise. And I have seen the way he looks at you since.'

Her mother was right in that, at least. Her betrothed bathed her in respectful but doting attention, taking her driving in Hyde Park, escorting her to the opera and behaving as though they had known each other for years and not days. She should be flattered. She was flattered—and excited—by his attentions, but they also filled her with a strange combination of guilt and unease. At last, she blurted, 'That is just the problem,

Mother. Why does he behave so? I have done nothing to earn even a jot of his affection.' Anyone who had been in town for any length of time had at least formed suspicions about the Banester family, its eccentricities, profligacy and rumoured bugbears. But it seemed Lord Kenton was too new to the country to know why they could not marry. Or perhaps he was too rich to care.

Her mother gave a quick scan of her body and toyed with the lace on her own bodice. 'You have inherited certain assets that make even strong men malleable. When I was your age, I had admirers aplenty. When I performed, half the young lords of the day threw roses on the stage and the rest sought out my changing room. But then I met your father...'

'No stories, please.' Thea dropped the lace in her hands and put them over her ears to forestall any more of her mother's ridiculous anecdotes about the ardent courtship of young Sir William. Her mother's previous career was not quite a secret amongst the *ton*. But it had taken all her charm and much of Father's money to make the truth fade into insignificance. Now that the fortune was gone, they could not afford to have the old scandal resurrected.

'Very well.' At forty, her mother's pout was every bit as pretty as a girl half her age. 'But allow me some pride. If you have charmed Kenton without effort, it shows that the apple has not fallen far from the tree, no matter how we wished to change your nature.'

'I am no actress, Mother. I have no desire to dazzle the man with illusion.' It was why she had brought the gun. Using a weapon had not been fair, but at least it had been cold, hard and real.

Her mother sensed her weakening and took up the fan again to give her another tap on the wrist. 'Do not waste time feeling sorry for him, Thea. A gentleman should have seen the risks of taking a young lady out in the garden alone. What happened to him after was his own fault.'

'Perhaps he is not quite right in the head,' Thea suggested. That made more sense to her than his sudden, willing attachment. 'His behaviour has been rather odd, has it not? So many men seem to return from India with tales of fever and malaise. But he is tanned and hardy.' And very handsome, if Thea truly wished to be honest.

'His complexion indicates nothing more mysterious than a strong constitution,' her mother replied. 'It guarantees virility, which you will appreciate soon enough, if you do not already. If the kiss I interrupted was any indication...'

'Mother!'

Her mother gave her an innocent smile and laid a finger to her lips to indicate a shared secret. She had been hinting since the first night that she had caught more than a brief glimpse of the way Kenton had behaved and the eager way Thea had responded to him. Her approval was no more maternal than Thea's response had been maidenly. It was all very inappropriate.

'I meant,' she corrected, returning the conversation to a safer topic, 'that Kenton's stories of his travels are almost too grand to believe. All wild adventures, narrow escapes, tigers and tea.' And, more worrisome, he spoke of bejewelled ladies and hinted at romantic escapades while veiling the details with Oriental silk. The stories were very exciting, but she'd had more than her fill of exaggerated anecdotes from her mother. She should have learned better and sought something more mundane in a marriage partner. Instead, she was sighing over Kenton like the silliest girl in London. 'If his life was as wonderful as it seemed, then what brought him home?'

'I expect it was his father,' her mother answered. 'The Earl of Spayne is seldom in town, though he lives only a county away. His health is rumoured to be failing. He could not have been comfortable with his heir spending half a lifetime away from home. Continental education and exotic travels are quite all right, but they should be taken in moderation.'

Thea raised an eyebrow at the disapproval in her mother's voice. It was a rather parochial sentiment from a woman who'd spent her formative years in a travelling band of players. 'I merely wonder if he exaggerates the happiness of his past. He seems a most contented fellow. Perhaps he is simply choosing to ignore or forget some hardship.' Or else he was too stupid to understand the things that had befallen him. Her pathetic attempt at kidnapping had made no impact on his mood, unless one could count this total and in-explicable infatuation.

Even more frustrating was her illogical desire to believe him. Before forming her recent plan, she had thought herself immune to his looks and charm. She had managed to resist them the better part of the Season. It had been easy when she could keep a distance from him. In close quarters, his speeches inflamed her curiosity and she'd become a rapt listener.

And his kisses inflamed something else entirely. Had she ever thought that her first kiss would be accompanied by reverent and impassioned poetry? She did not dare to share the details with her mother, who was already too willing to give her advice on the matter, based on the scene she'd witnessed. Thea could imagine the frank response she would receive if she announced that the man she intended to marry had heaped praise on her breasts and demonstrated his approval of them so strenuously that her heart had almost hammered its way out from under them.

Of course, then she might learn if all men

kissed as Kenton did. His lips had been as hot as the Indian sun and had left her just as dazed. She did not really need a husband for anything other than the fortune he possessed, but she could not help but be a little grateful that he offered so much more.

She felt another prod from the fan. 'And you are gone again. Really, my dear. I said it was normal to be so distracted, but that did not mean I encouraged it. You must keep your wits about you when you meet the man's family. Perhaps you did not realise that Kenton's uncle is Mr Henry de Warde. If you could manage to make him aware of the difficulty he's placed us in...'

'The idea had crossed my mind,' Thea said, all thoughts of romance fleeing from her mind. 'It will be a challenge not to tell him what I really think of him, when next I see him face to face.'

'You must exercise diplomacy, my dear. And perhaps just a touch of the charm you used to snare Kenton.'

Thea thought of the pistol, which must still be tucked between the cushions of the gazebo bench, unless Kenton had retrieved it for her after Mama had hustled her away. 'If I am given the chance to make my case to Mr de Warde, I shall use persuasion even stronger than that.' She would gladly put a ball between the man's beady eyes if it meant that she could restore even a fraction of the money that he had swindled from her father.

'I doubt your new husband would allow that, dear. Much stronger persuasion than you used on Kenton would have you uncovered to the waist.'

'Mother!'

Lady Banester sighed. 'I merely approve of your choice of gown when you finally decided to arm yourself for the hunt. It was quite lower than your usual necklines and you notice it had the desired effect on your quarry. We must choose lingerie for you with similar results in mind.'

Thea blushed. 'Surely once we are married that will not be necessary.'

Lady Banester held a swatch of champagne silk to the light, so that Thea could see her hand clearly through it. 'This should do the trick. And remember to stand with the firelight at your back. Once you are married, you must still keep the man's attention, my dear. It is so much easier when they do not stray. You have only to look at your father…'

'…to see just how horribly wrong that plan might go,' Thea said firmly. 'It is high time that he thought of more serious matters, Mother. Both of you. Really. You are very near to forty.'

'And still you have no brother,' her mother pointed out. 'Not for want of trying, of course. But with all the money caught up in the entail, we might as well have nothing at all to call our own. I was at a loss as to where we would get a dowry now that we can hardly pay our own bills. Thank goodness you have saved us that worry.'

'You will not have to worry about anything. I swear.' She would get the money from Kenton to make things right for her parents, no matter what was required of her.

Her mother took note of her silence and held up the silk again. 'As I said before, we will shop for nightclothes and you will be breeding in no time. That is what Lord Kenton wants, and Lord Spayne as well. The future must be provided for. A round belly is the quickest way to win the heart of the father. And what the son wants…'

Her mother smiled as though that should be quite obvious. 'Once you have given it to him, perhaps you can persuade Kenton to talk to Mr de Warde. If we explain the situation…'

'No!' The whole story was mortifying in the extreme. She could not imagine sharing the worst details of it with her new husband. 'I will tell him as much as he needs to know, so that he will pay the debts we have incurred. And then I will go to Mr de Warde and appeal to his sense of decency. He will surely return the bulk of the sum he has taken once he realises that we are now family. And there will be no further need for trickery or seduction.' Or even pearl-handled pistols in the moonlight.

'Of course, darling,' her mother said in a soothing voice. 'There is no need to become overwrought. Let us collect our things and go have an ice.' And then, with a shake of her head, she added the transparent silk to the pile of purchases.

Chapter Three

Miss Cynthia Banester was a beautiful bride. Of course, she was Lady Kenton now. She had Jack to thank for that. And she did seem inordinately pleased. Since they'd been seated, she'd made sure that his plate and cup were never empty as though seeking any way possible to show her devotion. 'Champagne, darling?' She smiled up at him.

'Thank you, love.' He smiled back as she saw to the filling of his glass. Jack felt a not entirely appropriate swelling of pride at how well things had turned out. The ceremony had felt real enough, with a licence and a vicar, and the good wishes of her family heaped upon them.

But she was his wife for only as long as he played at being Lord Kenton. Then he would go on his merry way and they would both be the better for his departure. He would have the money. She would be safe in the keeping of the earl, who was a fine old gentleman, for all his quirks. And she would be spared a lifetime of him as a husband. Jack doubted that she would continue to smile after she learned of his true character. Other women had assured him that he was fickle, shallow and faithless. He doubted that money, a false title and an equally false marriage would change that.

But that was a future he need never face. Today, his darling Cyn was frowning into her glass. She gave the smallest of pouts and he felt a sudden urge to kiss it away. He had to force himself to remember that he was as likely to grow tired of her as she would of him. The feelings of infatuation seemed real enough at the moment, but there was no way that they could outlast the honeymoon. He must be sure to be gone before they faded. Better that she should have bittersweet memories of the dashing Lord Kenton, the adoring husband who was taken too soon, than any introduction at all to plain old Jack Briggs.

Today, he was still Kenton and eager to show his mutual admiration. 'Is something the matter, my sweet?'

'I had hoped that we would see your father for the wedding. I quite looked forward to meeting him.'

It was a predictable expectation on her part and Jack answered it smoothly. 'He was detained in Essex. Business with the estate, I think. Travel is difficult for him. But I have written to him about you. He is very pleased with the union and eager to meet you. He sent the ring you are wearing now.' He paused dramatically to make the next words sound more like sentiment than a quickly constructed lie. 'It belonged to my mother. It was a great favourite of hers. I remember it well, though I was so very young, when she...' He sighed.

She looked around for something with which to distract him from his grief. 'Toast, Lord Kenton?'

He grinned at her and accepted the proffered bread. 'Thank you, Lady Kenton. And no need to be formal, now that we are practically as one. Kenton is fine. Or you might call me by my Christian name.'

'John?' she said hesitantly, as though trying the word for the first time.

He gave a silent thank you to the late John de Warde for being so conveniently named. 'Or you might call me Jack. It is what my friends call me. And I very much wish to be your friend.' He glanced down the table. 'I wish to be friends with your family as well. I must talk to your father before the day is through. He has spoken of a settlement, but we could not manage to find time to discuss it until now.'

'Tongue?'

Hells, yes. She was leaning forwards, over the tray of cold meats, in rapt concentration as though it took any great thought to choose the best piece for him. The tip of her own pink tongue protruded ever so slightly from between her teeth, and the set of her body gave him a tantalising glimpse down the front of her gown.

His body shot to attention as his mind instantly focused on the wedding night, which, as far as he was concerned, could begin any time after noon. Was it normal to be so utterly fixated on bedding one's own wife? There was probably some quote in Shakespeare's canon about delayed pleasure being sweeter, but for the life of him he couldn't think of it.

Because his wits were addled by lust. It had been three long and very respectable weeks since he'd offered for her. In that time he had done nothing to shock or annoy. He had played the part of a perfect gentleman and played it to the very hilt. Now, if they could just get this interminable breakfast behind them, he would get Cynthia Banester alone and fall on her like a condemned man at his last meal.

At least Jack Briggs would have done so. Lord Kenton would be a connoisseur. And if ever there was a dish to be savoured, it was the new Lady Kenton. There would be plenty of time later for risky and hurried couplings, after he had initiated her into any of the conventional arts that she was not yet familiar with. If the lady proved willing and true to her initial response, they might have no end of fun together before it was time to part from her. Several months as a doting husband to this redheaded pocket Venus was almost, but not quite, an ample payment for his services to the earl.

She stood beside him now, looking up through gold-tipped lashes, a shy smile on her face. 'My dear,' he said, surprising himself with a sincere sigh.

'Jack.' She leaned forwards again, giving him an even better look down the front of her bodice.

He leaned closer to speak into her ear. 'Have I thanked you yet for bringing me to this pass? I had not thought to offer for you, but now I cannot imagine my future with another.'

'I am relieved to hear you say that,' she said, sighing as well. He could not help but admire what a deep breath did to his wife's anatomy.

She reached out a finger and traced it lightly down the back of his hand. 'Many men would not have been so forgiving of my impudence. I very nearly tricked you into this marriage.'

He put an arm about her shoulder and pulled her close, planting a kiss upon her forehead, even though they were still in plain sight of both her father and the vicar. 'Let us speak no more of that…unless it is as an amusing story to tell our children.'

For a moment, the woman cuddling at his side seemed to evaporate and was replaced by a harder, shrewder but equally beautiful version of herself. 'I'd rather die. I mean…' she dissolved into softness and innocence again '…children often find tales of their parents' courtship to be more shocking than romantic. And describing the interlude in the gazebo with any sort of detail…' She stopped again. 'You are a compelling storyteller, Kenton, but some things should be kept secret.'

So she was embarrassed by her ardent response to his wooing. It was really quite flattering. 'As you wish. The circumstances of our meeting shall stay a secret.' The point was moot, after all. If there were children, it was not as if he would be there to spin tales for them.

And there would be no risk of them at all if he could not manage to say farewell to the girl's plaguey family and get her alone. He took a final sip of his wine and wiped his mouth with the napkin. 'I think it is time I spoke with your father, my dear. And then we shall retire to the Kenton town house and you may begin your new life.'

Her hand tightened on his suddenly and he patted it in reassurance. 'You have nothing to worry about, sweeting. Did I not promise you, on the night we met, that I would give you nothing but pleasure?'

'It is not that.' She attempted another melting gaze and leaned so close to him that he could feel the side of her breast pressing against his arm. 'Can we not go now? You may speak to my father on another day, when things are not so busy. I swear, he would hardly notice if we left together right now.'

From his other side, he heard Lady Banester give a knowing chuckle. 'The eagerness of young love.' The older woman touched his other arm, and for a moment Jack had to remind himself of the marriage that had just taken place and the sublime beauty of his bride. It was clear that Cynthia had inherited the charms of her mother. The woman was a stunner in her own right. And though clearly devoted to her husband, she was not afraid to wield her beauty like a weapon.

'You must forgive my daughter's impetuosity, Lord Kenton. Although with such a handsome husband, I can certainly understand it.'

'Thank you, Lady Banester,' he replied, remembering not to be too flattered. 'And your daughter has done nothing in need of forgiveness.'

'But it is plain that she wishes to see her new home. And you gentleman have things you must discuss.'

'Mother.' The single word from his wife was clearly a warning, although damned if Jack knew what it meant. The air between the two women crackled with tension. Occupying the space between them was like being caught in a battle of sirens.

'I am only trying to help.' Lady Banester pouted and Jack felt an illogical desire to agree to whatever she might suggest. 'And I have a suggestion that will please you both. While you and Sir William talk, I will escort Thea to your home, so that she might prepare herself for your arrival.'

'You will part me from my husband on our wedding day?'

He turned back to his wife with what he hoped was a firm but benevolent smile. 'Only for an hour, dearest. And then I shall return to you and we might continue our celebration.'

In bed. By then, he would have money in the bank and a promise of continued support for the lovely Cyn, in exchange for the use of various Stayne properties and the prestigious connection with one of the oldest families in Britain. Sir William was nothing more than a humble baronet. But since he lived like the plumpest pigeon in London, Jack assumed the level of gratitude would be substantial.

Between the equally generous rewards he would receive from Stayne and the fringe benefits of a buxom and affectionate wife, John de Warde, Lord Kenton, was proving to be the nicest role Jack had ever played. He would be sad when the farce had to end.

It had been more than an hour. More than two. And at last, more than three. In fact, it was nearly time to dress for bed, which was quite ridiculous. Thea had donned the négligée her mother had pressed upon her at half past one in the afternoon. It was getting rather chilly.

Her mother had assured her she would be well out of the thing by now. Thea had allowed the final scraps of embarrassing advice, because she had assumed that they would be just that. Final. No matter what occurred between her and Kenton, it would not have to be coached, described or dissected by a too-curious female parent. It could be a secret, between her husband and herself.

If Father had ruffled his feathers with precipitate demands for funds, there might be more than an unusual number of secrets to keep. While she knew more than a maiden should about the activities of the marriage bed, she lacked the experience to be a seducer. But she was prepared to be as willing and enthusiastic a pupil as a disgruntled husband might wish.

As soon as Kenton came home, at any rate.

How much had Father demanded of him? And how long could it take to write a bank draft? Thea had a mortifying fancy of treasure caskets changing hands. Or, worse yet, sheep and goats. Somewhere in London, her worth was defined in livestock and chattel. She must hope that her value was sufficient to fix the mess they were in.

From somewhere down the hallway, outside the closed bedroom door, she heard a thump. And then another and another. As the sounds came closer, they formed an irregular pattern. Booted footsteps? Perhaps if the visitor had a wooden leg. There was something not quite right about them.

The door to her room burst open, slamming against the opposite wall to reveal her husband leaning lopsidedly in the door frame.

'Kenton?' It was him, she was sure. But judging by the noxious stench accompanying him, he was disguised by gin. A quick examination of his boots revealed the reason for his uneven gate. At some point during their wedding afternoon, his champagne-polished Hessians had been abused to the point where one heel was missing. He had walked halfway out of the other and had been staggering along on the calf, trying to free himself as he walked. As she watched, he gave a final kick and the offending footwear sailed across the room to land beside the bed.

'Kenton. John. Jack.' She tried to settle on a name for him that best suited the situation. 'Shall I call your valet?'

'No, thank you,' he said, and, for a moment, he sounded almost like the man she'd expected. His voice was beautiful, as it always was. Clear, resonant and compelling. It was the sort of voice to melt hearts and reservations. And if they could get this difficulty behind them, she would happily listen to it for the rest of her life.

'Do you wish me to help you?' She crawled towards the edge of the bed, the silk of her nightdress billowing about her. 'You appear to need some assistance.'

He threw a hand dramatically in front of his eyes. 'Do not help me, you…succubus. Do not help me ever again.' He seized his remaining boot, hopping about a bit before managing to free himself of it and then tossing it after its mate.

'I do not understand.' She sank back on the bed, painfully sure that her last statement had been a lie.

'Don't you, now.' He struggled out of his jacket and pulled a bundle of papers from the pocket before dropping it on the floor. 'And you knew nothing of these, I suppose, when you decided it was urgent that you marry the first man stupid enough to be trapped by you.' He dropped the familiar invoices on the mattress beside her.

'I have no idea what you mean,' she said, hoping that she looked sufficiently guileless.

'Then I will tell you. These are a wedding gift. From your father. Your settlement. The one he promised to give to me, after we were wed.'

'Oh.' Now the storm would break for sure. And no amount of transparent silk would hold it back.

'Of course, foolish man that I am, I went to him, imagining it would be something akin to a small estate, or a rather large bank draft. Instead, I find—' he brandished the first paper '—the bill for the wedding breakfast. And here is another, for your wedding clothes and your mother's as well. Tailor's bills, grocer's bills. Butcher's bills, for God's sake. And they are a month old. Am I expected to pay for chops that I have not tasted?'

'Recently, there have been difficulties,' she said. It was a huge understatement.

'Difficulties?' There was a slightly hysterical

edge to her new husband's lovely voice that took her by surprise.

'Well, yes. My mother has always been prone to extravagances. But of late, a miscalculation on the part of my father has led to misfortune.'

'Misfortune?' The tone of this, if possible, was even higher than the last statement had been.

'But I am sure that they are nothing that you cannot handle, as heir to Lord Stayne.'

'Ahhhh.' And this was the strangest sound of all. One-part confirmation, and two-parts wordless oath, followed by a sharp slap to his own temple and a collapse into the nearest chair. 'I see it all now. The ease with which it was possible to catch you. Your sudden, devoted interest in me, which my own vanity made me want to believe. And damn me for a fool in that. Stayne will have my neck back in the noose as sure as your eyes are green.'

'Noose?'

'Where were my eyes? Where was my brain? And why, Lord, why must it be so easy for a ginger-haired girl with a magnificent bosom to trick a trickster?'

'A trickster.' He was hardly speaking to her any more. But since all he'd spoken before appeared to be lies, it was just as well. The last little speech had been so full of information that she could hardly take it all in. He was a trickster. He feared hanging and he feared Stayne.

Apparently, he admired her eyes and certain other portions of her anatomy. It was nice, but not germane.

'Why would your own father want to see your neck in a noose?' But he'd said, *back in a noose.* 'And why was it ever there in the first place?'

Lord Kenton stared back at her with a bitter grin. 'I have no idea what my father would want. I've never met the man.' He reached for a flask in his pocket, opened it and took a healthy gulp of the contents.

It was her turn to sit down suddenly on the nearest surface, collapsing back on the bed and hugging a pillow to her chest to conceal everything she had meant to display. 'But that means that you're...'

'A bastard,' he replied cheerfully and offered her the flask.

She waved it away. 'Then you cannot be Stayne's heir.'

'I am not even his natural son,' Jack replied. 'At least, I do not think I am. My mother was none too clear on the identity of my sire. I did not press her on the subject.'

'And I married a man of no birth, no consequence...'

'And no fortune,' he added, taking another drink. 'And there you are, hoisted upon your own petard. Since I married an heiress with no fortune, I have no sympathy for you.' He stood, walked to the fireplace and tossed her father's bills one by one into the flames.

'You cannot,' she said, dropping the pillow and hurrying across the room to retrieve them.

'You are clearly unaccustomed to having debts. These are but first requests. They will send others. I speak from experience.'

'A bastard with unpaid debts.' She folded her hands across her chest, trying to draw the spider's web she was wearing into some semblance of modesty.

'And do not forget the near hanging,' he said, wagging a finger at her and taking another drink.

'I cannot forget something that I know nothing about.'

'It is a very interesting story,' he said.

'I imagine it is. Would you share it with me?' *Your wife. Who would not have been such had she heard any of this a scant day ago.* She glared at him.

Her anger had no more effect than her near nudity was having, for he was lost in drink and the story he told. 'While it might be possible to dodge a London tailor, some of the more provincial innkeepers are less forgiving. When I elected to leave an establishment suddenly, by a window at the first light of dawn, the ostler caught me and had me up on charges of theft. When Stayne found me with his interesting proposition, I was on my way to the gallows.'

'As well you should have been. You were stealing from the innkeeper.'

'As was he from me. I should think the stirring performance of Shakespeare's better soliloquies was worth the price of a room and a dinner. He hinted at such before I began. But when I had finished, he claimed he did not care for tragedy and presented me with the bill.'

'A bastard, a thief and an actor!' The last was the worst news of all. She grabbed for the pillow and swung it at his head, and kept swinging until the leading edge was trailing feathers.

He dodged the final blow with a bow worthy of Covent Garden, then straightened, seized the pillow and thrust it back into her arms. 'At your service, miss. Or shall I say madam. You are a married lady now, after all.'

'I am most certainly not. I cannot be held to a marriage entered into under such fraudulent circumstances.'

'Fraud?' He pointed an accusing finger at her. 'You dress in silk and have not a feather to fly with.'

'That is merely money,' she said waving a dismissive hand.

'The words of someone who is used to having it,' he countered.

'It is nothing, compared to the lies you told. I thought, when I agreed to marry you, that I knew who your family was. Now it appears that you do not know them either. There must be a law that covers this.'

'You have but to make this disgrace public and find out,' he offered with an expansive gesture towards the door. 'Perhaps you can tell the next fellow you trap that this marriage does not matter. Here, take the licence with you.' He tossed a mud-spattered scrap of paper at her. Their signatures were still legible through the many boot-prints that marked it. 'But I doubt another man will be as stupid as I was, once the story of this mistake gets around.'

It was a horrible truth and one she had not yet considered. Once the truth was known, she would have no choice but to take de Warde's despicable offer that she repair her father's fortune with her virtue. 'You've ruined me!' she shouted, throwing the pillow back at his head.

He caught it easily. 'You've ruined yourself, darling. Do not expect me to feel sorry for you. Spayne hired me to do a spot of play-acting. I was to find a rich wife, bring her and her fortune back to Essex. My very life depended on success. What is to become of me now?'

'If he does not hang you, then I will. I will be a widow,' she said with narrowed eyes. 'That suits me well.'

'I was planning to give you just such a wedding gift before we discovered the truth about each other.' He gazed off at an imaginary and happier horizon. 'When all the settlements were made and your non-existent fortune was in the earl's bank, I was to meet with a tragic accident. Punting, perhaps. Although the water is too shallow to do the job right.' He framed the scene with his hands. 'Sailing. My boat would be found, dashed against the rocks. But alas, no body would be recovered. My father? Heartbroken. And you, the beautiful, young, rich widow, would weep openly over the empty coffin.'

'That will never happen,' she said, mouth set in a grim line.

'After how I meant to treat you in the months before the tragedy, I dare say you would have.' He gave her a long hot look that said she'd have been on her back by now and he seemed to think she'd have enjoyed the process. 'You would wear black for a year.'

'Six months at most.'

'Followed by half-mourning,' he insisted. 'I see you in lavender, wan, fragile and appealing.

'I see myself in red, dancing on your grave,' she said. 'You meant to bed me, cheat me and leave me a bigamist.'

'Spayne would have taken care of you. For all his idiosyncrasies, the man is a gallant gentleman at heart. He'd have seen to it that you were re-launched, remarried and none the worse for the experience.'

'But that happy future will not come to pass until you have the courtesy to die,' she said. 'I suggest you get about it.'

'Without your fortune, the earl has nothing to offer you. Adding two ciphers does not make an appreciable sum. If I were to die now, you would be a poor widow on the morrow.' He held his hands out again and pulled a frown. 'I see you in shabby black, tinged with the green of hard wearing. Perhaps you will take in sewing and live on the charity of the church.'

'I will not!' she shouted back at him. 'I could not make nearly enough by sewing,' she added softly, resigned. Then a thought occurred to her. 'I don't suppose there is a real Lord Kenton somewhere. Perhaps I am not married to you at all.'

Jack shook his head. 'Died as a child along with his mother on a trip abroad. Spayne kept the illusion alive because he did not want to be troubled by his family to produce an heir. But the foolish deception has gone on too long and, of late, his brother was clamouring to see the prodigal son.'

'Henry de Warde,' Thea announced bitterly.

'You know of him?'

'Only because he is the reason for my family's poverty. He sold my father a certain...' What would be an appropriate description? 'A fraudulent artefact,' she decided.

'That your father was willing to spend the whole of the family fortune to gain?' Her *faux* husband was eyeing her with suspicion, waiting for the rest of a story she had no intention of telling.

She ignored the unstated request for detail. 'It was no more unwise then Spayne's mythical son.'

'Probably true,' Jack admitted.

'I spoke to de Warde about it. I pleaded with him for mercy.'

'And he suggested that you work off the debt on your back.'

It had been the single most revolting moment of her life. But now that she had destroyed herself, it was likely to be the first of many. 'How did you know?'

Jack was staring at her with something almost like sympathy. 'Because it's what any sane man would have done.'

Now he seemed to be assessing her value and she wondered if he would have behaved the same, had he been de Warde. A glance at her reflection in a nearby cheval glass told her that it was too late to protect her modesty from him. A single pillow could not have hidden enough. 'I refused him. But now...' she looked at the man in front of her and resorted to complete honesty, which her teacher, Miss Pennyworth, had assured her was the shield and bulwark of any virtuous young girl '...I don't know what I shall do.'

He continued to stare. 'Suppose I were to suggest another way.'

'Anything.' She'd spoken too quickly. This was a man willing to steal from innkeepers, trick her into wedding him and fake his own death. He had made no mention of seeking a marriage in name only, at any time in his plans. There was no telling what scheme he intended now. 'Anything within reason,' she amended.

'I do not know how reasonable my plans are,' he admitted. 'But recent actions proved that we are both willing to consider unreasonable options to gain success. The kidnapping was an admirable twist,' he added, nodding with approval.

'Thank you.' She frowned. 'I did not think it would work.'

'A more timid tactic might not have got me. And you were not the most convincing actress I have seen. But the combination of beauty and risk was irresistible.' He paused dramatically. 'As I suppose my performance was to you.'

Silently, she cursed all actors and their perpetual need for approval. 'Actually, it was your relationship to de Warde that attracted me. Any man would have done.'

'I see.' She watched as his excessive pride deflated. Then he rallied. 'It makes me wonder what we might achieve by working together against a common enemy. There is more to Spayne's story than I have told you. And you are still keeping secrets as well.'

'I?' She tried to look guileless.

'You,' he said with a shake of his head. 'And why did I not see it before? But it is clear that Henry de Warde is at the crux of both troubles.'

'What do you think you can do about him?' It was unlikely that the man before her had a simple solution to her problem, but a forlorn hope was better than no chance at all.

'I will not appeal to his better nature, that's for certain. I doubt he has one. If we are to get anywhere with the man, we must do it in the same way he's got one over on us, using base trickery, lies and chicanery.' He walked past her to the bed, undoing the buttons of his waistcoat. 'But the details can wait until after we have spoken to Spayne. If we must travel tomorrow, an early night is in order.' He stretched out upon the mattress and patted the space at his side.

'Certainly not,' she said. Then she remembered what her mother had said about the transparency of nightwear and did her best to move out of the firelight.

He smiled invitingly and his voice, though slurred, was still as soothing as warm honey. 'You were not so ungenerous this morning.'

'That was when you were Kenton.'

'And you mean to hold out for nothing less than a viscount.' He sighed. 'My loss, I suppose. But you are wise to have standards.' He picked up the pillow she had thrown and tossed it back to her. 'I suggest you remove yourself from the vicinity of my bed, before I forget what you have done to me and take advantage.'

'And where am I supposed to sleep?'

'The house is large. Call a servant. They will find you a place.'

'They will know that we did not...'

'Then take the couch on the other side of the room.'

She glared at him. 'A true gentleman would leave me the bed.'

'As we have established, I am not a gentleman,' he said with a smile. 'But at least I have my wits. I have survived on those and little else for thirty years. If you wish me to apply it to this situation, I will need to be well rested. Good night, my dear.' And with that, he rolled so that his back was to her and closed his eyes.

Chapter Four

In the company of her new husband, the imposter Jack Briggs, the ride to Essex was proving intolerable. Instead of the sweet afterglow of a honeymoon, the day after Thea's marriage was rather like waking with a bad head from too much wine. Her brain ached from trying to comprehend what had happened to her. Her body was stiff and sore from a night spent without sleep on the hard couch in her husband's room, muscles rigid and teeth clenched with anger and frustration. The Kenton carriage was well sprung and roomy, but she might as well have been travelling in an open dog cart for all the comfort it gained her.

It was precisely the condition that the false Lord Kenton should have been experiencing. He had snored his way through the night, wrapped in a cloud of cheap spirits and the monogrammed linens of one of the finest families in England. Instead of waking the worse for drink and racked with guilt at how he had treated Thea and her family, the morning found him happy, relaxed and quite pleased with the way the day was going. When she had pressed him for an explanation, he had been unwilling to share the reason for his good mood. He acted as if lying about his life and identity, marrying some unsuspecting girl and being sorely disappointed in the result was an activity that happened every day.

Perhaps, to him, it did. The idea that she might be one of a string of similar Lady Kentons was more than disturbing. He did not seem the sort to travel from town to town, ruining innocents and stealing fortunes. But until last night, she'd have sworn that such a thing as had already happened was quite impossible. How could she be sure?

And he was whistling. Thea could not identify the tune. But she suspected, judging by the look in his eyes, that the lyrics were inappropriate for female ears.

She glared at him. 'Stop that incessant noise.'

Jack stared back at her, all innocence. The whistle paused. 'You do not like music?'

'That is not music. It is precisely the opposite. If you had any manners...'

'And the kind of breeding and education...' he said, in a pompous tone, waving a hand. 'We have already established that I do not. You were the one who wished to marry me. Now you must learn to make do.' He went back to whistling.

'It is vulgar,' she said with desperation.

'And so am I.' His eyes were narrowed, as though it had been possible to hurt him with a statement of truth.

'I have no doubt that you are vulgar, after your comments of the previous evening. But it is all the more reason for you to stop. You should aspire to be something better than you are.'

'As you do?' He folded his arms across his chest, waiting for an answer. His cheerful manner disappeared. He was looking at her, for all the world, as though he were the one who had been wronged by her scheming.

'Is this some veiled reference to my willingness to—' her mouth puckered in revulsion as she parroted his words back to him '—hold out for a man of sufficient rank?' It was as if he thought her no better than a whore for marrying him. 'There is nothing wrong with seeking a decent future through marriage.'

'For a woman, perhaps,' he said.

'You were quick enough to do it yourself.'

'I was doing it in service to another,' he said firmly.

As was she. Her family would have seen the benefit, had her plan worked as expected. But his comment rankled. 'You are little better than a servant to Spayne, then? If so, I order you to stop whistling.'

'I may be a servant to Spayne. But to you?' He grinned. 'I am a husband. And humble though I might be, it is not your place to command anything of me. As I remember, it was you who promised to obey.'

'But not to obey you. I said the words when I thought you were Kenton. I promised loyalty to a man who does not exist.'

'The majority of women who marry would say

the same thing. I fail to see why I owe an alteration of my behaviour to you, if you were not aware of the fact that marriage changes everything between us. Now hush, woman, and cease your nagging. I am trying to think.' He leaned back in the seat and closed his eyes with a blissful smile upon his face.

Marriage changed everything. He was right in that, at least. For the moment, it left her completely dependent on the man across from her, for she could think of no way to explain away what had happened without making matters even worse than they were. Jack had stopped whistling, though she doubted it was in an effort to spare her nerves. But she found the silence even more annoying than the noise had been. 'What are you thinking about?' she said at last.

He opened one eye. 'Are you to be one of those women, then? The sort that is continually trying to pry out the contents of a man's head for their own entertainment?'

'It is not entertainment that I desire. I merely wish to know what you have planned for our future together.'

'Together?' He laughed. 'I do not plan any such thing. I am taking you to Spayne, just as he wished. He will explain as much or as little of his situation as he chooses. Between us, we will see if there is anything that can be salvaged of his original plan. You will help us. And when it is through, I will return to my life. Beyond that, we have no future together.'

The glee with which he contemplated the end of their connection hurt, although why it should she had no idea. She wanted to be rid of him as much as he wanted to break with her. 'You seem to be angry at me, which is hardly fair.' Had she not worked long and hard to mould herself into the perfect wife? The least he could do was appreciate her effort.

He was having none of it. 'You deceived me.'

'Only because you wanted to be deceived,' she reminded him. 'At no time did I promise you wealth, or an adequate settlement. Nor did my father. It was you who chose to assume that there was money rather than debt. I, on the other hand, had no reason to believe that you were not

Viscount Kenton. I trusted your word as a gentleman.'

'Just as your father trusted de Warde.' He snorted. 'The gentry is far too trusting, in my opinion. But you are right. I was a fool. Your sort have been lying to me my whole life and it was only now that I chose to see truth where there was none. I apologise for my bad temper.'

'Apology accepted,' she said uneasily. Had it been her imagination, or had she just won an argument with the man? Truly not, if she had to do it by claiming herself a liar. 'But I did not lie to you. I merely omitted certain key portions of the truth. I took a gamble to gain your full attention. But I never claimed to be rich. You merely assumed it.'

'Of course I did. You were well dressed, seen at all the finest parties and your father spent freely.'

'Just as everyone else in society,' she responded. 'If you scratch the surface, you will find many in a similar predicament. It is hardly unusual.'

'You claimed that you needed to marry. You pretended to be fond of me.'

'But that was true,' she insisted earnestly, glad

that he was finally understanding her. 'I did need to marry. And it would have been difficult to gain your attention any other way than kidnapping. You were the most sought-after man of the Season. Even if I'd have caught your eye, your interest would have waned when you realised that my family was inappropriate.'

'As it did,' he admitted. 'Though it might have faded more slowly had I the chance to enjoy your favours, as I'd expected to.'

She gave a little gasp of shock to hear him freely admit that he'd meant to use her so, knowing full well that it would be a trick.

It did not seem to bother him in the least. He was still too focused on his own selfish complaints. 'You did not need to claim an attraction where you felt none.'

But she had been attracted to him. There was no way to escape that, for he was a most handsome and charming fellow. And the kisses he'd given her, when she'd allowed it, had been quite wonderful. But she would not give him the satisfaction of knowing so and allowed herself a small white lie, by avoiding the accusation with a scoff. 'You would have noticed no difference had we married.'

'And this is what honesty is worth,' he said with a dramatic gesture. 'The least you could do, now that you are trapped with me, is to spare my feelings and pretend that you once liked me.'

She had not intended to hurt his feelings, not that she truly believed he had them. 'I liked you as well as any other man,' she allowed. 'I have always known that the match I would make might be decided after a brief acquaintance, and based on fondness rather than grand passion. Had we married in truth, I would have given you the same wholehearted devotion that I'd have given to any other man.'

If possible, he looked even more injured. 'It is faint praise to know that any man could have taken my place and received similar affection.'

'You would not have minded, I assure you.' She raised her head with pride at her one accomplishment. 'I have been properly educated on that score and would have made you a fine wife.'

'This I must hear,' he said with a lascivious smile. 'Tell me what sort of education you have that would lead us to be in the situation we are sharing. Did it involve tricking men into having you? Or are there other skills I might appreciate?' He gave a waggle of eyebrow to imply the sorts of things her mother had all too candidly explained to her.

'I have no idea what you are talking about.' She did her best, but the thought that he might see easily through the falsehood was acutely embarrassing. 'I know all that is important for a wife to know. I can sing and dance and play the pianoforte. My watercolours are deemed to be quite good. I can net a purse and embroider with silks. I can manage the servants of a large household and plan all sorts of entertainments. My manners are impeccable, whether on a morning visit to a friend or a court presentation. In addition, I am quite well read, can speak and understand French and read a bit of Italian. Most importantly, I am willing to be led in all things by the wisdom of my husband. What more could a man expect?'

'I stand corrected,' Jack said with an ironic smile. 'Apparently, you are all I could want. The fact that you are poor as a church mouse and cannot hide your contempt for me does not enter into the equation.'

'The poverty cannot be helped. It was not my doing. And I hold you in contempt because you lied to me,' she said. 'You pretended to be someone you were not. Your name, your family, your stories of India—not a word of it was true.'

'I was acting,' he insisted. 'I played the role I was hired for.'

'But I believed in you and your stories.' And she was most thoroughly disappointed to find that the man she had convinced herself she could love did not exist at all.

He brightened. 'Which is proof that I am a better actor than I have been given credit for. I wish, my dear, that I could take you to meet some of my critics and show to them how completely convincing I am in this part. They would take back what they said about my performance of Mordaunt Exbury in *Love and Fashion*. They said I was not lordly enough,' he added indignantly. 'And some wag in the audience had the nerve to throw a rotten potato.'

'I hope he hit you, you miserable cur,' Thea said with sincerity. 'You stood before God and lied through your teeth about staying with me until we were parted by death.'

'And as far as you knew, we would have been.' He thought for moment. 'It is almost the truth, when you think about it. A real Kenton existed. But he is, in fact, dead.' He smiled at her in encouragement. 'Perhaps you are already a widow.'

'But I did not wish to be *his* widow. I wished to be his wife. And in any case, I did not marry that man, rest his soul. I married you.' She raised a finger in a dire gesture of accusation, hoping that he would see the difference and the dilemma it put her in.

He caught her hand out of the air and pressed it to his lips for a quick kiss. 'And we must endeavour to make the best of that unfortunate mistake. We are just coming to Spayne Court. Let us tell all to the earl and see what he makes of it. I am sure that, once he has explained the advantages of the situation, you will be a most happy widow.'

'Once I know you better, I am sure I shall.' She snatched her hand back from his, ignoring the tingling in the fingers where his lips had touched it, and hurried to exit the coach as soon as the servants could open the door.

Chapter Five

Even before she'd set her cap for Kenton, Thea had known that Spayne Court was as venerable a house as one could hope to find in England. As the guidebooks had assured her, it looked like a castle. And that was what it had been when the first earl was awarded the land and title. The current Spayne was rumoured to be an enigma. He made few trips to London for Parliament, and none at all for social reasons. By turns the gossips described him as frail, in ill health, and healthy but suffering tragically from grief after the death of his wife, though this had occurred some ten years earlier. The *ton* speculated that the sudden appearance of Kenton was a sign that he was failing at last and the coronet was likely to be passed sooner rather than later.

But the man that greeted them when they entered the great hall seemed spry enough. He was healthy, well groomed and barely past middle age. He was also smiling broadly at Thea and gave no evidence of debilitating grief.

She could see from the first why he might have chosen Jack to imitate his heir. Though the resemblance was not strong, their blond hair, straight noses and sparkling blue eyes were close enough to alike that it was not hard to believe them father and son.

'Jack.' Spayne stepped forwards to clap the back of the mock Kenton, as though there were nothing strange or unfamiliar about him. 'Back from London at last and with your lovely bride. Let me have a look at the girl.' He stepped away again, turning to Thea and giving her a thorough, head-to-toe examination before holding out his hands to her in what seemed to be a sincere gesture of welcome. 'My dear Cynthia.'

'Lord Spayne.' Her knees buckled instinctively into a curtsy and her head bowed in respect, even as she reminded herself that the man had been instrumental in her recent undoing. No matter her personal feelings about his scheme, he was a peer and her training would permit nothing less than total respect.

He took her hands and lifted her back to face him, beaming. 'You were certainly right in your letters, Jack. She is magnificent.'

Jack cleared his throat as though embarrassed to be caught in praise of her. 'I said she was well suited to your needs.'

Without looking away from her, Spayne corrected him. 'That is not what you said at all.'

'I think, if you were to read the letter again—' Jack said, sounding rather desperate.

Spayne cut him off. 'Sometimes it is better to read between the lines to find the meaning. Yours was quite clear. The girl is a great beauty, you were smitten and so you presented her as the logical choice for my needs.'

'That is not at all what I…' For the first time, her *faux* husband seemed totally out of countenance, and perhaps a little in awe of the man before him.

The earl held up a finger. 'I do not blame you for it. One has but to see her to understand.' But he did not understand at all. As Jack had taken pains to remind her, she was not the daughter he had wanted at all. After all the effort she had taken to be otherwise, it was distressing to be such a disappointment to the father of the man she had thought to marry. Rank and honours aside, he did seem to be a most personable gentleman.

Beside her, Jack cleared his throat again. 'My lord. If we could speak in private for a moment. The situation has grown rather complicated.'

The earl looked at him with a tip of the head.

Jack glanced around to make sure the servants were not so close as to overhear. 'After our wedding, I had a most enlightening talk with Cyn's father. It seems I misunderstood much of our courtship. The man was seeking a settlement from me.'

There was an agonising silence in the room, as Spayne contemplated the meaning of that. Thea held her breath, waiting. His response, when it came, was not the angry outburst that she feared. The man blanched white, his welcoming smile frozen on his face. He said nothing. And though she felt an almost convulsive tightening on her hands, he did not release them.

Jack continued. 'I have explained to my lady wife much of my recent history. But I think further discussion is necessary.'

That pause continued a moment longer, then Spayne seemed to thaw, returning almost to the lively gentleman he had been only a few moments ago. 'Things have not gone to plan, have they?' He gave a slight sigh and released her hands. 'But that is the way of things, in my experience. They are never what they seem.'

'I agree,' Jack said, with a touch of asperity.

'No matter. It cannot be helped.' Spayne's response was firm, and showed no judgement against her, though it seemed to hold some unspoken warning to Jack. 'Let us go into the library. There is an open brandy bottle and a stout door to keep the world at bay. Just the way I like things.' Absently, the earl wandered towards a door to the left and Jack followed at his heels.

They would retire to the library to decide her fate and she would be excluded from the decision. Miss Pennyworth had assured her that it was a woman's lot to be treated thus, hammering away at her unfortunate tendency to behave as her mother might, insinuating herself into the situation, offering opinions and speaking altogether too much.

But it irked Thea that she was to be at the mercy of the scheming men who had hatched the plan that had got her married to Kenton. They had also left no instruction as to what she must do while they retreated. The least they might have done was call for a maid to take her to a parlour for a small glass of ratafia to steady her nerves.

Then, the earl, who was framed in the doorway of what must be his sanctum, glanced back at her and gestured. It was the merest twitch of a finger, inviting her to follow. 'You must be a part of this discussion, my dear. After all, you are family now.' There was no irony at all in his voice.

Perhaps that meant he was a better actor than Jack.

Thea hesitated, then followed a step or two behind, as the earl led them to the library and closed the doors behind them. It was a comfortable room full of well-used books and deep soft furniture, almost Oriental in its opulence. She had the impression that this place, rather than a more formal study or office, was where Lord Spayne spent the majority of his time. 'Come, sit. Refreshment, Jack?' He gestured to the decanter. 'It is rather early. But I think, under the circumstances, a good stiff drink is in order.'

Jack looked longingly at the bottle—and then refused. It surprised Thea. Of the many qualities he possessed, she would not have counted self-denial as one of them. It seemed that being in the presence of Lord Spayne intimidated him. Or rather, that he treated the man with the sort of respect an actual son might give to a beloved father.

'My dear?' Spayne looked at her now. 'Do you enjoy brandy? Or something weaker, perhaps.'

'No, thank you, my lord.' Now that the man had made the offer, her desire for a restorative vanished. It put her quite in sympathy with Jack. If there was to be punishment for the muddle they had made, better to get the truth out of the way quickly and have the drink after.

'Very well, then.' He turned to Jack. 'I sent you

to marry for money. It seems you have failed and married for love instead.'

'No, my lord. Not love, certainly.' Jack was waving his hands in denial, as though embarrassed at the idea that he had failed so completely in following what should have been simple instructions.

'Infatuation, then. But I do not blame you. I know, more than many, of the dangers one treads when following the call of one's own heart. Only one question remains: what is to be done now?'

Jack seemed to relax a little, once he was sure of the earl's mood. 'There is more. The lady, herself, is in distress. She married me, expecting your money to rescue her family from difficulties caused by your brother.'

'Damn!' It was the first time she'd seen Spayne act with anything less than aplomb and it startled her. Then his calm returned. 'I am sorry, my dear. But it upsets me to know that my brother has caused you bother. Henry is a villain and has been so for as long as I can remember. It is bad enough that he gives me trouble, but unforgivable that he hurts others. If you could explain the nature of the problem, I will find a way to rectify it.'

'But Jack said you could not.'

'It does not matter what Jack said, or that I have no fortune left to spare. Henry is my brother and my responsibility.' His words should have encouraged her, but suddenly Spayne looked a little older than he had when she had come into the room. It made her feel bad for burdening him. 'Please, tell me what he has done now.'

Jack gave an encouraging nod and Thea sighed. 'He has swindled my father out of a great deal of money. And though I have pleaded with him to relent, he has refused.'

'He made an offer of protection,' Jack added.

Spayne made a huffing noise as though he was disgusted, but not particularly surprised.

'And while I do not doubt her, she has been less than forthcoming of the details of the transaction that has caused all the trouble.' Jack turned suddenly to her, and it felt as though she were standing trial and guilty of some horrible crime. 'Just what artefact did your father purchase that could have been worth so much?'

Spayne looked at her expectantly.

'It is very complicated,' Thea said, not knowing how best to start.

'We have time,' Jack said, folding his arms and settling into a chair. Both men were staring at her now and the silence was nearly as pregnant as it had been when Jack had revealed her lack of funds. It was clear that they were not going to say another word until they had heard her story.

Very well, then. If she must tell it, she had best make a clean breast, start at the beginning and give them every last embarrassing detail. 'It all began,' she said, 'when my father married an actress.'

Spayne laughed.

'An actress?' For the first time since she'd met him, Jack was caught flat-footed, unable to respond with more than two words and a gaped-mouth stare.

Thea looked around carefully, to be sure that no servants could hear. It was hardly a secret, but the less said on her mother's career, the better. 'Mother has worked very hard in the last twenty years to put it behind her and, for the most part, she has succeeded. The scandal is nearly forgotten. Although, when we are alone, she is more candid about her past than is proper.'

'Twenty years,' Jack repeated, as though the passage of time had some added significance. 'When she performed, was she, by any chance, one Antonia Knowles?'

'How did you know?' It had been a long time since someone had recognised her, but it seemed that the past was impossible to bury.

Jack smiled at the memory. 'Because I saw her perform. She did Ophelia. And I wept buckets when she died.'

'You saw my mother? On the stage?'

He closed his eyes, his head raised to the ceiling as though giving thanks for an answered prayer. Then, a sigh of ecstasy escaped his lips.

And as she sometimes did, Thea felt an odd prickling annoyance at the attention her mother garnered so effortlessly. It was common, earthy and certainly nothing Thea herself aspired to. But men other than Father seemed to find her near to irresistible when she made an effort to call attention to herself. The fact that it came from the man who would be her son-in-law was more an-noying by far than any past irritations. 'She is much older now,' Thea reminded him.

'But still a surpassingly handsome woman,' Jack replied, unfazed by her tone. Then he ex-amined her as though it was their first meeting. 'You hold many features in common with her.'

'Because she bore me,' Thea snapped. 'It is hardly a surprise that I favour her.'

But Jack was no longer looking at her, but at the woman on the faraway stage. 'Antonia was the most radiant, most beautiful, most talented woman I had ever seen. I fell quite in love with her that day. It was hopeless, of course. She had many admirers, older, richer, more powerful…'

'And she married my father,' Thea said, firmly. While it was some comfort to think that her mother was as talented as she claimed, she had no wish to think of the men that might have come before her father in her mother's affections.

'Ahh. Yes.' Jack finally recognised the awk-wardness of the situation, staring contritely at Thea as though that would be enough to mollify her. But Spayne still chuckled in the background.

Thea continued her story. 'Father's family was less than approving of the match, although he has never regretted it. But at that time, Grandfather set the majority of Father's inheritance aside until such time as he produced a son to carry on the family in what they hoped would be a more respectable fashion. Many provisions were made for the rearing and education of Father's heir, and the money still sits, waiting, drawing interest for my brother.'

'And do you have a sibling?' Spayne asked.

'Unfortunately, no. My parents have done their best to raise me in a way that would be sufficient to allay Grandfather's concerns. I was educated in a boarding school of his choosing, so that I might have all the graces, skills and manners of a proper young lady.'

'And a head just as empty,' Jack added, availing himself of the brandy and pouring a drink far too generous for noon.

'I was as far removed from my mother's past as it was possible to be.' She glared back at Jack. 'Until recently.'

'How nice for you,' Jack said with no trace

of apology for his true identity. 'But it did your family no good. Your father still needs his inheritance?'

'Unfortunately, Grandfather is in some degree right about my father's profligacy. Over the years, he spent lavishly to be sure that my mother was welcomed into society. Their entertainments were grand and well attended. He spent even more on governesses and schools for me.' And in the end, it had done her no good, for she had fallen into the same trap as her father. Perhaps it was some sort of genetic predisposition. 'There was money enough left, of course,' she added. 'But they have always lived in the assumption that there would be more in the future. It has been twenty years since their marriage. While it is not impossible that my mother might have a child, with each passing year it becomes more unlikely. When Mr de Warde made his suggestion, Father was only too eager to believe him.'

'And that suggestion was?' Spayne prompted.

Thea winced. 'A certain statue that was guaranteed to increase fertility and fecundity. It is an Indian god, I believe. Mr de Warde said that to possess it would most surely result in the birth of a male child.'

This time, it was Jack who laughed. 'All this bother over an aphrodisiac?'

She could feel herself blushing from toes to hairline. 'I know it sounds foolish. That is why I did not tell you before. It is intensely painful for me to admit…' *that my parents are such idiots.* She hoped he understood. And then she added with more sympathy, 'But considering present circumstances, *you* must understand the lengths that one might go to when moved by desperation.'

That, at least, silenced Jack's mirth. She added, 'Mr de Warde was most convincing.'

'Oh, I have no doubt of that,' Spayne said with narrowed eyes. 'And I am quite sympathetic to your father's need for a male child.'

'I see. Is that why you need Jack to play your heir? Because you cannot provide one for yourself?'

Now there was another embarrassing silence. And Thea remembered Jack's reticence to reveal the whole of Spayne's story. Despite the manners and graces she thought she possessed, she had blundered badly in asking this powerful man to tell her what were probably embarrassing secrets. 'I am sorry,' she said quickly. 'I did not mean to pry, for that is no concern of mine.'

'That is all right,' Spayne said with a kind voice that put her immediately at ease. 'You are part of the family now and there is no need to keep the truth from you.'

Since Jack was not really his son, the earl owed her nothing at all. 'But…'

The gentle-spirited man looked firm, younger and resolved. Though a mild manner might be deceiving, he was every bit as powerful as she had expected him to be and his look intimidated her to silence. 'I will never think of you as anything less than a daughter, no matter what might happen in the next weeks. You married a man who I have claimed as a son. The rest is of no consequence.'

It would serve no purpose to argue her way out of the connection, no matter what the truth of the matter. She lowered her head in respect. 'Thank you, my lord.'

Spayne smiled, as though happy to see the matter settled. 'Now that we have established that you deserve to know the rest of my story and how I came to be hiring a son.' He gave a fond smile to Jack, as though it might actually be possible to buy family. Then he continued. 'It is not as if there has never been a Kenton. I provided one right enough, marrying when I was young, as was expected of me. Family and friends saw the boy when he was born and can attest to the fact that he existed.' Spayne sighed. And now, along with the lines of age on his face, Thea could see a deep and old sadness. 'The boy was never right. Weak of lung and weak of intellect as well. But a sweeter child you would not hope to find. My wife and I took him abroad to Italy for his health. But he sickened and died, as did his mother.' Spayne stared into the fire. 'I thought I'd lost everything that day. And I meant to give myself over to vice.'

'Surely not, my lord.' Although she could quite believe it of his brother, there was nothing about the man before her to indicate a taste for dissipation.

He gave her a fond smile. 'Fear not, my dear.

I was not nearly so wicked as I thought. After several years in Italy, I came to the conclusion that, when all was said and done, I simply preferred the company of men.'

'My father often says that the company at his club is quite bracing and he can understand why some men spend so much time there,' Thea responded, not quite sure why Spayne's innocent admission would be delivered in such hushed tones.

There was yet another prolonged silence in the room. Then, Jack laid a hand on her shoulder. 'That is not quite what Spayne means, Thea. He prefers men in the same way that I prefer the company of ladies.'

Now she was blushing again as she remembered some of her mother's more inappropriate stories of her equally inappropriate friends. 'But that is illegal. And immoral.'

'So we are told,' Jack agreed. 'But then, so is cheating your father out of his money. And that is something that hurt you and your entire family. Any harm Spayne might cause is limited to the people participating. It is hardly fair, is it?'

She gave a hesitant shake of her head.

'And that is why I did not immediately tell you the whole of Lord Spayne's story. It was not my job to share the man's secrets without his permission.'

'Too many know them already,' Spayne agreed.

'But no one learned of the death of your son,' Thea prodded. 'Why did you keep such a secret as that? Were you ashamed of him?'

'Do not think that by my change in behaviour, I mean to deny a moment of my marriage to my Catherine, for I loved her as best I could and was faithful while she lived. I loved my son as well.' He said it hurriedly, as if he could not wait to reassure her. Then, there was another guilty pause before he began again. 'But when I returned, it seemed easier to tell no one that I had lost my little boy, along with his mother. There had always been rumours about my habits and doubts about my commitment to the marriage. I knew I was obligated to provide an heir to carry on the name and title, and I had done so. But I had not the heart to do it twice.'

'But you did not have to marry again, or to

have another child.' The *ton* would hardly be surprised to find that the child had died along with the mother. They had been halfway to convincing themselves that Spayne was a victim of tragedy. What would one more detail matter?

'I could make Henry my heir,' Spayne said with disgust. 'He has always chafed under the unfairness of being the second son. You cannot imagine what it is like to know that your own flesh and blood sees you not as a brother, but as an obstacle.' Spayne frowned. 'Things eased when he was removed one further step from the title. But then, I lost little Jack… I knew, when my brother heard of it, all the troubles would start again. But if people thought that I had a delicate child who was being educated abroad…' He shrugged in embarrassment. 'At the time, it seemed the lesser of two evils. It was foolish. I was wrong. The more time passed, the more difficult it was to admit the truth. And then Henry demanded to meet the man that stood between him and the title. He had become convinced that the real Kenton was dead. And he began to apply pressure to me.'

'What sort of pressure?' Thea asked, truly curious what there might be that could frighten a man with so much power.

'At first, it was merely an exposure of my habits.'

'It is a crime,' Thea agreed. 'You could hang for it.'

'But that is not likely.' Spayne gave her a knowing smile. 'That part of my nature has been an open secret for some time. Since I know certain facts about others, we are all agreed to keep mum and look the other way. While Henry might think he could ruin me, he is mostly a nuisance. But it would be an embarrassment to have my own brother making accusations. So I paid to quiet him, increasing his monthly portion each time he threatened. Over the years, Henry's silence has grown into one of my largest monthly expenses.' Spayne frowned. 'But of late, he would not stop asking about Kenton. And his insinuations have taken a much darker tone. He was hinting that my son was dead and that I was the cause of it. If I did not give him all I have, he would see me swing for murder.'

'Blackmail?' Thea said, shocked.

'I was sure it would not be enough. He wants the title—and for that I must die.'

'You owed him nothing,' Thea insisted. 'The accusations are false.'

'I have been lying about so much for so long, it would be laughable to stand in court and reveal, on my word of honour, that the boy is dead, but I am innocent of it.'

'And so you found Jack.' Thea rubbed her temple, trying to organise her thoughts. It was a mad plan. But the more she listened to it, delivered in the patient voice of the Earl, the more sensible it seemed. All the more proof that Miss Pennyworth had been right. Honesty was the jewel in the crown of character if lying caused so much trouble. 'Oh what a tangled web we weave,' she muttered.

Jack made a face. 'Leave off quoting Scott, my sweet, and go back to Shakespeare. "Assume a virtue, if you have it not."'

'And that is what you are doing?' she said, eyeing Jack with suspicion. 'It sounds more like deception to me.'

'Either way, it has been quite effective,' the earl said with a smile. 'Henry can prove nothing now that I have produced the heir. There is little point in hounding me into my grave, only to see my son take my place.'

'And I am just married,' Jack said with a grin. 'Perhaps there will be a child to put Uncle Henry one step further away. I expect the thought makes him livid.'

'A child?' If the truth had not been revealed on their wedding night, she might very well have… The shudder that resulted from the thought left her body with a strange, nervous energy. She firmly dismissed it. 'You will certainly not get a son from me. Even if you did, he would not be the heir, because you are not really Kenton.'

'Do not worry, my dear,' Spayne said, reaching out to pat her hand. 'Such extreme measures are not necessary. I could not hope for a better son than I have found in Jack.' He smiled at the other man, and Thea wondered, for a moment, if the man had forgotten that he had no relationship to the actor. 'He has performed admirably in all I have asked of him.'

'All things save one,' Jack reminded him. 'I have not, as yet, repaired your fortune. Nor have I given de Warde the punishment he truly deserves.'

Spayne looked worried. 'As I have explained to you, that is a difficult matter.'

'It will not be solved by giving him more money,' Jack replied. 'For now, he is content with bleeding you. But he wants the title. He will not be satisfied until all who stand between him and it are gone. The only way you will be sure is to remove the threat permanently, just as he wishes to do with you.'

Spayne looked at him with the aristocratic coldness Thea had expected from the first. 'You are still speaking of my brother. If I resort to, as you put it, permanently removing him, I am become the thing he threatens me with. I will not stoop to violence, nor do I wish you to do so on my behalf.'

'Very well, my lord.' Jack bowed his head in sincere respect. It was clearly an argument they'd had before that Jack did not expect to win. 'But

I have a suggestion that might remedy the fact. My wife...'

The look Thea gave him made him pause and correct himself. 'Miss Banester has a score to settle with de Warde, just as you do. The source of all troubles is de Warde. Amputation is not an option, but all the same, we must treat the disease and not the symptoms of it. Your brother must be given a taste of his own medicine.'

'And how do you mean to do that?' Spayne looked interested.

'We will trick him into giving us his money. And then we will discredit him, to remove the teeth from his accusations against you.'

'And how will we do this?' Spayne asked eagerly.

'The first step will be to return to London and organise a ball to celebrate our recent marriage. You must come as well, Father. No begging off as you managed with our wedding.' Jack grinned. 'We must be as one big, happy family.'

Thea imagined the addition of her own family to the mess that had been created and gave a delicate shudder of horror. 'Such a public display is unwise in the extreme and quite beyond our financial reach. Have you forgotten? We have no money.'

'But we still have credit.' Apparently, the state of their finances, though it worried her to no end, did nothing to render Jack any less cheerful. 'It must be resplendent. Spare no expense, for we will be inviting my dear Uncle Henry. I think it is time that he got to know me.'

'So we are to go further into debt, parade our sham marriage before the *ton* and invite the deplorable Mr de Warde into our home as we do it. What is the next step in this wonderful plan of yours?' Although Thea was almost afraid to hear it.

'I will tell you the day I know it,' Jack said with a smile worthy of the stage. 'For now, it is a work in progress. Little more than an improvisation.' He gave a dramatic gesture, as though he was building castles in the air.

Thea groaned in exasperation, but Spayne gave a satisfied smile. 'Well, do the best you can with it, boy. I am sure it will come to you after dinner and a good night's sleep.' Then he looked from

Jack to Thea expectantly. 'Now you must go and refresh yourselves. I am sure the journey from London was tiring, and you will have things to discuss between yourselves that do not concern an old man. I shall have the cook send something to your room.' With that, he picked up the book upon his desk and settled himself into a chair by the fire, giving every indication that the interview was at an end.

Chapter Six

'That went better than I'd hoped,' Jack said, pushing his plate away and wiping his mouth on a napkin. They'd withdrawn to the rooms allotted to them by Spayne, which were adjoining suites in the master wing of the house. By the time Thea could be changed from her travelling dress, the servants had brought them an impressive display of cold meats and a wine that proved Spayne's cellars were as old as his title. Then they'd arranged it neatly on a table in her sitting room and departed as quickly as they had come.

The single rose in the vase between them was most likely a commemoration of their recent wedding. It gave Thea a sick feeling to think that their complete privacy was given with the assumption that the newly married couple would be wishing an early bedtime and no help preparing for it. She could not decide which bothered her more, the false intimacy or the idea that Jack had been unsure of his welcome. If he had expected the earl to throw them both into the street, it was irksome to think that he had led her into it with no warning. 'You anticipated trouble?'

'Not really. But then, I am never sure of Spayne. His whole plan is so outlandish it is a continual shock that he chooses to stick to it.' Jack looked back at the door, as though he could see through it, and back to the ground floor. 'In fact, everything about him is a surprise.' He seemed not so much frightened as honestly puzzled by the way things had gone. 'I keep waiting for him to wake up and see things for what they are.' He looked back at Thea and smiled. 'Or to wake myself and find that it has all been a strange dream. It would make far more sense if I were to find myself back on the gallows, feeling the rope tighten as the stool was kicked out from under me.'

His expression was open and unguarded, almost innocent, compared to the worldly assurance she was used to seeing from Lord Kenton.

It came upon her with the same sudden tug and loss of breath that he was describing, that she might be seeing the real Jack Briggs. For all his big talk and roguish threats, he did not seem to be such a bad fellow. He was just as handsome as Kenton, but with a vulnerability that she had not expected. And he displayed a sincere affection for his benefactor. 'Spayne seems to allow you much latitude in your behaviour.' She had expected to find something akin to servitude. But what she had witnessed in the library was closer to partnership between the two men. It might even have been considered friendship.

'When he rescued me, I had not expected that, either. For weeks, I waited in apprehension, expecting to find the hidden trick that would land me in a worse spot than I'd occupied.' He smiled at Thea. 'Since I'd already faced the hangman, it took some doing to guess at a more grim scenario.'

'You might still be hung, drawn and quartered,' Thea offered. 'That is the punishment for treason, is it not? Or perhaps they will only hang and behead you. I am not sure if it signifies. But impersonating the son of a peer must have some punishment more severe than death.'

Jack gave her a pained look. 'Thank you for a possibility I had not yet considered. And please remove the look of hope from your face. Consider that Spayne might be punished as well for his part in it.'

'That would be a shame,' Thea agreed. The man, for all his faults, was being kind to her, which was more than could be said for his brother.

'He is more than a little barmy for getting himself into such a predicament. But he did not seek this wild hare of an idea to harm you or anyone else,' Jack reminded her. 'He approaches his difficulties with his brother in the same haphazard way he deals with his finances. I have done what I can to set those right. His situation is not irreparable. Had we enough time and no interference, I would have the coffers full again in a year or two. But with his brother's continual meddling, it will be quite impossible.'

'He allows you to handle his money?' If possible, this was even stranger than that the man had lied about his own son. It appeared he had turned the running of a sizeable estate over to a stranger.

Jack guessed her thoughts and responded with a mocking tug on his forelock. 'While I may not be educated in a manner that you respect, your ladyship, I know how many beans make five. And that is more than can be said for Spayne, who cannot seem to grasp that a small economy like eating a mutton dinner instead of beef saves enough to fix a tenant's roof. He does not think further than the moment ahead. In short, he needs a keeper and the job has fallen to me.'

'He must be a fool, indeed, to trust an itinerant player who deserved to be hanged as a thief,' Thea said.

'Or perhaps I am just a man who is grateful that I have a chance to help my rescuer,' Jack corrected, all trace of mirth gone from his face. 'You may think what you like of me, but I would caution you not to take my admission just now as an invitation to show Spayne anything less than the total respect he deserves. I might also remind you that your own father is no wiser, for he spent all he had on some Indian novelty to make him potent.'

Thea fell silent.

'And as for my career? You have no right to look down your nose at me, considering the identity of your mother.'

'Mother was an actress,' Thea admitted, 'but that was many years ago. Now she uses those talents to navigate in society. Her play-acting goes no further than that, because it is improper to be so false.'

'You had no desire to follow in her footsteps?' Jack asked, interested.

'Certainly not. I am my father's child as well, and my grandfather's. I was properly schooled to take my place in society. My understanding of the rules and boundaries of my place is excellent.'

'Which was why you married me,' he said, with a grin.

'I married Kenton,' she reminded him, shaking her head. 'They were very clear at school of how things were supposed to be. I knew how to address everyone, from the king to the lowliest servant. I knew who I was not to speak to or acknowledge at all.' She gave him a pointed look.

'If you believed all they told you, you'd be forced to cut your own mother,' Jack reminded her. 'And Spayne should be hanged for being a molly. But the same people would allow de Warde to pass amongst them unpunished.'

Thea remembered the acute embarrassment she'd felt as her school friends had talked of their noble families and she'd remained silent, afraid of what they might say if they knew the truth of hers. They would not have given the time of day to Jack Briggs. Yet any one of them would have married Spayne's heir, or even Spayne, if the opportunity had presented itself. The rules had all made sense, until she had tried to put her training into effect. 'Nothing is as it seems and no one is as they appear to be. You are not Lord Kenton. The earl has been lying about his entire life. De Warde lied to my father. In turn, my father lied to my mother and me, until we had no money at all on which to manage. Nothing I knew was true.' *Except me*, she reminded herself. *I know who I am—and that must not change.*

'It is a rude awakening for you.' He patted her hand. 'But I will help you. It will be clearer after you've had a good night's rest in a real bed.' He gave her a gentle, encouraging smile. 'I doubt you slept well last night and I did not make it easy for you.' He stood up from the table and walked to her side, offering his hand. 'I am sorry for that. Despite how it may seem, I mean you no harm.'

Hesitantly, she put her hand in his. He was right. She was tired, which explained her current confusion.

'With your help, I will make things better for you and your family, and for Spayne as well. And you will never again have to endure the advances of Mr de Warde.'

That would be no small thing, for she had seen the look in his eyes when he talked to her, and known there was something much darker on de Warde's mind than a simple business transaction. 'How can you be sure?' she whispered.

'Because if he tries anything, I will take care of him.' Jack flexed his arm and she saw the muscles tighten beneath his coat sleeve. Perhaps stage fencing and mock fighting were not as impressive as a true duel, but they had not left him a weakling. She remembered the way his arms had felt when they'd danced, before she'd known the truth about him, and the easy way he handled even the most spirited horse in Hyde Park. The thought of intimacy with powerful Kenton had left her breathless with excitement. Jack Briggs might not have the title, but his body was the same one that had held her. The knowledge that he would use his strength in defence of her was strangely appealing.

She reached out and touched his arm. It was the first tenderness she'd shown him since their wedding breakfast and it made him smile. He pulled her to her feet and into his arms, just as he had in the weeks before their marriage. For a moment, she closed her eyes and pretended that he was still Kenton and could take all her problems away.

His head was near her ear, his voice barely a whisper. 'Whatever happens, and whatever I might call upon you to do, you must not worry. You will be safe.'

Without thinking, she dropped her head so that

it rested against the front of his coat. 'That would be nice.'

He was stroking her hair and she allowed it. It was an innocent gesture, no different than comforting a child. But then he touched her chin with the tip of a finger and tipped her face up to look at his and the smile on his face was something much different. He closed his eyes, leaned forwards and pressed his lips to hers in a kiss so chaste as to be almost brotherly.

But it did not feel innocent to her. It felt like the first kiss of a long evening and a reason to set aside all the rules and follow where ever the night led. When he withdrew, the warmth, the tingling and the sweetness of his lips stayed with her.

And then he changed. The light in his eyes died and he spoke with a casual tone that told her this was of no importance to him. 'There, there. Feeling better?'

'Yes. I think I am.' She was better than better. Not as good as she would have been, if the kiss had been longer, but that would have been most unwise and he was right to end it.

He slipped an arm about her shoulders, gathering her closer in a way that should feel fatherly and unthreatening, but even at this brief contact her body was beginning to respond. Her knees felt watery. Her heart beat faster. Her body felt hot and constricted by her gown.

Then he turned her body, kissed her lightly on the forehead and released her. 'Sleep well, Thea. We will talk again in the morning.'

'Goodnight, Jack.'

Then he was gone through the connecting door to his suite. And she was alone.

What the devil had that been about?

Jack passed through his own rooms and kept walking out into the hall, down the main stairs and towards the brandy decanter waiting in Spayne's library. As Kenton, he could have rung for a servant and had a glass brought to his room. But right now, it seemed important to put as much physical space as possible between himself and Lady Kenton.

Or else to close the distance completely. He still was not sure what he wanted. She'd been sleepy and willing in his arms with a bed scant feet away. As on the night of their marriage, she'd been wearing some ridiculously frilly dressing gown that had given little more than an illusion of decency. And he had not even bothered to take a decent look. He had done the gentlemanly thing and gazed into her eyes.

When in thirty years had he ever been so foolish? Common sense told him that weakness was to be exploited. He was only playing a part. If he did it well, then he would be rewarded by a night or two with a woman, who, if not the very image of perfection, was a blood relation to it.

But Kenton looked away, damn him. The man was a paragon. And he was praying on Jack's nerves. It was good that the role would be ending soon. If Jack stayed too long in it, he might make a permanent and rather foolish change of character, like that thoroughly depressing fellow he'd known who could not seem to play anything but Hamlet.

But rather than mooning about, talking to skulls, Jack'd be trapped as a gentleman. It would be almost as suicidal. He would be the sort of fellow who would not press the advantage when the lovely Cyn was at her most vulnerable. He would tell himself that a simple kiss would be enough. His soul would sigh over it, as it had tonight.

Rubbish. As though a passionless peck meant anything. It was no different than those he'd given to dozens of actresses in the final scene of the insipid comedies that amused the masses.

But this kiss had tried to change him. As he'd taken it, he had been worrying that she would never allow even this small liberty. They had been close to real intimacy on their wedding night, bare hours away. But the affection of their engagement proved both brief and ephemeral. At the time, he had not taken it seriously. And then he had lost it all in an instant. Should it come again, he would remember to appreciate it.

After tonight, he could imagine that there would be more. And he had a very good imagination. He was seeing not a brief passion, but a lasting and sincere affinity. It was almost as bad as his delusion that Spayne was anything like a real father.

He must remember the hollow sound the gallows steps had made as he'd climbed them. That had been the last real sound he'd heard, before this farce had began. And he would not come to that place again. At the first sign of trouble, he would run and leave the girl and the earl to fend for themselves.

Reassured and returned to himself, he continued down the hall and pushed through the doors of the library, relieved that it was dark and quiet. He went to the brandy decanter and poured a stiff drink, tossed it back and had another. Far smarter for him to enjoy Spayne's liquor, and Kenton's house, his clothes and, if the chance came again, his woman. He would hold the pleasures close, but keep the genuine feelings as far away as was possible.

'Trouble with your wife?' The voice behind him came as a surprise. Apparently he had not bothered to check the shadows to be sure that he was free of company. Spayne was reclining on a sofa by the fire.

And worse, the man was meddling with his mind. Their arrangement gave him no right to, and Jack had been foolish to encourage any closeness between them. 'What makes it your business?'

'Nothing, I suppose.' Spayne yawned and sat up. 'But when a man is given to bolting brandy at this hour, it is often the result of a woman.'

'You are lucky not to bother with them,' Jack said bitterly.

'Men are no better when they decide to be difficult,' Spayne said, holding out his glass to be refilled. 'But tell me what you are making of the lovely Cynthia.'

'I can make nothing of her at all,' Jack grumbled. 'The woman is a mystery. Soft as a kitten one moment and ice cold the next.'

'And you are attracted to her.' The earl gave a nod of approval.

'What sane man would not be?' Jack said a little defensively. 'You saw her. I know she is not your type, of course.'

'I have preferences,' the earl corrected, 'but I am not blind. Nor am I dead to all feeling. I did manage to have a son.' He thought for a moment. 'One son that I am sure of. I was young once and got up to as much trouble as I could find before becoming set in my ways. But enough of me. We are speaking of you and Thea. She is a beautiful girl.'

'As sweet as an unplucked berry,' Jack agreed.

'It is no surprise that you fancy her. But it is more than that, isn't it?'

Jack grunted in disgust.

'You like her.' The earl smiled again. 'That is hardly surprising as well. She is a most pleasant girl.'

'Pleasant?' Jack erupted and snorted again. 'Clearly you have forgotten whatever you once knew about women. She is bigoted and shallow. Worse yet, she is proud of these qualities. She is one of the most disagreeable females I have ever met.'

'I have not forgotten all that much. She is contrary. Those are often the sort that are the most desirable,' the earl said with confidence. 'You like her, and you want her.'

'I want the girl I thought she was,' Jack allowed. 'All sweetness, like a honey pot. But while the body is all honey, the tongue is like being stung by the bees.'

'Too much honey becomes cloying. But I've found that an occasional bee sting can be a god-send,' the earl commented, flexing his fingers. 'It gets the blood flowing in the veins and feeling back into the extremities.'

Jack narrowed his eyes. 'I have no trouble with feeling in my extremities, I assure you. I can get that from any woman. And I would be far smarter should I seek the tingling with a professional and not that harpy that I have married.'

'*Harpy*? Surely that is too strong a word.'

Jack rubbed his brow. 'Perhaps.' He knew it was. She had been soft and sweet just now when he'd left her room. Why was it so difficult to give credit to the girl who was in as difficult a spot as he was? 'She aggravates me. And there is nothing I can do about it.'

'Nothing?' The earl raised an eyebrow.

'Nothing she will permit,' Jack amended.

'Then things have changed since I last knew a woman,' the earl announced. 'At that time, wives were not allowed to permit or refuse. They acquiesced.' He gave Jack a sharp look. 'Of course, a gentleman made sure they acquiesced graciously. He did not give them a reason for refusing.'

'I?' Jack gestured broadly to himself. 'I gave her no reason to refuse me, other than that I am who I am. When she thought I was Kenton, she was as smooth as butter. It was only when she discovered my true past that she closed the bedroom door.' Of course, he had been the one to close the door tonight, but details hardly mattered.

'Can you honestly say that you'd have found her as appealing had she been a poor woman?'

'Of course I would. As I said before, just look at her. I simply would not have married her. Before or after. We'd have had our fun and that would have been the end of it. But now?'

'You are trapped together,' the earl affirmed.

'Until we can sort out the mess that you have made with de Warde.' It was no mess of Jack's and they had all best remember the fact. He could leave at any time. If he wished to, of course. But for some reason he was loathe to go.

'And you cannot find a way to make the best of this? I would think, with your skills as an actor and your claims to romantic ability, you'd have made some progress by now.'

Jack stared at his make-believe father, wondering if he had understood correctly, for it almost sounded as if the man advocated seducing the lady. 'That would hardly be proper.'

'Pish,' the earl said, dabbing at his nose with a handkerchief. 'You are married, my boy.'

'But am I? Really?' Strangely, he had given no thought to the eyes of God and the law when getting involved in this scheme. But now that he was in the thick of it, the idea chafed at him.

'What is marriage, really, but a commitment between two people?'

'Two people who are using their true names to marry,' Jack added. 'As far as I know, she is married to Kenton. And at such time as that man comes along, I will gladly give her up to him.'

Spayne laughed. 'In the words of your favourite playwright, "What's in a name?" You stood at an altar. I suspect God knew who you were when you said the vows.'

That was almost more disquieting to think about, for now Jack could imagine the Deity watching over and blessing and rendering irrevocable a commitment he had not meant to make. 'Then he will see when I break them and leave her.'

'As long as you stay, you are married. But when you stray?' The earl shrugged again. 'My brother has gone through the ceremony, of course. And some might call it more real than yours was. But you have not seen the way he treats his wife. The poor thing is little more than a cipher, trailing after him when he needs to seem respectable. But she is forgotten at home for the rest of the time, alone, childless and forced to turn a blind eye to his villainy.'

'Childless,' Jack said, as a wisp of an idea began to form in a dark corner of his brain. Then he focused on Spayne again. 'You are right, in any case. Mrs De Warde is a fine example of what I would not wish on any woman.' He brightened a little. 'In comparison, Thea is lucky to have me.' It was not as if he was some seducing rake, should he succeed with her. Her child would at least appear legitimate. It was more than his own father had left for him.

'And it is not as if I will not take care of the girl and her offspring should anything unexpected occur,' Spayne reminded him. 'I should think, when she marries again after you are gone, that a maidenhead on a widow would be much harder to explain than the absence of one.'

'I would probably be doing her a service by dispensing with it and saving her the awkward explanations, but, no. I cannot.' And where had that last come from? Kenton, of course. Diddling with the pretty was exactly what Jack had planned to do when he had chosen her. And now he could not bring himself to do it. 'Damn you, Spayne. I fear you have given me scruples.'

The earl laughed. 'You speak of it as though it were a disease, my boy. As if I have given you measles along with a name.'

'It might as well be. Unless the woman proves more willing than she has, I feel a moral obligation not to act on my desires, despite what the physical side of me might feel.' He glared at the earl again. 'Hence the bees. I am stuck with an arm up to the shoulder in the hive, the honey is on my fingers and I do not dare stick them in my mouth. Damn you, and damn the woman as well for being as sweet as she is.'

Spayne laughed at him, showing no mercy whatsoever for his difficulties. 'Mark my words, boy. The time will come soon enough when the prospect of getting stung will not be enough to stop you from a taste. And when it does, you have nothing to be ashamed of. Neither of you will come to harm by following your hearts.'

'Brave words from a man who should know better,' Jack said bitterly and tossed back the last of his drink. 'The sooner I am done with this and gone away, the better. Although it is vexing at the moment, in the future I will see that the girl is right to reject me. In the meantime, the safest course will be to keep my hands to myself.'

Chapter Seven

The return trip to London was quite different from the outbound trip, with none of the sparring and megrims of the day before. Spayne saw them off after a hearty breakfast with a promise to follow as soon as they could assure him of a real need for his presence, since he refused, even now, to spend any more time than was necessary in the same town with his brother.

But this left Thea alone with her husband. And despite the tenderness of the previous evening, there existed a kind of wary silence between them as though neither could decide upon the next move. At least today he was not whistling, apparently having decided to fall back on the part of Kenton so as not to provoke her.

In turn, she chose to behave as she thought

Lady Kenton would, polite and reserved, receiving his courtesies as though they were sincere and responding to them with respect. It made the trip easier, as well as her re-introduction to the servants at the Kenton town house. It was clear that they held their master, if he was such, in a sort of awe. He might as well have been the Duke of Wellington, for the scraping and bowing of the footman, the rigid posture of the butler, round-eyed looks he got from the matronly housekeeper and the flounced skirts and pouting lips of the housemaids, which he magnanimously ignored.

She would have thought that, if a common actor was given such utter devotion from a gaggle of young ladies, he'd have taken advantage and worked it to his own ends. But from the disappointed looks on some of the faces, it was clear that he had no dalliances, no favourites, no scandals, and had done nothing to render his image any less shiny.

It seemed he meant to play Kenton as the sort of honourable gentleman that one hoped for but seldom saw in true society.

Then she remembered the way he had treated her on the previous two evenings. She had been convinced he was nothing more than Jack Briggs, once the bedroom door had closed and the facade could be dropped. And yet, though she would hardly call him polite, she had felt no fear for her virtue, or the sense that he might try to trick her into an intimacy she did not welcome. While not always to her liking, his actions were at least totally sincere.

But for the moment, he was being Kenton. And Kenton disappeared into his study, once they were through with the formalities. It was not her job to question what her husband did with his time, if he did not choose to spend it with her. He had requested that his man of business be sent for and was assured that the previous day's mail awaited him on his desk, just as he liked it. It appeared that spinning wild tales of India in London ballrooms was only a facet of what his life had become since Spayne had found him. The rest, though mundane, was carried out with the same care and diligence.

And she had her job to do as well. She gave a

few hurried instructions to the cook and house-keeper about dinner and a warning that there would be plans for a ball. Then she retired to the grand rooms provided for her use, which adjoined the master's bedroom.

Once there, she found that her maid, Polly, had followed from her old home and was laying out a familiar day dress on the unfamiliar counter-pane. It was a change she should have welcomed. Had she not been waiting for years to be truly out from under the roof of her parents, starting a new life in a house of her own? But if that was true, then why did she feel something not unlike vertigo, as though her whole life had slipped vio-lently to one side, trying to throw her off balance? And why was a tear rolling down her cheek?

Without a word, the maid offered her a hand-kerchief. Thea returned a wet smile of gratitude. 'I do not know what's come over me.'

'Nothing to fear, your ladyship.' Polly gave a little grin as she said the carefully rehearsed hon-orific, which was another reminder that she was no longer Miss Cynthia Banester. 'It comes over brides sometimes like this. At least my sisters say so, for they are both out of the house and properly married. It is a very big change, after all.'

'You have no idea,' Thea said.

'Might I suggest a visit with your mother? It'll be a great comfort.'

Comfort was the last thing she imagined when speaking with Antonia. Over the years, she had spent more time soothing her mother's nerves than receiving comfort. But she surprised herself by saying, 'That would be nice.' And once she decided upon going, it did seem like the only answer. In the carriage, she found her emotions even more tumultuous than they had been at Kenton House. By the time she reached her parents' doorstep, she was touching her face regularly with the damp handkerchief. And at the first sight of her female parent, Thea could not help herself. She launched herself into her mother's arms, weeping like an infant with a wail of 'Mother'.

'My dear,' the woman responded, gathering her close. For all her foolishness over some things, her affection was genuine and Thea welcomed it now. 'Whatever is the matter? And why are you not on your honeymoon? I did not expect to see you back in London for some weeks.'

'Honeymoon.' She let out a fresh wail, trying to remind herself that the lack of such had been more of a narrow escape than a denial of reward. 'There will be no honeymoon. Because there is no marriage. My husband is not truly Kenton.'

'I do not understand. Is he cruel? Did he hurt you?' Her mother pushed her away, searching her face and arms for signs of abuse.

Thea shook her head. 'He is not even real. He is an actor, pretending to be a gentleman.'

She felt her mother stiffen and glance hurriedly around the hall to be sure that they had not been overheard. Then she pulled Thea into the drawing room and shut the door.

'We are alone. Now quickly, tell me all. What did Spayne have to say on the matter? Or did you not go to his house as you were planning?'

'He knew all along. It is terribly complicated.'

'Well, then, there is nothing to worry about.' She could feel her mother slump in relief. 'If Spayne acknowledges him, then who will dare to doubt? And if we know it? What is a little secret between families?'

'You do not mean to tell me that you approve?' Thea pushed away from her. It was just the sort of morally suspect advice she should have expected from her mother.

'It is simply that I admire a part well played,' her mother said with no little awe. 'I never would have suspected him. And I, of all people, should be able to spot a false coin. He acts as grand as any viscount of my acquaintance, and I have known a good number. Although he is more personable and more handsome than most,' she said thoughtfully. 'But those are hardly faults, my dove.'

'He tricked me,' Thea said indignantly. 'He has no money and no name.'

'Neither do you,' her mother replied. 'I believe you were perpetrating a similar trick upon him when you forced him to offer for you.'

'It was not the same at all,' Thea insisted. 'He did this for money. And I was trying to save my family's honour.'

'I really do not know why you bother, little

one,' her mother said, honestly puzzled. 'This is but a temporary annoyance, I am sure. We will come right, one way or the other. If all else fails, I will take to the stage again.'

'Nooooo.' It was an old threat and seemed to return, like a nightmare, whenever things looked darkest. 'You will ruin me, Mother. No decent man would marry the daughter of an actress.'

'You are married already,' her mother reminded her. 'Therefore it is no longer an issue. Now tell me…' she leaned closer '…is the mock Lord Kenton as much a stallion as he appears? Or is that an act as well?'

'Mother!' She looked around, worried, even in the privacy of her old home, that someone might have heard the question.

Her mother scoffed. 'You needn't fuss so. Now that you are a married woman, you are allowed to be more candid about such things. You are still so skittish, one would think…' A cloud of suspicion crossed her face. 'You are still acting like a schoolgirl, Cynthia. Tell me you did not deny your husband his marital rights?' Her mother was looking at her in shock, her tone outraged. It almost made Thea feel that she had done something wrong.

'He is not my husband, Mother,' she said emphatically.

'If not he, then who?'

'No one, I suspect.' Although she was still not totally sure. 'There was a ceremony, of course,' she added doubtfully, 'but it can hardly be called legal.'

'And do you expect us to take him before the courts, tell the whole truth and ruin the reputations of everyone involved, including your own?'

There would be no way to sort it out legally without revealing everything. 'I suppose there is no way that the blame can fall only on Jack,' she said with a sigh.

'You are quick to wish that on him. You liked him quite well enough a few days ago.'

'That was before I knew who he really was,' she said testily.

'And every bride, since the beginning of time, has said something similar after the knot was tied. Most of them not as early as you, of course,' her mother added with a shrug. 'But all of us, even I, have sometimes looked at the man we married and wondered what in the world possessed us.'

'You and Father?'

'Of course,' her mother said with a surprised smile. 'The man bartered away everything we owned for a dusty doll with too many arms to be Christian. On the day I realised what he had done, could you blame me for doubting?' And then she smiled again. 'But we muddle on, my dear. We all muddle on. A disappointment is not the end of the world. Nor is it the end of the marriage. Sometimes, it is the beginning of true understanding.'

'And how could that be?'

'After a few short days of acquaintance, you know your husband for who he truly is.'

'He is a liar,' Thea said in disgust.

'All men are. And not as good at it as they think. We women are forced to look the other way and pretend that we are fooled. But we know the truth. Jack owned his untruths on the very first night.' Her mother smiled. 'It is quite an achievement on your part. You unravelled all his secrets while he was still fully dressed. Were you wearing the nightdress I selected for you?'

'That is immaterial.' As was the gown, or very nearly. And it reminded Thea that Jack Briggs knew far more about her person than a stranger should. 'You talk as if you expect me to forgive him.'

Her mother thought for a moment. 'I expect you to give him a fair hearing. And to pay attention to how he treats you, now that you know the worst.'

'I do not think he likes me very much,' Thea admitted, almost in a whisper. It had been easy to dismiss that yesterday, when she'd thought him the worst man in the world. But after last night, she was not sure.

'Have you given him reason to dislike you?'

Other than denying him her bed? And why was that making her feel so guilty when it was the most sensible decision she could have made? 'I am often short tempered with him,' she admitted.

'Then try to be sweeter,' her mother said, as though this would solve all.

'There is no amount of sweetness that will make up for our differences. I suspect he would much rather have married you. He saw you on stage once, but he did not recognise you until I admitted the truth,' Thea added with more than a little relief.

'He knows of me?' her mother said, totally missing the point of the problem.

'He seemed quite…impressed,' Thea admitted, remembering the dazed look that had come over Jack as he'd thought of Antonia Knowles.

'I knew that he was a sweet boy,' her mother said, pleased again. 'You should be kind to him, if for that alone.'

'But it does not solve the problem at hand. He thinks he will be able to trick de Warde out of the money he has taken from Father. What if he wants me to help him? I am no actress, Mother. And an actress is what his plans are likely to need.'

'A pity, but 'tis true,' her mother agreed. 'You really are quite hopeless, Thea. And it is my fault for trying to raise you to be so much my opposite. But do not fear. Do the best you can. And if it is impossible, then you must come to me for help.'

'I am sure that will not be necessary,' Thea said, dreading what that help might entail.

'In any case,' her mother said, glancing in the mirror as though to be sure her reflection was still as fetching as it had always been, 'you and Kenton must visit, if only so that we might speak of old times.'

'Of course,' Thea said, vowing that she would do nothing of the kind.

Chapter Eight

When Viscount Kenton announced that he wished a ball to honour his happy marriage to his lovely new wife, the house threw itself into the preparations with vigour, polishing silver and dusting chandeliers that already gleamed with careful tending, handing Thea suggested menus and already prepared guest lists, all awaiting little more than her suggestions and approval.

It had been explained to her in school that being the lady of a great house was no different than being the general of an army. And her troops were properly marshalled and eager for battle, after too many years of peace and quiet.

It was some consolation to know that, when Jack was gone, she would keep her place here until she remarried. Before they'd left Spayne

Court, the earl had pulled her aside and reiterated that her place as dowager was secure. Once her mourning had passed she could entertain as often as she liked.

If there was the money for it, of course. She must trust that Jack's plan, whatever it was likely to be, would turn out successful and that the fresh string of debts she was accruing could be paid in the near future.

But when she was dowager, Thea doubted that she would wish to stay here. Lacking a master, the house would be rather lonely, no matter how fine the hospitality. During the day, there was a lack of closeness between them that, while understandable, kept the house from being as warm and pleasant a place as it might have been.

But he greeted her each evening at dinner with a kiss on the cheek. And over a fine meal he would regale her with his adventures in India. Though she knew them to be complete fictions, they were no less entertaining than they had been. Sometimes more so, for now she asked questions that might lead him into greater and more amusing fictions, and she never found him at a loss for words. It was really most diverting. When they retired to their separate rooms, they parted amicably. Kenton gave such life to the house that she would quite miss him when he died.

She stopped in mid-breath at the thought, confused as to how he had managed to bedazzle her, just as he had the staff. In just two short weeks, she had come to accept him as the man he pretended to be.

She could not miss a man that did not exist. When Jack Briggs pretended to die and Kenton disappeared, the house must be empty of her as well, no matter what the earl had promised. To entertain here at all would be awkward, for she was unsure how long she could keep up the pretence that she was anyone's widow. The whole truth would likely come pouring out of her with the first glass of champagne. Better to remove quietly to the country and do her best to forget that any of this had happened. But first she must get through her partner's scheming with as much grace and as little participation as possible.

Now it was the night of the ball and Jack still had not told her what he planned to do. For her part, she meant to smile and nod and do nothing that might give the game away. If she did not interfere, she could not spoil the result and it would be over all the quicker. Then her life could return to something akin to what it had been before that fateful night in the gazebo.

She was wearing her best new gown, a pale-gold silk overlain with embroidered net and banded with satin. The effect must have been spectacular. When Jack saw her, his careful composure faltered and he stood in the connecting doorway between their rooms as though frozen in place, his mouth slightly open in amazement.

'Does it suit?' she asked, giving a half turn and pretending that his reaction had not pleased her.

'Oh, I say. Yes, it does.' He did not seem to be looking at the dress at all, but the generous, expansive cleavage displayed above it.

'I should hope so. It cost you dearly. Or it cost someone. I expect you will be long gone by the time the reckoning for it comes.'

'I suppose I shall be.' He said it with a sigh that almost sounded sincere, but he was still ignoring the dress and focusing on her exposed skin.

She laid a hand across her bosom to obstruct his view. 'If we are to go through with this, you had best stop ogling me. We are supposed to be married, you remember. You have seen me before.'

'Even so, I would still enjoy looking at you.' To put her at her ease, he looked up into her face. 'Tonight, we must be sure that others look at you as well. Let us decorate you in a way that will have de Warde's full attention. Although I suspect the old lecher will be giving you enough of that, even without the Spayne emeralds.' He produced a padded jewel box from behind his back, stepped forwards and set them on her dressing table. 'Stand still a moment and let me help you.' He opened the box to reveal a parure of brilliant green cabochons. There was a necklace of chained rosettes framed by clusters of diamonds, matching earrings, a tiara and a suspiciously blank space that must have contained a ring.

She touched the ring on her hand nervously and found it hard to take the next breath. 'I have been wearing *that ring*?'

He smiled. 'You have heard of it, then?'

'Everyone has heard of the Spayne emeralds. They were a gift from Henry VII. A heavy girdle of stones, with matching clips, buckles and stomacher. They were lost briefly under Cromwell's rule, found, restored, reset...' She ticked off what she could remember of their history on her fingers. 'Unlike most stones with a long and storied provenance, they are thought to be lucky. They are more famous than the earl who was entrusted with them. But the current Spayne said nothing about them when we visited.'

'Well, he must have been thinking of it,' Jack said with a shrug. 'He brought the lot of them down from the lock rooms in Essex when he came to town yesterday. Said we would have need of them if we truly wished to play at lord and lady.'

She gave the actor an incredulous look, for he was speaking of the famous treasures as though they were nothing more than costume pieces. She looked down at her hand. 'When you gave this to me, you did nothing to indicate that this was *that ring*. You said it belonged to your mother.'

Jack shrugged. 'I said all kinds of nonsense

when I was eager to get you into bed.' He put a hand on her shoulder and turned her, so that he could better reach her throat. She felt the warm touch of his fingers at her nape. 'I did not expect you would remember. And that was almost accurate, if I had actually been Kenton. Spayne said his wife did quite like wearing the ring. She complained the rest was too heavy.'

As he adorned her with it, Thea could sympathise with the late Lady Spayne. 'They are.' If his hands had not been there to steady her, she would likely have fainted from the shock of wearing them, for she certainly did not deserve it. If he was not Kenton, then she had no right at all to touch them. 'They are also the showpiece of the entail. They are a symbol of the family. Even when I thought I was marrying Kenton, I did not think to see the ring on my finger every day, even as a joke.'

'Tonight, you must wear every last stone, no matter how much they weigh.' He pulled her body close to his, her back against his chest, his arms around her waist. And for just this once, she would allow it, if only to steal a little of his irrational self-confidence. 'We want everyone to know that you are the symbolic vessel of the future Earl of Spayne.' His hands were on her belly and the gentle pat on her stomach raised butterflies in it. He was talking of her womb, full with his child, and her mind drifted nervously to the activities that would make it so.

'We especially want to impress de Warde. If his goal was to force the earl to disgrace and suicide, it will infuriate him to see how far afield his plan has gone. I expect it will bother him even more so when you tell him that your mother is pregnant.'

Chapter Nine

'When I what?'

His arms were suddenly empty as she jerked away from them. It was a shame because he had been quite enjoying the round, soft, full feeling of holding her. Now she was turned to face him, all cold chill and sharp corners again.

He smiled, trying to lull her back to what she had been. Then he set the tiara on her head so that it rested crookedly in a nest of curls. 'Tonight you will tell my esteemed uncle that your mother is most blessed with fecundity, due to the idol he has given your father.'

'But my mother is not pregnant. Even if she was, I would not be so vulgar as to announce it at a public gathering to a gentleman.' Her hand was fluttering at her throat as though she might choke on the outrage.

He watched the fingers for a moment, toying with the chained emeralds dangling at the delicious hollow of her breast. 'That is not important,' Jack said, pulling his eyes away and trying to focus on the matter at hand. 'You will be telling him that she is. And you will insist that I have told you it is a boy, using arcane skills I picked up in the mysterious East.'

'But that would be lying.' She was staring at him with her beautiful green eyes and a worried expression, as though it mattered in the slightest what happened to de Warde, as long as they succeeded. Had her mother taught her nothing about dissembling?

Then he remembered how easily he had fallen for her tricks and looked at her, eyes narrowed to see the schemer before him and not the tasty package that held it. 'When did you discover such morals? You lied to trap me and it did not bother you then.'

'That was merely a deception. Evasion. Half-truths in the moonlight. Certain latitudes must be taken if one wishes to catch the attention of a man. But this…'

'Is to trick de Warde,' he said, frustrated. 'He is your enemy, is he not?'

'It does not matter who he is. I cannot say such a thing.'

'Do you want him to go unpunished?'

'I do not wish to sink so low as to discuss my mother's…' She gave him a helpless look. 'Not even to see justice done.'

'Yet you were willing to marry a stranger to repair your family's fortune,' he reminded her. 'And that would have required far more than discussion.'

'Of course,' she replied, 'because the stranger was a viscount. How else would I have helped my family? Taken in washing?'

As though a little manual labour was the worst fate that could befall a woman with financial difficulties. Jack could think of at least one career for such a voluptuous female that could have netted a pretty penny. 'And see how well that worked for you. Next you will tell me that it is more honourable to give yourself to de Warde, like some kind of martyr.'

There was a hint of desperation in her expression, as though she might actually consider it. Then she shook her head. 'That would be totally different. We were married. Mr de Warde could not marry me, as he already had a wife.'

Jack clenched his fists at his sides to keep from pulling out his own hair. Her combination of wide-eyed innocence and cold-blooded social climbing was maddening. 'Perhaps you are right and I do not understand people of your class. There is nothing particularly intelligent about taking the honourable course as the nobility do. It is littered with male suicides and ruined women. Do you have no sense of self-preservation at all?'

She was still looking at him as though he was talking gibberish. If he was smart, he'd have turned and run at that moment. Since there was no saving her, he would be better to save himself.

There was the faintest twinkle in her eye, caused by a single unshed tear. She was not stupid, for his own vanity insisted that no stupid woman could have caught him. And the trick she had used was a clever one, he had to admit.

But she had been unlucky enough to have the rest of the sense trained out of her to make her acceptable to society. It was as if someone had taken a diamond, then forced it into an inferior setting. He had but to pry it out again and set it right.

He took a deep breath and schooled himself to patience. Hard experience had taught him the lessons needed to stay alive. The current circumstances would force this woman to fight unarmed against a man who did not share her high ideals. She needed to learn life's true lessons all at once, and he must be her teacher.

'What you are saying, that you do not wish to lie and cheat to get what you want, is an honourable and worthy thing,' he began. 'It is cruel of me to taunt you for it. But you must have realised by now that de Warde is no gentleman, no matter his birth. He has shown no respect for you, for your family or for your honour.'

'And now I will be forced to sink to his level.'

'Only long enough to beat him at his own

game,' he promised. 'We will use his greed against him. It is only in grasping at things that do not belong to him that he will overbalance and fall.'

'You are saying that, if he were a proper gentleman, we would not be able to defeat him with lies?' she said hopefully.

Her own father had been brought low by them quick enough. It was a spurious argument, but it seemed to console her. If Jack lied now, it was a small white one that would save her fragile pride. 'Indeed. For all his good birth, my dear Uncle Henry is as base a villain as any I have met. That will be his weakness in the end. But I will need you to help me if we are to prevail.'

She sighed. 'Even if it goes against my nature.'

'It is nothing worse than a little play-acting,' he coaxed.

'And that is just the trouble with it. I have tried so very hard not to be like...' She bit her lip.

Jack had little experience with sincerity. It was a shame that she was not acting, for he'd have found it even more appealing had it been on stage. As she nibbled her lower lip it pouted, full and lusciously kissable. He could not tear his eyes from it, nor keep his mind focused on the urgency of the situation. But it proved again why his reaction to her had been so sudden and so irresistible. After seeing Antonia, he had been waiting all his life to meet a woman very like her. When one appeared before him and beckoned him towards the garden, what chance did he have? Now he could not seem to help himself and reached out to clasp her hand. 'To be like who, Cyn?'

'Whom,' she said, softly. 'It is more properly said whom, I think.'

'And while correct, it does not answer my question.' Although he was sure he knew the answer. 'Who do you fear to emulate?'

'My mother, of course.'

'But if the great Antonia is your mother, then you have no need to fear this little charade. You have the ability to beguile bred deep in the bone. We have but to bring it out of you.'

'That is exactly what I fear,' she said with a wail. 'I do not want to be an actress. I have seen what they are like. Flighty, mercurial, altogether inappropriate for society.'

'Is your mother cruel to you?' he asked, praying that it was not so. After so many years, it would be a shame to discover that his idol was less than worthy.

'Not really,' she admitted. 'She loves me well enough, in her own way. But she was not the sort of person likely to marry a man like my father. She was quite far below him in birth. In fact, I doubt she even knows the identity of my grandfather.'

'Then you do not love her,' Jack guessed. Her vehemence surprised him, for at the wedding she'd seemed quite fond of her mother.

'That is not true, either. She is my mother. How could I not love her?' Her eyes were gloriously round, deep and green, and as he stared at them, he felt his mind wandering again. 'I simply do not like being her daughter.'

'Eh?' Apparently, this was another of Thea's subtle distinctions that he could not follow.

'She is rather a force of nature,' Thea explained. 'There is no changing her, any more than it is possible to erase her past. People like her well enough. But even when she tries, she cannot manage to behave as the mothers of the other girls I know.' Thea gave a helpless wave of her hands. 'She is altogether too…too…too everything. She laughs too much, talks too often about things that are best left unsaid and is altogether too visible.' Thea frowned. 'I am not like that. I favour Father, I think. That is why we decided that it would be better if I were educated away from home to bring out the qualities that would most please Grandfather.' She smiled fondly at the thought. 'I attended Miss Pennyworth's Seminary for the Education of Young Ladies.'

'It sounds dreadful,' Jack supplied.

'It was not.' She gave a sigh of relief. 'It was so much easier. There was order. Peace. The other girls were quiet and well behaved.'

'Seriously?' Jack arched his eyebrow.

A slight flush crept up the graceful column of her throat. 'Well, they should have been. It was most vexing to the teachers when they were not. I sought to be a good example and followed the instructions of the mistresses to the letter.'

'I suspect you did.'

'And no one told me stories of—' her lips pursed in disapproval as she whispered '—things no young lady should know.'

'What sorts of things are those?'

'My mother sometimes... It is just that...' She blushed scarlet. 'She and my father, after so many years, are most ardently affectionate to each other.'

'Your father is a most fortunate man,' Jack agreed.

'But if he is, I should not know of it. Nor should I know if he is not. I should not know anything at all about that part of life. And I especially should not know about that part of marriage.'

Jack smothered a smile. 'I should think it would be a comfort not to live in ignorance.'

'But the other girls all were,' Thea said. 'They knew nothing about anything. And they seemed far more content than I was. Miss Pennyworth did not say a word on the subject. We were given educating tracts, scripture, sermons and all necessary skills. But nothing was said about...'

It was a horrifying prospect. Innocent girls

married to the sort of worldly gentlemen he knew inhabited the *ton*, going to their marriage beds in terror. 'Did you take it upon yourself to question her? Did you demand to know the truth?'

'Certainly not. Nor did I enlighten the others with what I knew. If we needed such information, then surely someone would have given it to us.'

Of all the things he had expected, when making the offer to the passionate creature who had caught him, it had never occurred to him that his lady would be a self-righteous prig. Her response on that night had been more than ardent. And with her heritage considered, he'd have used words like 'temptress' to describe her. 'But your mother told you everything, of course.'

'And I spent two years at boarding school, doing my best to unlearn it. I was not about to be brought up in such a way. I hoped that Father's father would approve of my efforts,' she said earnestly. 'If I could manage to persuade him that my mother's influence had done me no harm, then perhaps he would relent on the matter of Father's inheritance.' She sighed. 'And when I came back...' She gave another helpless wave of her hands. 'Chaos. Just as I feared. Just as it always is when I am home.' She stared into his eyes, worried.

Jack could not help the feeling creeping up his spine to help, to protect, as though nerves and sinews stood ready, despite the healthy scepticism in his brain, to rush to the aid and comfort of the poor girl who needed him. Ginger hair and a fine bosom, he reminded himself firmly and stayed his hand. They had tricked him before.

'I want to be just the opposite of my mother. Honest, polite and exactly what I appear to be. And I have succeeded. Until now.' She pointed a dire finger in his direction. 'Until you.'

So he was the fault, was he? He thought in disgust of what would have happened to her had she been wed and bedded by a spurious gentleman like de Warde. It would be no less than she deserved. 'As soon as I am gone, you can go back to being just as you were,' he assured her. *Ignorant and silly.* 'In just a few short weeks, we will have finished with Uncle Henry. It is the best I can offer you, really.' *And good riddance.* 'A small sacrifice on your part will mean success for your parents, and for Lord Spayne as well.'

'If there is no other way...' He watched her bosom rise and fall in a huge and very theatrical sigh that would have done her mother proud. 'Tell me what I must do.'

'It will be simple. You have but to do as I tell you and say what I ask you to say. There is really nothing to acting but remembering words in the right order. If you were good in school, you will be good at this. Pretend it is poetry. I suspect you've memorised your fair share of that.'

'But how will I make people believe the lies?'

Jack tore his gaze from the swelling breast and the pouting lips. 'People will believe you, I am sure. Men, particularly. De Warde especially. He has but to look into your eyes...' And then he realised he was doing just that and thinking of things that had nothing to do with the matter at hand. He cleared his throat and cleared his head. 'Where was I? Acting lessons. Yes. When the story is sad, you think of a sad thing. When it is happy, think of the moments that have brought you joy. Let your mind go to memory as your mouth speaks the words. Can you do that?'

'I will try.' She gave him another worried look, and he felt his heart melting.

With enough tutelage she would be every bit as convincing as her mother had been. But tonight would be a difficult evening. 'Remember, you are not doing any of this for personal gain. You are helping others by it.'

'That is true,' she said, brightening a little.

'Think of poor Lord Spayne, at the mercy of his brother.'

'That is quite awful,' she agreed.

'And your parents, unfairly persecuted by him.'

'The man is truly a villain,' she agreed.

'And think of what will happen to me if you fail.'

She looked as though she'd come back to earth with a bone-jarring thump. 'Nothing less than you deserve. You are as great a trickster as he is.'

'Then do not think of me,' Jack corrected, annoyed that his lovely wife had not an ounce of sympathy in her for his poor neck. 'Help the others. Help yourself. When you meet de Warde at the ball, tell him the story I shall teach you, just as I give it to you. Think of it as the first step in being rid of me.'

She gave a resolute nod and he began his instruction, irked to know that an end to their marriage seemed almost as desirable to her as regaining her father's money.

Chapter Ten

Jack had sometimes thought of Kenton's London digs as if they were a person: old, venerable and dignified. Perhaps the town house was not the first stare of fashion, for there had been no viscount in residence since Spayne had been a young man, but at that time he had appointed it with care. The place still looked expensive, but it had a comfortable shabbiness that put Jack at his ease.

But now that there was a Lady Kenton, such seediness was not to be allowed. Thea had changed a curtain here, a painting there, making a host of subtle alterations to the whole house to bring it up to date, and then going hammer and tongs at the ballroom, adding festoons of fresh flowers, champagne fountains and music. When dressed for company, the town house was splendid, and the ballroom even more so.

His old self goggled at the sight of it, wanting to rush to the refreshment room and fill his pockets with cakes, hide wine bottles under his coat and perhaps tuck bread and cheese up his sleeve, then run before the nobs got wind of his presence and tossed him back into the gutter.

Instead, he took a sip from his wine glass and gave a spare smile and approving nod. Such luxury was nothing less than Kenton expected. It was good to have the help of a wife, to make the ball go as it should. And Thea, bedecked in a silk gown the colour of the champagne he was drinking, showed no agitation. He must take his cue from her. 'It looks well,' he said.

'Is that all you have to say for it? Well?' He had said something to offend her, but for the life of him did not know what.

'It looks as a ball thrown by the Viscount of Kenton should look,' he replied cautiously.

'Of course it does,' she agreed. 'Such entertainments and their preparation do not intimidate me. This one will be a highlight of the social Season.'

She gave a critical glance to her surroundings, showing none of the hesitance that she had displayed when Jack had attempted to school her in her part of their scheme. Perhaps things would go better than he expected. The creature before him was beauty and confidence personified, and not the scared little girl he had seen in their rooms an hour ago.

Then she gave him an angled look of disdain. 'That is, of course, if I can refrain from choking each time someone calls me by my title.'

From her other side, the Earl of Spayne leaned closer and murmured, 'If you do, I shall simply tell them that you cannot believe your luck. And that I am quite charmed with you, despite the idiosyncrasy. Accept it or not, my dear, you are my daughter-in-law.'

Thea smiled and, for some reason, Jack found it annoying. Hadn't he told her the same often enough? No matter who he was, she was safely Lady Kenton. Apparently, the words coming from 'an actor' meant far less than those coming from a peer. He swallowed his irritation and smiled back at her, smothering the strange, boyish eagerness to catch her attention again. 'There, see? You have nothing to fear, just as I promised.'

'Other than debtor's prison, of course.'

'I am Kenton, just come from the East with pockets full of riches. This evening is nothing we cannot afford,' he reminded her.

'You are an actor, aren't you?' she said, with a sarcastic flutter of her fan. 'To tell such lies with a straight face.' The look she turned to him was pleasant, but distant. So much colder than it had been when she'd agreed to the marriage, but totally appropriate for a society couple. Even if they were newly married, polite people simply did not make fools of themselves over their own spouses.

He squeezed her hand and smiled as though her snub did not bother him. 'Come, let us greet our guests.'

They lined up properly beside the earl and went through the laborious task of greeting the people invited into their home. Jack put on his best smile, reminding himself that this, as all things were, was a performance. He was Kenton. And Kenton was a gracious host.

And his guests responded well to it. He thanked

God on several occasions that, after memorising as many plays as he had, keeping straight the names and titles of the *ton* was hardly an effort. On several occasions, he even managed to correct his wife, who had memorised *Debrett's* as a schoolboy might learn his Latin.

It was not until the earl's brother appeared that he felt his character wavering.

'Henry.' Spayne's bow was stiff.

The man before him was a younger, paler copy of the earl, blue eyed and fair haired, but with none of Spayne's easy charm. On de Warde, the blue eyes looked cold and the hair was smoothed back with Macassar oil until it seemed as dark and unctuous as its owner. De Warde answered with a nod. 'George.'

And how was Jack to play this? His plan required that he be the *naïf*, eager to be led by his worldly uncle, so that he might turn the tables unexpectedly later.

But as he watched and his wife blanched at the prospect of facing the man, Kenton, damn his chivalry, would not be contained. The vermin before him had blackmailed his father near to bankruptcy, tricked his father-in-law and made vile suggestions to the woman who had become his wife. He was suffered at this event for the sake of the family connection, but it was little more than that. Kenton allowed his natural distaste to shine through the courtesy. 'Uncle de Warde, how nice to see you, again. Aunt de Warde.' The woman beside him looked almost colourless, her lips thin and bloodless, thinning even more at the sight of Cynthia, who she must know was a rival, even if an unwilling one.

'Kenton? In my memory, I have not seen you at all.' Uncle Henry was cold in response, making it equally clear that there would be no love between them.

'It is hardly a recent acquaintance,' Jack said with a tight smile. 'I do not remember it, but Father assures me that you attended my christening.' Let him think that Jack viewed the separation as rudeness. 'And, of course, you know my wife.'

'The lovely Cynthia.' The lecher smiled a little too broadly at the sight of her. Instead of warmth, the grin gave him a wolfish air that obviously made Thea uncomfortable. But manners won out and, though she insisted she did not like to lie, she managed a more lifelike smile than Jack could have done. 'Mr de Warde.'

'And how are your parents, my dear, dear girl?' He continued to hold her hand as he spoke, as though prepared to receive bad news and offer comfort.

'Quite well,' she said, smiling brightly. Again, it was a social lie, a falseness that did not trouble her. 'They will be here tonight.'

'They are probably happy that you have made such a fortunate marriage. And to so prestigious a family.' The man was staring at the Spayne emeralds now, where they rested on Thea's breast, looking for all the world like he could not decide whether he wanted the frosting or the cake beneath.

'It was a love match,' Jack said drily. 'We are both very happy for it. And they have had other good news as well. They are soon to be blessed.'

There was the slightest twitch of surprise from de Warde, as though he wondered what the secret might be. But Jack made no move to elaborate, looking past him to the people behind. 'Now, if you will excuse us, Uncle, there are others waiting to speak with us.'

'Of course.'

When de Warde had moved on, and Thea could manage a word, she half turned to him and muttered *sotto voce*, barely moving her lips lest another might hear, 'You were very rude to Mr de Warde.'

'Because I do not like him.' And neither did Kenton. It was quite the easiest part of the role. 'But you will go to him shortly and smooth his feathers again with your good manners, just as it is your instinct to do. Apologise for my temper. Make peace with him. Then, remember what I have told you to say. Get the story out as best you can, then you are free of my plot.'

'That is all,' she said like a muttered prayer.

'That is all.' For tonight, at least. But she must take the hurdles one at a time. There was no point in frightening her with the whole course, just yet.

Thea waited until all the guests were properly welcomed and enjoying themselves, then allowed herself a moment to survey the scene again. It looked just as it should be. It made her wish that Miss Pennyworth could see her and assign some kind of a grade to it, for it was proof that all her education had served a purpose, no matter what Jack might think. She was sure that he could not have managed it, even with the help of his loyal servants. And it surpassed anything her mother might have managed, for the Spayne name had opened the guest list to the heights of society that her father's meagre title could not access.

Would that it were all that was expected of her. She was quite exhausted already, wishing only that she might lie down after, or at least enjoy what she had done. But how could she, knowing that the worst of the night was still ahead?

She scanned the mob for Henry de Warde, remembering the lines that Jack had written for her and the need to deliver them spontaneously, and yet word for word. The ideas seemed to contradict each other. How could a rehearsed scene appear fresh? And why was not the consummate actor here to help her through them? She glanced furtively about, praying that he would come back for the end of this. But he was already out of the room and halfway down the hall. He had been no use in the receiving line, of course, behaving exactly the opposite of how he had promised her he would, putting de Warde on guard against them and making her job even more difficult.

But now that her husband was out of sight, dear Uncle Henry was leering at her from across the room as though her recent marriage and earlier heartfelt refusal of his advances had meant nothing to him. She supposed that Jack would have viewed this as more opportunity and not a social disaster. Instincts and training promised that she was allowed to cut him, even if he was family. And he certainly deserved it.

Instead, she put on her best hostess smile and approached him, noticing the slight widening of his eyes in surprise. 'If I might speak to you alone, Mr de Warde, just for a moment.' It was the last thing she wanted and she was sure that it must be obvious to him.

'Alone?' Did he suspect her already? 'Is that necessary?'

'Perhaps not.' She glanced about her quickly,

hoping the other guests were distant enough so as not to hear her bald-faced lying. 'I merely wish to offer an apology to you for my husband's behaviour just now. I am sure, with your renewed acquaintance, he will warm to you, just as a dutiful nephew should.'

'Is that so?' He gave her a pitying look in response, as though her optimism proved how little she knew of the subject.

'I am sure of it,' she said, giving an overly enthusiastic nod that made her feel like a badly operated puppet. Jack had ensured her that such enthusiasm was necessary. Of course, he had been staring at her bodice as he'd said it. She was quite sure that he could not have known how ridiculous he was making her.

De Warde gave little notice of what her head was doing, focusing much lower in response to her movement.

'I, myself, have recently discovered that I owe you an apology,' she added. 'And can think of no better time to give it than now.'

'You do?' His face tilted upwards again, brow

furrowed as though he could not quite be sure what he had heard.

'For the kindness you have done my father.' The words sounded too flat, compared with her enthusiastic movement, and not very convincing.

'Kindness.' Clearly, the man could not think what he had done that might be described as such.

'I did not think it so at first, of course, but Kenton has shown me how wrong I was. When I accused you of tricking my father,' she added, throwing Jack's words aside and padding her part so that it might be more clear. 'When you sold him the idol that did not work. But then, it did.'

'I beg your pardon?' de Warde seemed to be getting more confused, and not less, as she explained herself.

'I probably should not reveal too much, since it is supposed to be a secret for some time.' For ever, perhaps. She could hardly expect her mother to accept the congratulations of society for a sham of a pregnancy.

Now de Warde looked as though suspicion was dawning. 'You are not saying that…'

No, she was not. She could not. It was simply

too embarrassing. She skipped ahead in the prepared speech, avoiding the most difficult line that
he would have had her blurt in its full and embarrassing detail. 'Indeed. I had my doubts at first.
But now that Jack has explained it, and supplied
the missing idol, and we have seen the wondrous
results…' She ploughed through the words as
though they were so much rocky earth. 'It was
most kind of you, sir. My family thanks you. I
thank you. And, of course, my father thanks you.'
Her own voice in her ears sounded as though she
were acknowledging condolences and not cele-
brating a blessed event. 'But I must say no more.'
Because she could not manage another word.

'No, please…' de Warde reached to take her
hand, and she did her best not to shudder at his
touch '…I must know everything. Surely, if I
have been so instrumental in your good fortune,
you must tell me the details.'

She looked desperately across the room for her
husband, praying for rescue, wondering how long
it would take before she lost the last of her nerve
and told the truth.

Chapter Eleven

Jack played at being the gracious host, visiting with gentlemen in the card room and escorting ladies out on to the floor. But at the back of his mind, he was continually aware of the presence of his wife somewhere in the room. He caught occasional glimpses of her, like a bird in a forest, more glittering, more beautiful and altogether more graceful than her already magical surroundings.

He thought of the flowing red hair, the green eyes and full lips of his wife, but transposed on to another, faraway performance of Hamlet that he'd viewed as a boy. This was even better than watching from a distance. Tonight, he was sharing the stage with a woman very like his ideal.

The real Antonia was there, of course, almost

as lovely as she had been. But now that Thea had admitted the truth, Jack could almost understand her difficulties with such a mother. Lady Banester had given him a look as she'd said his name and touched a finger to the side of her nose, as though to reveal that she knew all, but would keep the secret. But once that was done, she'd made several sly references to the truth to remind him of it. Rather than letting it go and keeping silent, she could not manage to resist the joke.

Thea had survived a lifetime of exposure to her mother's wit. Though not really hurtful, it probably wore on the nerves of a girl with more natural reserve than her mater.

But it did not seem to bother Lord Banester, who Thea thought she resembled. In light of his recent change in understanding, Jack reexamined his bride's father. Despite what Thea claimed, the man held little in common in looks or personality with his daughter. He was short, round and balding, and the remaining hair was the colour and texture of straw. He was not as shy as Thea, nor as boisterous as his wife, but obviously good humoured. Given what he'd known of

Antonia Knowles, Jack would have assumed the man who caught her would be both rich and powerful. But it was clear that this was not the case.

Jack sidled closer to his father-in-law, leaning down to catch his ear. 'The evening is going well. I am most pleased with the way Thea has handled it.'

The man tented his fingers and drummed them together, as though he had accomplished the matter himself and was well pleased with it. 'Indeed. It is most gratifying to see my daughter making a success of it.' He gave Jack a cautious sidelong glance. 'Given your reaction on the wedding day to the state of our finances, I worried that this would not be the case. It was never my intention to trick you into an inequitable match.'

Jack swallowed the response he wished to make in favour of something more diplomatic. 'Of course not. The matter is all but forgotten. It is trivial compared to my feelings and the acceptance of my father. He adores Cynthia, as do I.'

Banester gave a sigh of relief. 'That is good to know. Really, I expected no less.' He smiled with pride in the direction of the viscountess. 'She is all I could have hoped for in a daughter: duty combined with beauty. And manners that are the equal to any you might meet.' He had omitted breeding, of course. But then Jack could hardly complain about it.

'She is a jewel,' Jack agreed. 'As is your wife.'

'Indeed.' It was now that Jack saw the real man behind the doting father, for when he looked at Antonia, he seemed younger, straighter and less foolish. There was something beyond the lust that one might expect in such an unequal match. Nor was it precisely adoration, although there might have been a component of worship. It was love, plain and simple. Even after twenty years, it all but glowed from the man as he stared across the room at his wife.

As though she could sense it, Antonia raised her head and turned to look back at him with an expression that mirrored his. Then she floated across the room to his side, as graceful as a girl, to put her hand on his arm. As she moved, the room underwent a subtle change, even the most jaded members of society looking on with a sort of wistfulness that Jack had not seen in them before.

There was no doubt that the match was a success, in the home and in the *ton*. How could anyone, other than perhaps Banester's stiff-necked father, refuse entrance to such a couple?

'A dance, my dear?' Banester said it not with the hopefulness of an unworthy suitor, but as a man used to getting his way, and Anontia responded with a giggle, tugging his arm to bring him to the floor.

As though he could guess at the contents of his mind, he turned to Jack before going. 'Over the years, I have been fond and foolish, particularly of late in regards to a kinsman of yours. But really, who can blame me? There is little I would not attempt in an effort to preserve my marriage and my family. I have been most prodigiously blessed in those areas, have I not?'

'You have indeed, sir.' Jack gave him a small bow of admiration. And the lovebirds were gone, out on to the dance floor, weaving gracefully between the other couples, but staring at each other as though they were the only two in the room.

Which made Jack search again for his own wife. Considering their recent marriage, they should be the ones playing the young lovers. Just for a moment, he imagined an adlibbed scene between them, standing close, exchanging whispered confidences and perhaps a kiss.

Then he remembered the need, on this of all nights, to stick to the script as he had written it. She was having problems enough performing to his instructions without him complicating matters further. When he found her, it appeared that she had been trapped by her quarry and not the other way around.

Henry de Warde had her sequestered in a corner, and even from where Jack stood he could see it was not going well. Thea fairly twitched with discomfort as she told the man her tale of fertility. Jack had thought her claims of being a poor player were nothing more than false modesty. Hadn't she reeled him in with little effort and outlandish behaviour? This should be no different. Easier, perhaps, for she only needed to say a few words and let him handle the rest.

But watching her now, he suspected her physical charms in the moonlight were the only things that had led him to believe a word from her. That and the gun, of course. Tonight, unarmed and candle lit, it was clear that she could not talk de Warde into giving her the time of day, much less into believing the unlikely story he'd given her to deliver. Dear Uncle Henry had a grip on her arm, pushing her to reveal more and wearing the smile of a sceptic suspecting a trick.

Yet the man continued to listen to her, probably for the same reason that Jack had. He wanted her. Even with his own wife scant feet from them, he was undressing Thea with his eyes, trying to force her to reveal something that he might use against her later.

Jack suspected that this had been the man's plan from the first. Taking money from her father had been incidental. Surely de Warde did not need it. He got all he could possibly want from Spayne. Instead, he had wanted this girl, rendered vulnerable and unable to refuse his advances. Even now, he was watching Cyn intently, fairly licking his lips at the flush on her cheeks and the rise and fall of her bosom as she tried to escape him. The fact that she was now married, and to a member of his family, did not bother him any more than his own pale wife, waiting in the corner for his attention. His weakness for her was a cause for celebration, for it marked something that could be used against him.

Instead, Jack felt a seeping, creeping guilt at the knowledge that he'd sent Thea out, unprepared, against such a rogue. She had told him that she was not up to this task and he had ignored her, allowing her to struggle alone against the man who tormented her. Added to the remorse was his sympathy for a fellow player at a loss for words and alone on the stage.

Even worse, there was the distasteful prospect that de Warde might take the coronet by playing the long game, trying to seduce Lady Kenton and putting his own bastard third in line for an earldom. That was simply not to be borne.

But stronger than all was the idea that his wife…Kenton's wife…was being ogled by that *roué*. It was utterly abhorrent. De Warde was touching her, gripping her by the wrist as she tried to withdraw gracefully without calling attention to the problem, but she could not seem to get away from him and was forced to endure it.

The jealousy it raised in the man he was pretending to be was an utterly primal thing, as his distaste in the receiving line had been. Jack could feel his fists balling, the desire to strike warring with the knowledge that a gentleman would not take such brutal vengeance. A duel, perhaps? Or merely a snub. Family or no, he outranked the man. His uncle could not be permitted to harass Cynthia, especially since the man's attentions clearly bothered her.

Jack wiped a hand across his face, trying to clear the thoughts from his mind. It was all well and good to play a character, but one must remember not to become the character. Cyn was not his wife. Even if she was, he doubted he had a right to be jealous of her. He'd always suspected, should he find a woman wily enough to tie him down, the relationship would not be exclusive on either side. And here he was, after less than three weeks, thinking he cared about whose bed this one slept in.

Or desiring to spare her the minor discomfort

of talking to a man she did not like. She knew as well as he did what was at stake with this one. She'd best make an effort to play the part correctly.

But without thinking, he was moving towards them. And when he arrived at the side of the pair, it was Kenton who was in charge. Jack could manage little more than a clipped, 'Uncle de Warde?' They stared at each other in silence for a moment and Jack could feel the struggle going on between them. De Warde demanded respect, did he? Well, he would get none, since none was given. Even if the part required it, which he suspected it might, he could not manage to like the man, not even in pretence. Suddenly, his own acting skills were as bad as his novice wife's. It was another disconcerting surprise and, even worse, it did not bother him nearly as much as it should. He reached out without a word and disentangled de Warde's fingers from his wife's gloved wrist, tucking her arm into the crook of his.

Then all his attention fell to his wife as he assured himself that she was no worse for the contact. She was looking exceptionally fine this evening. And she was his. 'I think you have talked quite long enough with him, Thea. Dance with me.' He placed his other hand over hers and stroked it.

'But…' Her eyes widened as if to say, *I do not understand. Is this part of the plan?* 'The music has already begun.'

'It does not matter. Come.' It was not a waltz, which was a shame. He wanted to hold her in public, where de Warde could see and know that he would never have her. 'We will join at the bottom of the set. There is room for one more couple, I am sure.' He pulled her arm and she came with him after a weak smile and confused shrug in the direction of de Warde.

She took her place in the row opposite Jack, smiling in relief. She curtsied to his bow, met each advance and turned gracefully under the hand he offered to her. He'd always prided himself on being an excellent dancer, but it was all the better to have a good partner. Even before their marriage, he'd learned that Thea was as skilled and graceful as any girl in London.

He could feel his own breast swell with pride,

as though each time he touched her hand it was a sort of claiming, an announcement to all, and especially to Henry de Warde, that she was safe from his advances for ever.

Or until it was time for Jack to leave. The rational mind reminded him that it was not wise to become too attached to things as they stood. They could not last. If the girl would not let him bed her, what good was she? All the same, he wanted to stuff her in his pocket, steal her away and feast upon her in private.

He sighed. It was ridiculous. It did not further his plans to behave like a starving man at a banquet, gorging himself. Even if it did, she would not allow it. She was a woman, not a sweet shop.

Although he could see the similarities. The few kisses he had got from her had been sweet enough. He could not help a smile when he thought of them.

All the same, he was likely to get more satisfaction a bite at a time than to gobble her down in one sitting. Kenton, had he existed, would have had the sense to charm her into bed rather than forcing her, as de Warde was attempting. Come to think of it, Kenton had done a damn fine job just now. Her demeanour was changed, relaxed and as happy as she should be on her first triumphant appearance as the Viscountess of Kenton.

Even if Jack could not have her, he liked looking at her, just as he did the ballroom. As long as he was Kenton, she was his, just as the house was. He could see, in his imagination, their long and happy life together, the passionate evenings and the languid mornings. He could create that reality in his mind and carry it with him to revisit on lonely nights in the future.

But for now? He could not like the idea of de Warde being anywhere near her. So he danced with her again—and tried to stand up a third time until she laughed and reminded him that they had other guests to partner.

Then a shadow flickered in her eyes that made him wonder if it was the whole truth at all. Perhaps she had liked him even less than she claimed and did not want to prolong contact. If that was true, then he had no idea how to read truth from fiction in her character. She made as if to walk away from him, but as she passed he caught her hand again, pulling her away, backing towards the door to the hall. 'Come with me.'

She looked back toward the dance floor. 'You said you wished to dance.'

'And now I wish to be alone with you.'

'But our guests…'

'Can spare you a moment.' He pulled her out into the hall, around a corner and behind a potted palm.

'Jack,' she said in warning, but her voice was not so stern as it usually was and she gave a playful push against his chest.

'Remember,' he whispered. 'we are married and newly wed. An occasional show of affection is quite appropriate, I'm sure.'

'Not really,' she replied. 'A marriage licence is not an invitation to behave without decorum in public places.'

'Clearly a rule written by someone who was not married to you,' Jack responded, pulling her even closer.

'Neither are you.' She tried to push him away again, but her hand lingered, toying with his lapel. Then she whispered, 'Married, that is. To me.'

He touched a finger to her lips. 'Do not talk nonsense, Lady Kenton,' he said. 'Of course you are mine. And I want de Warde to realise the fact so that he ceases drooling on you.'

'Is he…?' She leaned to look around him, worried that they were observed.

'Just play your part and do not concern yourself.' What harm would it do to let her think they were still acting, if it convinced her that this intimacy was necessary? He could not stand to wait longer to claim what he craved. He pulled her hip to hip and lip to lip, and took her mouth.

Why had he not done this from the first? She was as sweet and good as anything he had imagined, like wine on his tongue, each breath perfumed with fruit and spice, and a body that a man could fall into like a soft bed. Even the moralistic Kenton whispered in his ear that he must rid themselves of these annoying guests post haste and spend the rest of the night, and possibly the rest of life, taking pleasure with this goddess.

And she seemed to agree. She tangled her hand in his cravat, mussing his evening clothes so that she might kiss his throat, burying her face against the vee of skin that she had exposed so that she might lick him there, nestling close under his chin and making his pulse race. 'Jack,' she whispered.

He twined his hand in her hair, knocking the tiara askew and feeling the curls wrap his fingers as though they could draw him closer and whispered back, 'Oh, God, Thea. Oh, sweet Lord.' Then he kissed her eyes, the tip of her nose and her lips again, and the hand that had been in her hair was clutching her breast. The fit was natural, as though his hands were made for nothing more than to caress her. His fingers slipped down the neckline of her gown and found a nipple and she moaned eagerly into his mouth, her body responding as instantly to his touch as his did to hers. The tip was trapped between two of his fingers and he squeezed, imagining his lips there. His body was hard where it pressed into her belly and close to exploding like some foolish schoolboy with his first woman.

It was a maddening, dizzying feeling, wanting everything from her and knowing that this was neither the time nor the place for more. Tonight, when they were in bed…

Suddenly, she pushed away from him, looking around quickly to see if anyone had noticed their absence.

'Cyn?' The withdrawal caught him by surprise, making him wonder if she had read his mind, or simply been so in tune that she had reached the same conclusion and then rejected it.

'Well, that was interesting,' she said breathlessly. 'But I think that was quite enough affection for now.'

'Not nearly,' he said, lunging for her again.

She evaded his arms. 'Too much. I am sure anyone who saw us was probably scandalised. And now, if you will excuse me, I feel a chill.' She glanced down and gave her bodice a sharp tug upwards. 'I must repair myself, then I will be returning to the ballroom.' She did not wait for an answer, merely straightened her clothing, turned and ran.

When Thea could manage a thought, it was that she liked kissing Jack, probably because he was very good at it. The night they had become engaged, he had been fulsome in his praise and eager in his affection. When she'd realised that her plan was succeeding, she had been overcome by relief and allowed him to take liberties. Very quickly, she'd found herself overcome by another feeling entirely.

This time, there were no flowery speeches as his lips met hers, only a sudden surge forwards and the feel of his arms around her and it was more than the sheltering caress she'd expected. He was holding her tightly, almost painfully so, and his lips pressed hard on hers. She opened her mouth to his tongue and thrust back at him as he clutched her to him. He needed a shave, for his whiskers scraped against her cheek. She had followed the rough skin down his throat, kissing at the saltiness of it, tearing at his neckcloth like a hungry animal so she might bury her face against him, smelling and tasting.

When she had come to her senses and fought free of him, he had looked as dishevelled and confused as she felt.

He was not following, but it took an effort to

slow her steps. It felt rather like turning one's back on a threatening animal, knowing that at any time it could take to its feet, pursue and catch her, knocking her to the ground.

She would fall on her back with him on top of her. The thought sent a sudden rush of pleasure through her, telling her just how far gone she was. She wanted more. She wanted him. When he'd been the real Lord Kenton, there had been no harm in such thoughts. But she knew who he really was, and it was more than unwise to continue.

What had come over her?

She hurried past the ladies' retiring room, down the hall to the library. There was a mirror there over the mantelpiece. She could fix her hair in privacy and call for the maid if necessary. A single murmur of the name 'Kenton' would bring a smile and a nod from Polly, who had hinted that, with such a handsome husband, she was both surprised and disappointed that Thea had not been rendered to this sorry state already.

She arrived at her refuge and closed the door behind her, slowly and politely, working hard to maintain her composure even though there was no one there to admire her.

'My dear?' Lord Spayne looked up from the book he had been reading. 'Is something the matter?'

'No. Of course not.' Jack was forcing her to lie, even when he was not at her side.

'So far from the ballroom, on this of all nights?' he said with a sceptical smile.

'As are you,' she reminded him.

'But I have done my part, been properly seen and admired,' he reminded her. 'And I do not much care for cards or dancing. The quiet here suits me well.'

But when she glanced to the table at his side, she saw two brandy glasses. Had there been a discreet tête-à-tête, or merely a conversation between similarly antisocial friends? After a moment's thinking, she decided that she did not really care to know.

Clearly, he was not so easily put off. 'I might retreat, my dear. But you are the hostess and most certainly cannot. What brings you so far from the party, I wonder?'

'I was…looking for a book.' Because why else would she have come here?

'It must be a very exciting one to make you flush so.' Spayne gestured to the couch at his side. 'Perhaps you would like to sit for a while and talk with me. You need not be worried that I will tell anyone. I am generally very good at keeping secrets.'

If that had been true, he never would have needed Jack's help. But it did no good to argue with the man. She collapsed into the place he had offered and struggled to compose herself.

'It is Jack, isn't it?' he said without warning, then reached up to straighten the tiara and reset an emerald pin that was near to falling from her coiffure.

'He is very…personable,' she admitted cautiously. Although it made no sense, the earl seemed quite fond of the actor and it would be a shame to disillusion him by complaining that the man was a rogue.

'Indeed, he is.' Lord Spayne smiled. 'That is a good part of why I chose him. He reminds me of myself at a younger age. Back then, I was quite the rake-hell.'

'Have you changed so very much?' she asked in surprise.

'I am satisfied with house and home, and a few select friends,' he admitted. 'I only go to London when forced by duty, for there are many here who would prefer that I kept to myself. It is easier on all concerned that I not raise any more scandal than necessary.' Spayne frowned. 'That is the difficulty with Henry. He is really the only one not satisfied with the way things have gone. But enough of me.' He paused and tipped her chin up, dabbing with a handkerchief at the smudged powder on her cheek. 'Tell me what you think of Kenton. When he sets his mind to something, he is rather hard to resist.'

'What he wishes does not concern me,' Thea said firmly. 'It is nothing less than what any man wishes, when he is thinking of his own satisfaction. It is foolish of me to be influenced by his desires.'

'Why ever so?' Spayne seemed surprised by what, to her, was obvious.

'Because there is nothing permanent about them. He will tell me any lie he can think of, if it furthers his ends. He is an actor. And they do not change. They are always looking for a better, more exciting version of the truth.'

'You really believe he cannot be sincere?'

'He has not been truthful to me since the moment we met.'

'But he cares for you.'

'He cares only for himself and the money. He has told me so.' But perhaps he cared for Spayne. He did seem to think highly of the man and recognised the debt he owed. And that had nothing to do with her.

'If that is what he claims, then you are right,' Spayne nodded. 'He is even lying to himself. If he cared only for his own skin, he would have run by now. And if he wishes money, he needn't wait for the conclusion of this game to receive it. He could steal whatever he wished from me and I would not even notice.'

Thea thought of the ring on her finger, a price-less heirloom released casually into the hands of a thief. 'You allow him to settle your business for you?'

Spayne smiled, unflappable, then eased back into the chair and took another sip of his brandy. 'When I can convince him to do so. He is dashedly good with it, you see. It is a shame that he does not mean to stay, for I would happily turn the estate over to his care, should he wish to remain.'

'And he would swindle you blind for your troubles,' Thea reminded him. 'He has no bond of blood with you.'

'He could steal no more than my own brother has managed,' Spayne replied. 'Nor could he make a bigger mess of things than I have myself.' He leaned closer to her with a fond smile, retying a bow on the shoulder of her gown. 'It is a sad thing to admit, but such titles as mine do not always fall to the wisest, the bravest and the most deserving. An honest history will show that I am far from the best of my line. Not as despicable as my brother, of course, but too craven to take the reins and make a good job of it. It does not do to be intimidated by one's own tenants.

If they continue badgering me, I am like to tell them that their roofs leak because I have not the money to fix them. But Jack always comes up with something. If he cannot find the money, he can at least make a decent excuse.'

'You mean he will lie to them,' Thea said.

'No more than was necessary,' Spayne replied. 'He has a natural talent for dealing with difficult situations, probably since he can be all things to all people. If he must refuse a request, he does it in a way that keeps hope alive and sends the petitioner away with a smile. Strangely, it seems that they are more productive when happy, even when I can offer nothing more than his hollow reassurances.'

When put this way, it did make a sort of perverse sense. 'But he is doing none of this by choice,' she reminded him. 'He fears he could be hanged if he returns too soon to his old life.'

Spayne laughed. 'For what? I paid his debt and he has done more than enough for me to work off the amount. It is far more likely that he will be hanged if he stays. If his true identity is discovered, it would be easier for me to claim myself as his victim than to admit my part in the scheme.'

'Then he stays for no logical reason?'

'If he loved being Jack Briggs as much as he claimed, he'd have gone back to it by now. Instead, he is spinning a more elaborate role than before. And he does so out of his fondness for us.'

'Fondness.' That went some small way towards describing what he had said the night they had spent at Spayne Court.

'And he wishes to bed you,' Spayne added bluntly. 'But I prefer to focus on the bonds of affection.'

'So would I,' Thea replied with a gasp. 'He might wish to bed me, but I certainly will not allow it.'

'You do not want him as well?' Spayne asked, eyes wide and innocent. She opened her mouth to respond, and he added quickly, 'Remember, you are quite adamant about the need for honesty in all things. Do not think to lie to me about your lack of desire and the need to maintain your reputation. I live far from London specifically so that stories of my antics may not escape to the city.

The current situation with Henry is difficult, but not so dire that the pair of you could not adjourn to Spayne Court and enjoy a proper honeymoon. Even if anyone takes note of your behaviour, I seriously doubt that comment will arise from a husband and wife sharing a bed.'

'It would be wrong,' Thea insisted, although it had felt like an excellent idea when they'd tussled together in the hall just now. 'He lusts after me, of course. That is only natural.' As was her corresponding animal attraction to him. 'But he is only pretending to be fond of me because Lord Kenton would have been had he married me. And he is such a good actor that he can convince even himself.'

'I doubt it requires very much convincing to be fond of you. You are a very nice young lady and one that I will very much enjoy having for a daughter.'

'Thank you,' Thea said, too tired to argue that she was not his daughter at all.

He took her by the shoulders and admired the work he had done to her costume, then gave an approving nod. 'As a second father to you, I have a bit of advice to offer. Give in to your desires.'

'Lord Spayne!' It was the sort of shocking thing her mother might say to her—and exactly the sort of advice she'd spent her life fighting against.

'I know that society tells you otherwise. But I also know the pain it causes to heart and mind to fight against who you are. If you want Kenton, or Jack Briggs, you may have him. There is no crime in it, no sin. Forget the name, forget the past. Remember only how you feel when you are with him.'

'Frustrated. Angry. Confused.'

'Confused,' Spayne said with a nod. 'Tell me—if he was so very wrong for you, why would you feel this confusion?'

'I should be able to resist him,' she agreed, wondering why she could not. She felt nothing but revulsion when Henry de Warde touched her. 'But he kissed me, and everything stopped making sense.'

'That is where the frustration comes from,' Spayne said with a smile. 'Yielding will take care of it.'

'It will leave only the anger,' she said firmly. 'I doubt I should be able to stand the man, should he use and discard me, as he is likely to.'

'Then you could make up your argument with him and be even happier than before,' Spayne said with a sigh, as though this were some sort of bonus.

Thea remembered the shoe-throwing tantrums her mother gave on occasion. Those outbursts had not weakened her father's affections for her, for all their violence, but Thea had no desire to emulate them. 'All the same, my lord, he is not someone I seek a closer relationship to. The sooner we are through, the happier I shall be.'

'Very well, then.' Spayne raised his hands to release her. 'Return to your party and see to your guests. Let Jack take care of Henry and do not worry yourself about it. As for the rest, I am sure your marriage will sort itself out with enough time.'

Given her extreme reaction to Jack, that was exactly what she feared and needed to guard most strenuously against.

Chapter Twelve

The last of the guests had strolled out of the large front door, and through the windows of the town house Jack could see the beginnings of dawn glowing above the houses to the east. He'd have cursed, if he could have managed to speak. But his voice was hoarse, nearly raw from too much chatting and breathing the smoke of the men taking cigars in the card room. The pain in his throat was coupled with the bitter taste of disappointment.

As a party, the evening had been quite successful, but as a part of his actual goal it had been a disaster. Cyn had barely managed to deliver his message and de Warde had looked at her like a wolf with a lamb dinner. Jack's own interference had done little to further the plot. He had been too lost in jealousy to keep the focus of his thoughts on the other man.

And then he had finished by very nearly ravishing the beautiful Thea in a public hallway. As pleasant as that had been, he'd have been much smarter to keep a cool head in the ballroom and seduce her later in the bedroom, when she'd have had no reason to break away. Instead, he had frightened her to the point where she'd kept a marked distance from him the rest of the evening. When forced into proximity, she had fallen into the banal courtesy she seemed to think society demanded for the spouse of a noble, beautiful and aloof, and not nearly so much fun as she'd been in the hall.

What had he been about in attempting this at all? There was not a chance of success. He had nothing more than a poorly written scene, a novice actress and his own insufficient education and experience, against an adversary who had already bested an earl and a baronet.

Better to admit defeat now and let the whole thing collapse. He would go upstairs and tell Cyn that she need not worry about a repeat performance. Or, better yet, he would tell her nothing at all. He could leave by the same door as the guests and be gone before the sun was fully up. Let the nobility sort out their mess tomorrow. It was none of his concern. It was the coward's way, he supposed, but it was the path he was most familiar with.

And then he turned to find the woman who had been avoiding him for hours collapsed like a rag doll on the bench beside the door. He could not walk past her with no explanation, but a few words would have to do. He held out a hand to her. 'Up you get, Thea. There is a matter we must discuss.' She would be glad to be rid of him, he was sure. It would be a mercy on his part to remove himself from her presence.

She gave him a baleful look, her society smile disappearing with the last of their visitors. 'Please, simply leave me alone. I am not well.'

As he looked at her, it did seem that she spoke the truth. But with her objection to convenient lies, was that any real surprise? She covered her face with one slender hand, as though the small amount of light shining through the leaded window panes was almost too much to bear. From what he could see of her complexion through the fingers, she was unnaturally pale. 'What ails you? Your stomach? Or is it your head?'

'Just a megrim. Such parties almost always bring them on. It is the stress, I am sure.'

'This was a particularly difficult evening,' he agreed. 'But you needn't have worried. You handled it all masterfully. It is a shame that you could not take more pleasure in it.'

'I was the hostess,' she said firmly. 'It was my job to give pleasure to others, not to seek it for myself.'

'My, but that is a grim assessment.' He had always assumed that, with money and rank, there came a sort of automatic pleasure. But Cyn made it seem like another set of worries. He must remember to be glad of his freedom, now that he meant to take it back.

'And, of course, there is the business with Mr de Warde. It was the point of the whole evening. But it went terribly.'

'Not so bad, really.' While she might stick at untruths, delivering a convincing lie was not all that hard for him. And if ever a woman deserved to hear one, it was his poor wife, who looked truly wretched as she remembered how it had gone. 'We will find a way around him, once I have a little time to think.'

He remembered how she had looked before the gathering had commenced and felt a stab of sympathy. 'For now, I know something that might help.' He stepped behind the bench where she was seated and leaned back against his legs.

She resisted at first. It was no wonder that her head ached, for her body was as taut as a bow string.

He pushed on her shoulders, forcing her closer to him. 'Close your eyes,' he commanded, then placed one hand on either temple and rubbed his palms in slow circles.

Almost immediately she sighed and he felt some of the tension leave her. 'I expect you are doing this so you can look down the front of my gown.'

'I expect I am,' he said and then surprised himself by not taking the suggestion. It was not that another glimpse of her breasts did not interest him. But, got this way, it was hardly sporting. 'At least you will gain something by it, so do not complain.'

'You are right. I should not be ungrateful.' She relaxed even further, melting into him like butter.

He pushed her head forwards and stroked the nape of her neck. 'You are forgiven. Now be quiet and let me help you.'

This was different. He could not remember ever saying such a thing to another human being. But it was nice, helping her. While the physical advantages of having a woman legally in one's bed were understandable, the idea of finding satisfaction in nurturing and protecting a person frailer than himself had never occurred to him.

Of course, he had never met Cyn.

And now she was nestled into him like a sleepy kitten. She sighed again. 'You are right. That is much better.'

He paused, expecting a dismissal.

'Don't stop. Your hands feel wonderful.' She had relaxed enough to be completely unguarded. If he was smart, he would press the advantage, turn the massage into a caress and gain what he

214 _Two Wrongs Make a Marriage_

had wanted from the first night. He could leave after and still be gone before the sun was fully up.

Instead, he ran his fingers through her hair, removing the tiara and loosing the pins that held the elaborate coif so that he could massage her scalp. This elicited an almost-unladylike groan. 'The late Lady Spayne was too right,' she murmured. 'Uneasy lies the head that wears the crown.'

'_Henry IV,_' he said with surprise.

'_Henry IV Part Two,_' she answered without looking up. 'There is much I did not seek to learn from my mother, but a knowledge of Shakespeare was quite inescapable.'

'And the quote is appropriate,' he agreed. 'You hair was bound so tightly it surprises me that you can think at all.'

She shook out the mane of red so that it fell free to her shoulders. 'I must dress it so. The curls run wild, otherwise.'

'And we mustn't have that,' he mocked, remembering the shocking profusion that her mother had allowed and the way she'd refused to powder it, even when roles had required it. In response her daughter seemed to have adopted a style that, while most fashionable, was the picture of restraint. But as he undid the braids, Thea's curls wrapped around his fingers as though they could tie him to her.

'Tonight, the braids were the only thing holding me up. Now that you have undone them, I swear, I am almost too weak to stand.'

'Then let me help you.' He pulled her to her feet and scooped her into his arms. She was a surprisingly easy burden, fitting perfectly in his hold.

She gave one sleepy murmur of protest before snuggling close again. 'What are you doing to me?' she asked, but it was hardly the demanding tone he'd grown accustomed to.

'Putting you to bed.' He turned and went into the house, down the hall and mounted the stairs towards their rooms.

'But I don't want to go. I want to stay here. With you.'

He might inform her that if it was togetherness she wanted, a bed was just the place for it. Instead, he said, 'You will not be so charitable once I am through with you, I am sure.'

'I shall return to detesting you when I am not so tired,' she agreed. 'And when you have not been so kind to me.'

'And I will go back to being despicable tomorrow.' Hadn't his plan been quite the opposite only a moment ago?

But leaving would mean leaving the delightful baggage who had twisted her fingers around his lapel and was now burying her face against his neck. 'Do not send me to bed like a child. Tell me what you are planning.' A touch of her old firmness was returning, now that her head was no longer bothering her. But it explained the real reason she wished to stay with him, even though it was not as flattering as the one he'd chosen to imagine.

'I hardly know myself,' he admitted. 'And no amount of thinking will force it from me tonight. I suspect I shall wake with some idea of what to do next. I will share it with you then. It will be over soon enough and then you will be rid of me.' Why did his impending freedom seem less appealing than it had only a moment ago?

'I shall miss you,' she replied. 'I am growing quite used to you destroying my peace of mind.'

They were at her door now. He fumbled with the handle. There were probably a dozen glib comments he could have made about what he would like to do to disturb her calm, but he could not manage to think of one. Instead, he carried her to the bed and set her down on the edge, then reached behind her to undo the lacing on her gown.

'I should call a maid.'

'No need, my dear. I assure you, I am quite an experienced dresser and not the least bit shy.'

'Actors,' she muttered with a laugh as he efficiently stripped her to shift and stockings, pulled back the coverlet and tucked her into bed.

'Sleep,' he answered, and planted a single kiss on the top of her ginger head before going through the door to his own room.

Chapter Thirteen

'Lady Kenton, you have visitors.' Polly drew back the curtains of the bed and let in the late morning light.

Thea yawned and touched her temple, surprised that her head did not hurt as it had just a few hours before. She had a vague recollection of being put innocently to bed by the man who, earlier in the evening, had been trying to remove her gown in the hall. One or the other of the recollections had to be a dream, for they did not seem to correspond.

She looked sleepily at her maid. 'Did you say visitors in the plural?'

Polly gave her a confused look.

'Are there more than one? And do these people realise that I did not lie down until dawn?'

'One of them is your mother,' Polly said. It explained much. Since she had returned to London, her mother had shown little sense of convention, coming and going as she pleased without invitation or announcement.

'And the other?'

'Mr Henry de Warde, my lady.'

At this, Thea sat bolt upright, gathering the sheets about her. 'Here? Already?' She squinted at the clock. 'It is barely ten o'clock.' She thought hurriedly. 'Have Graves put him in the library and fetch my husband to speak to him.'

'Lord Kenton is still asleep,' Polly said. 'And Mr de Warde wishes to speak to you. And the library is already occupied. Lord Spayne…'

'Does not wish to see his brother,' Thea agreed. Of course, neither did she. Damn Jack for sleeping when there was so much to be done. She had no instruction as to how to proceed. 'The drawing room for Mr de Warde, then.'

'And your mother waits in the morning room.'

'Keep the two separate,' Thea said, unsure what her mother was likely to do should she know of the man's presence. Worse yet, what embarrassing question Mr de Warde was likely to ask of her after last night's discussion. 'Refreshments for everyone. Dress me in the blue muslin. And for heaven's sake, send the valet to Kenton's room and get him downstairs to help me with this.'

A few minutes later, when Thea entered the morning room, she found her mother holding court over the maid that poured her chocolate, looking as regal as a duchess and grander by far than the earl hiding in the library. But then, Antonia Banester carried out every social call as though it were an opportunity to take centre stage.

Annoying as it was, Thea had to admit that it had served the older woman well. Her past should have been a damning blight on any reputation, but her mother had made it a sort of asset. She sat even the most common chair as though it were a throne and allowed gentlemen to admire her for her beauty and her vivacity, while acting as friend, confidante or sympathetic shoulder to ladies. As long as she was silent, she appeared to be the mostly gently bred of females.

It was only when she opened her mouth that Thea worried, for there was no telling what she was likely to say.

'Mother,' she said, her tone low so as not to carry to other parts of the house. 'What are you doing here?'

'I heard the most interesting rumour at the ball last night,' her mother responded, her eyes full of devilment. 'And strangely enough, it concerned me.'

'About that...' Thea tried to think of a logical place to begin the story.

'Lady Antonia.' Behind her, Jack fairly skidded into the doorway, still tugging his cravat into shape and pushing past Thea as though she did not matter. Then he stood before her mother, bowing deeper than he had before, as though she were truly a duchess and he a footman.

'My dear boy.' Though Thea felt sleep deprived and fuzzy, her mother was in fine form this morning, practically sparkling at the opportunity to make a fresh conquest. She waited for Jack to raise his face to her, then held out her hands to take his, pulling him forwards and kissing him lightly on the cheek.

To Thea's horror, the man who was supposed to be her husband looked up with a sincere and uncontrollable blush and the eyes of a sheep.

She set her teeth against each other until she could hear them grind, and clenched her fists to prevent the slap on the arm that he deserved and she most assuredly wished to deliver. 'Stop this nonsense, Jack. You have met my mother before, you know. You saw her just last night.'

'The ballroom was hardly the place to suggest what I had in mind. And I could not speak candidly, for we were not alone,' he responded without turning his head.

'You are not alone with her,' Thea reminded him acidly. 'I am here.'

'Of course, darling,' her mother said dismissively. 'We have not forgotten you. Now let the man speak.'

'Lady Antonia,' he said, wetting his lips as though nervous. 'I never thought to ask this of the woman who ensnared me from the stage when I was so young as to hardly understand what the feelings meant, but I find myself in need of an actress.'

'You wish me to perform again?' Her mother laid a trembling hand upon her breast as though shocked, a gesture which Thea knew to be false modesty. It amazed her that anyone was fooled by such, for she had learned almost from birth to be suspicious of it.

'It is a small part,' he said, staring at his feet and toeing the carpet, humble in response. 'Hardly worthy of you.'

'I have been retired for many, many years,' her mother responded with a sidelong, demure glance that she used when she wished someone to notice the green glory of her eyes. 'It is most flattering to think that there are those who can still remember.'

'How could I forget?' he said with a sigh.

'I am sure if you tried, you could manage it,' Thea prompted and poked him in the sleeve with a stiffened finger. 'We do not have time to reminisce right now. De Warde is in the next room.'

'De Warde?' her mother said, alarmed. For a

moment, the glamour seemed to fade and the older, worried woman underneath it was revealed.

'Jack forced me to tell the most outlandish lie about you last night. Now I fear we shall all have to answer for it.'

'There is no time to explain fully,' said Jack, staring past her in the direction of the sitting room. 'But we need you to beguile Henry de Warde.'

Her mother gave him a sharp look. 'I do not know what you think of me, my lord, but I am most devoted to my husband and do not wish to have anything to do with that odious man.'

'I understand,' Jack assured her. 'And might I say that Banester is lucky to have such loyalty from one who could have any man she chose. What we require is nothing more than a short conversation. A few words only, but delivered with the grace and confidence that I know you are capable of giving them so that he believes you utterly and completely. We need you to tell de Warde that you are *enceinte* and that it is the result of the statue he sold to your husband.'

Her mother gave a short, unladylike laugh that

quickly modulated into a seductively throaty chuckle. Thea could almost see the hair rising on the back of Jack's neck. When her mother used her charms to the fullest, as she tended to do when caught off guard, few men could resist. 'How utterly delicious.' She smiled winningly at Jack. 'I assume that you have some nefarious scheme afoot?'

'I would not call it nefarious, exactly.' Jack's eyes were downcast again, hands behind his back.

'It is wicked in the extreme,' Thea corrected. 'We mean to trick the man out of the money he has taken and hopefully we will leave him as destitute as he has left us.'

'Stronger than I'd have put it,' Jack admitted.

'Thea has always had a way of plain speaking. I could not seem to break her of it,' Lady Antonia said with pity, as though the truth were some embarrassing birthmark that could not be removed. 'But really, do you mean to cheat the man?'

Jack wove his fingers together. 'Just a bit, perhaps. Really, given the opportunity, he will do the work. As they say, give a man enough rope and he will hang himself.' Jack smiled at her mother, very near to being besotted.

'As well you should know, Jack,' Thea snapped. It was foolish to feel jealous of her own mother, but sometimes it was hard not to be.

'Do not worry. The circumstances do not bother me overly,' her mother said with a devious smile. 'The man deserves all that we can give him in the way of discomfort and embarrassment. I will be happy to oblige.' She reached into her reticule, produced a vial of hartshorn and waved it delicately beneath her nose. 'Please, Thea. Take me to the sitting room and allow me to rest. A woman in my condition sometimes has difficulties with morning visits and the sofas are particularly comfortable in that room. I cannot stay long. I am sure your other guest will understand.'

'This way, Mother,' Thea said, rolling her eyes at Jack and taking her mother's arm. It was nonsense, of course. But her partner in crime seemed almost convinced enough to offer assistance, even though he knew full well what caused the sudden indisposition. Before she went, he whispered a few quick words of instruction to Antonia and she nodded in agreement.

Jack remained behind and Thea led her mother the few short steps down the hall to the next room, where their enemy awaited.

'Please forgive my delay, Mr de Warde,' she said, relieved that she did not have to face the man alone. 'But I was receiving my mother and did not wish to leave her.'

'I much prefer the light in this room,' her mother said, fanning her face with a gloved hand. 'And the air is fresher as well. But enough of my delicacies. Mr de Warde.' Her mother held out both hands to him and, when he took them, leaned in to kiss him on both cheeks.

The gesture was so genuine, and so affectionate, that even the gentleman receiving it seemed surprised. 'Lady Banester?'

'It is so good to find you here.' Her mother coloured prettily, somehow managing to look both look delicate and pale beneath the flush. 'I am so sorry if I have treated you coldly in the past. My current happiness renders the previous feelings invalid and I hope that an apology will be enough.'

'Then am I to believe the news that your daughter offered was accurate?' This seemed to be the last thing that de Warde had expected to hear.

Her mother tapped Thea's arm with fingers. 'You naughty thing. We were keeping it a secret, were we not, until things had progressed further. Disappointments sometimes occur in the early months and I would hate to raise hopes only to dash them again. And, of course, we must inform your grandfather before telling the rest of the *ton.*'

This went in direct opposition to her current openness in speaking in front of their other guest, but then she lowered her lashes and gave de Warde a veiled glance. 'Of course, it is hardly necessary to keep the truth from one who has been as instrumental in our good fortune as Mr de Warde.'

'I have?' Knowing the magnitude of the fraud he had perpetrated on them, he was totally at a loss.

'Of course,' Antonia ploughed on, ignoring his

discomfiture, 'I thought it extreme at the time. But the little idol you found for my husband was well worth the price we paid for it. Although it was up to Kenton to find the missing piece and make the thing complete.'

'You say there is more?' He looked both puzzled and suspicious now. 'And what would Kenton know of it?'

'He lived in India, of course. Apparently, such altars are quite common in the remote areas he travelled.' Antonia smiled triumphantly. 'And he said that they must be bought, not given as gifts. That explained the fee you extracted from my husband. I am so sorry to have suspected you, sir. For a time, I quite thought you had tried to cheat us. But now...' she laid a hand across her belly and gave a sigh of relief '...all is clear.'

'Is that so?' De Warde's eyes followed her hand, and then returned to her face, still doubtful. 'And he claimed there was a missing element?'

'Indeed. Correct me if I am wrong, Thea.' She glanced to her daughter.

'I would not dream of interrupting,' Thea said, not needing to feign sincerity.

'But as Kenton explains it, Lakshmi, the girl—' Antonia gave a dramatic flourish of her hands to indicate a curvy body and multiple arms '—brings luck and prosperity. But she must be embraced by her lover, Vishnu, to bring fertility.' Antonia gave a coy purse of the lips. 'He is a blue gentleman, also well endowed...' she paused significantly and then added '...with arms.'

Thea gasped in embarrassment, but the frankness seemed to have no effect on de Warde other than adding to his dazed expression.

Antonia continued. 'I must admit, the pair of them together make a rather striking, one might say scandalous image.' She wrapped her own arms about her body in imitation of an erotic embrace.

'Mother!' Thea had no trouble pretending outrage at this latest lie. Whether she was speaking truth or lies, her mother managed to be equally outrageous.

'I expect it is seen as some kind of offering to the gods.' Antonia frowned. 'And I doubt the vicar would approve of it. It does not sound very

Christian.' She brightened. 'But it was amazingly effective, despite that.'

'And are the statues still in your possession?' de Warde asked. 'For I would most like to see them together.'

'Of course not,' Antonia said dismissively. 'Once one has used them, it is important that they be got rid of quickly. It gives others a chance at progeny and prevents...' she gave a giggle '...multiple blessings. While I should like to have one son, I seriously doubt, at this point in my life, that I should wish to have two of them. We had Kenton return them to the antiquities dealer where he found Vishnu.' She smiled at Thea. 'But I am sure he means to purchase them back again immediately, my dear. You have the succession to think of, after all.'

'Certainly not,' Thea said, forgetting for a moment that the whole conversation was a sham.

'But of course.' Her mother reached to pat her hand. 'I do not mean to imply that your husband is any less than fully capable in that regard, but it is sometimes better to be sure. And he says that the users of such icons invariably have strong sons, which is what Spayne will wish to see from you. Consider how long it took to secure the situation for your father and I.'

'I doubt that he expects such of me,' Thea insisted, though it made sense of his advice at the ball.

'Am I not right, Mr de Warde?' Antonia appealed to the man, as though he would be an ally. 'Spayne will want to continue the line. And other than Kenton, your family has no issue. I believe you and your wife are childless.'

De Warde's eyes narrowed ever so slightly. 'We have been married but a few years.'

'But your wife is older than you, is she not?' Antonia gave a sympathetic shake of her head. 'It is not always easy for a woman to produce a child as age advances.'

'Mother,' Thea said in warning, as her mother seemed to have lost what little sense of decorum she possessed.

Antonia covered her mouth with her hand. 'Oh, my dear, you are right. I am being terribly rude to discuss such things at all, much less in mixed company. Please, Mr de Warde, accept my apologies.'

'Of course, madam.' He gave a slight bow, but he was looking speculatively at her midsection. 'And congratulations to you and your husband on your impending success.'

Antonia reached out a limp but graceful hand and clasped his. 'You are too kind, sir. And after the unfair way we treated you. We owe you much. I can hardly…' Her mother gave a slight gasp, as though she could not contain her emotions, and then looked up at him with a watery, yet bewitching smile. 'I cry so easily now. I had forgotten the excesses of emotion one has, for it has been so long since I was expecting Thea. But thank you. A thousand times, thank you. Because of you, our fortunes are mended with the breach between William and his father. We will name the child Henry, in your honour.'

If he had been doubtful before, Mr de Warde now had the slightly panicked expression that men sometimes got when confronted by an overly emotional and expectant woman. 'It was nothing, madam. Really. I had no idea…' Then he remembered that he should have expected these results, cleared his throat and said, 'I had no idea that it would affect you so. But if these tears are happy ones, then I will not begrudge them to you.'

'You have done Thea and Jack a service as well. He had not expected to find Lakshmi here in England. And now that the divine lovers are united, he and Thea might—'

'Mother!' It was quite one thing to hear lurid stories about her parents' intimate lives—it was an embarrassment, but one that Thea had suffered over the years—but quite another thing indeed to have the stories extend to her.

Her mother had the sense to look contrite. 'Of course, my darling. I speak out of turn again. Mr de Warde wished to speak to you as well, did he not?' When Antonia looked at the man, it was with disapproval that was almost motherly.

And Thea had to admit that his request to meet with her, specifically and alone, was an unusual one and not altogether proper. She followed her mother's example and gave the man an innocent look. 'Yes, Mr de Warde, we have quite carried away the topic with our own concerns. What is the reason for your visit this morning?'

'I only wished to continue our conversation of the previous evening, which was interrupted, as you remember.'

She could remember no such thing. From her side, it had been a timely rescue by Jack from the attentions of a man who had already proven far too attentive. She hoped their brief exchange at the ball had not given him the idea that she actually wished contact with him. If that was the case, what was she to do with him once she had embarked on the freedom of pretend widowhood? 'I remember speaking, of course,' she admitted, 'but I had quite forgotten the topic.'

Mr de Warde looked from her to her mother and back again. 'Nothing important. I merely wished to welcome you to the family.' He gave her a particularly intense gaze that convinced her he had quite misread her desire for privacy on the last evening. 'Perhaps I might return tomorrow and find you less busy.'

'Or perhaps not.' Jack was standing in the doorway, a stern frown upon his face.

'Kenton.' Antonia fairly shrieked with delight at the sight of him. In Thea's opinion, it was rather excessive. But then, what part of her mother's performance had not been?

'Kenton,' de Warde responded flatly.

'Uncle de Warde.' Jack gave a tight nod of his head and stepped closer to Thea, laying a protective hand upon her shoulder. 'Do not think you need to take the welcoming of my wife on to yourself. My father and I have that quite in hand.'

'I am pleased to hear it,' de Warde said, clearly unhappy. 'And interested as well to hear more of the assistance you gave to Banester and his lady.'

'That—' Jack's eyes narrowed '—was a private matter and no concern of yours.'

'I disagree.'

As did Thea. If the whole point was to involve him, why could they not get it over and done with? 'But...'

Jack shot her a warning look. 'Thea, we will discuss the matter later.' His tone was full of the condescension she had expected from a powerful man towards a young and inexperienced wife. Miss Pennyworth had assured her that such behaviour was normal. But now that she faced it, Thea found it rather annoying.

Jack hardly seemed to notice. His hand tightened on her ever so slightly. It seemed more like a display of possessiveness than any silent explanation of his words. 'I think any more such calls on my wife can be made when I am at home to visitors as well.'

'Of course.' De Warde gave a tight bow and a look of purest venom to the man at her side. 'Good day, then.' He rose and took his leave.

Almost as soon as the door closed she heard Antonia's sigh of satisfaction. When Thea turned, it was to find her reclined on the couch like Cleopatra, sipping a glass of port.

'It is rather early, Mother,' Thea reminded her. 'Still not noon.'

'It might be morning for you, but it is the end of the work day for me,' her mother said with a moue. 'And I find a small glass refreshing after a successful performance.'

'Successful performance?' Jack said, still looking at her mother like a devoted puppy and taking no notice of her morning drinking. 'More than that. It was a masterwork.'

'You think so?' her mother asked.

'The bits you embroidered on to my tattered story have made a whole cloth of it.'

'Improvisation was always my strength,' Antonia said with false modesty.

'And it is a challenge for my talents to rise to yours,' Jack replied with a bow.

'What the devil are you both talking about?' Thea demanded, throwing aside her training and evoking the sort of common language that her mother used. 'The man hardly said a word.' She glared at her mother. 'Not that you left him space for one.' The reproof was useless. Her mother had never learned the art of listening more than one talked. So Thea turned her anger and frustration to Jack. 'And then you sent him away.'

Now her mother and her husband were sharing compliments and secrets like old friends. And, as usual, Thea was left quite in the dark.

Jack looked at her with surprise, almost as though he'd forgotten she was still at his side.

'My apologies, Cyn. We are not attempting to keep secrets from you.'

'But you are doing it all the same,' she reminded him.

'Then let us catch you up on what has occurred.' He offered a sweeping gesture to Antonia. 'Ladies first.'

'In the beginning, Mr de Warde was sceptical,' Antonia confirmed. 'The change of heart in our family seems quite extreme to him. He cheated us, after all. And now we are opening our arms and embracing him.' She gave Thea a sly look. 'Of course, he is still hoping that one of us will embrace him. Watch that one, Thea. He is a snake.'

'I understood that much, Mother. Now explain the rest of it.'

'The less we told him of the magical properties of the idol, the more he wanted to know of it.' She gave Jack a smile now. 'I was crying at the end and had him in the palm of my hand.'

'No man can resist your tears,' Jack said with a sigh.

'Which proves how stupid you all are,' Thea

said with finality. 'My mother is quite the most transparent creature, once you know her tricks.'

'Do not be jealous, Thea. It does not become you. And you are quite charming enough in your own right when you make an effort to be. See how easily you caught Kenton.'

'I did not catch him,' Thea insisted. But Jack was giving her a speculative and worried look, as though he feared being ensnared should she take it into her head to weep.

'Do not trouble me with semantics,' her mother replied. 'No matter how it happened, you are married to his enemy and it makes de Warde desire you all the more.' She gave Jack a warning look. 'And you must be careful with my daughter, sir. I will expose all if you think to sacrifice her to that monster because of some silly family argument.'

'Never.' Jack laid a hand over his heart. 'He will have to settle for the idol that I do not wish to give him.' He thought for a moment. 'Or idols. At an antiquities dealer, you said?'

'You could not very well keep such valuable items in the house,' her mother said with a smile.

'You have presented me with a challenge,' he said. 'But I am worthy. Let me take my leave of you. I must dress to go out.' He smiled at Thea. 'Since you wish to see the plan in progress, you will come as well.'

'Wherever are we going?' Thea asked.

'To the antiquities dealer, of course. To visit my idols.'

Chapter Fourteen

An hour later, Jack met her in the foyer and had the footman summon the carriage. He'd dressed in his plainest coat, setting aside stick, studs and fob. As he had recommended, Thea wore a cloak and a veil. It was hardly a disguise to fool a friend, but an acquaintance might not have recognised her at first glance.

And Jack appeared to be someone similar to Kenton. Was he distant family? A cousin, perhaps? He'd seemed to change his posture along with his coat. As he moved, his body became less rigid and controlled, moving through the world as though simultaneously seeking adventure and unsure of where the next step might land him.

They took the Kenton equipage as far as Bond Street, then Jack dismissed it, informing the driver that, since this was a fine day, they would very likely walk back. Instead, he led her a few streets away and hired a cab to take them the rest of the journey.

The little shop they stopped at was down a dark side street, far from the area she was accustomed to. But the sign above the door, with its three balls covered in flaking gold leaf, revealed it for what it was. 'A pawn shop?' she said suspiciously.

'Indeed,' Jack answered with some glee.

'Mr de Warde will never come to such a place.'

'He never has before. I am quite sure of that. And that is what will make it possible to gull him now. He will not know what to expect.' Jack grinned broadly. 'I, on the other hand, am quite familiar with the workings of such places, and this one in particular.'

'What a surprise,' Thea said, though it was no surprise at all.

He laughed again and squeezed her hand. 'Come along, darling. It will be another educating experience for you.' He pushed the door, which squeaked as it opened, and she heard the jingle of a bell. The tone was brassier than anything she'd heard in a nicer shop, sounding almost surly in its announcement of their presence.

She looked about her, taking in the strange surroundings. The little room was dimly lit, which gave it an even more mysterious appearance. But it was the stuff lining the walls that drew her attention. Bric-à-brac from hundreds of lives, abandoned and for sale: cavalry swords and duelling pistols hung from the walls, outmoded gowns and coats filled racks beneath them. The shelves beside them held trims: scraps of braid and plumes plucked from finery by light-fingered servants. Trays of gaudy jewellery heaped casually in plain sight to demonstrate their meagre worth, spilled from the drawers and counters of odd bits of furniture that she could not imagine displaying in any home. Taken as a whole, it was both intriguing and a little bit sad, as though the misfortune that brought the customers to sell the items left a miasma over them that could be felt.

A man appeared from a back room, sharp featured and with a rat-like squint, but with a well-roundedness that implied the success of his business.

'Joseph, Joseph, Joseph.' Jack spread his arms wide in welcome, as though the broker was the one who had come to him.

'Briggs.' It was clear that he'd been recognised and equally as clear that he was not welcome. 'What do you have for me today? And if it is nothing more than dirty lace and mismatched brass buttons passed for gold, then you may as well go out again. In short, do not expect me to pay for a good story.'

'So much more than that,' Jack said with a smile. 'It is not a story. It is a proposition.'

'A proposition?' The man's narrow eyes narrowed even further.

'A business transaction of a more lucrative type. I wish to rent your shop.'

The man laughed. 'My whole shop.'

'For a special performance.'

The man waved a hand. 'Do you see a stage here? Because I do not.'

'I will need it for a few hours at most,' Jack continued, as though he had heard no objection.

'An evening will do. Some time when you are normally closed. I will see to it that it does not interfere with your business.'

'So shall I. Because no such performance will take place.' Joseph pointed towards the door as though a gesture would be enough to eject them from the shop.

'You will be well compensated for it,' Jack assured him.

'For the chance to have you and your thieving friends strip my shelves? I would have to be well compensated indeed.' But the man did not refuse outright this time. Instead, he looked at Thea as though trying to decide if she had sufficient money to make this worth his while.

Jack held out his hands in a gesture of innocence. 'I will leave the merchandise alone. I merely need a suitable space to meet with an old friend. He will compensate me. And I will compensate you twenty pounds for each hour needed.'

The man considered. 'Thirty. And I will need the money up front.'

Jack mimed turning out his pockets. 'Unfortunately, that will not be possible. I am a bit short right now, but the return is guaranteed.'

'And you should know, from all the other times you have been a bit short, that that is not the way I operate.' He looked at Thea again. 'If you wish me to even consider this, you must give me some collateral.'

Jack looked at her as well, his gaze devoid of passion. It went on so long that she almost began to suspect, despite what her mother had said, that he was ready to barter her away. Then he grabbed her by the hand and pulled her out of earshot and behind a counter holding a collection of enamelled snuff boxes. 'Give him your ring.'

'My what?'

'Your wedding ring. Give it over.' He held his hand, palm out to receive it.

She grabbed his arm and tried to drag him back into the light. 'I most certainly will not.'

'You will. It is not as if we are actually married. There can be no sentiment involved.'

Yet there was. It felt as if he was rejecting her marriage, treating it as though it meant nothing at all to him. 'All the same, you gave it to me to wear and I will have it on my finger, even after your death. You cannot take it back.'

He stared at her with surprise, and she thought she saw his resolve wavering. In a moment, he would admit that he had no right to part her from her wedding ring and find some other less hurtful solution. But then his eyes hardened again and he said, 'You can have the ring, or the money that belonged to your father, which I will give to you when this scheme goes right. You cannot have both. Now give it over.'

It was a betrayal of the earl, but who had she known longer, him or her own father? And what did it mean of the marriage and of Jack? Without the ring, who was she? She twisted the emerald on her hand, still unwilling to take it off. 'What will I tell people who ask after it?'

'Tell them it is being cleaned. Or sized. Or reset to be less heavy. Tell them whatever you like. In short, make something up.'

'You would know how to do that far better than I.'

'And you are learning fast enough. You only need more practice,' he said, as though deception was a thing that came easily to her. 'Now give me the ring and keep quiet.'

She pulled it free of her finger and dropped it into his hand, and he walked back across the room and presented it to the pawnbroker. 'There you are. Gold, two large diamonds and an even larger emerald. Quite genuine, I assure you.'

'I will assure myself, thank you very much.' Joseph took out a jeweller's glass, fixed it in his eye and examined the ring first in silence, and then with a small sigh of satisfaction. 'Worth thirty pounds at least.'

Jack scoffed in disgust. 'Far more than that.'

'And it will be mine when your game falls through and you cannot pay.'

'Which it will not. Keep the ring for now and return it to me when we are done or I will have you up on charges. I will return when I know the hour and the day of our performance. At that time, you have but to give me the keys and remain absent until I summon you. I will collect the ring, pay you for your time and we will be through. There is no need to record this in your books. I think it might be better for both of us if it were easily forgotten afterwards.'

'Agreed.' Joseph offered a hand and the men shook once, eyes meeting as though gauging each other's honesty, then they parted and Jack offered Thea his arm. 'Come, my sweet. Our business has concluded.' He bowed deeply to the broker. '*Au revoir*, my dear sir.' His manner was a little too grand, as though he were not an actor playing a viscount, but a viscount playing an actor.

As they left the shop, Jack smiled as though the interview had been a success.

Thea had a much more critical opinion of it. 'He does not like you very much. Nor does he trust you.'

'He does not like anyone. And as for trust? He would not be as successful in his business were he any more trusting. But he is as honest as can be expected. And he knows that the ring was not mine to give, nor yours. It is obviously part of an entail. By law that means he should not have accepted it. He will not be asking questions because his risks outweigh ours.'

'Very well. He is our partner in crime. And what are we to do next?'

'Find another partner to play pawnbroker.'

'Another?' It was bad enough that the story had spread this far. 'You are making things unnecessarily complicated.'

'You must trust me to know what is best,' he said.

When they were seated in a rented cab, Jack pushed himself into a darkened corner opposite Thea, hoping that the shadows would hide the slight sheen of perspiration popping out on his brow. The brief visit to his old life had raised strange emotions in him, as did the sight of the beautiful woman hesitating to remove his ring.

He was probably reading too much into that, wishing for things that could never be. But when the moment had arrived to part with it, she had not given him the perfectly logical argument that he'd expected. The ring was entailed and not theirs to barter away on some wild scheme.

Instead, she'd said, 'You gave this to me.' As though he'd had any right to place it on her finger and as if the oath accompanying it had any meaning.

It made him wish that there were some other form of ready cash so that she did not have to remove it. Why had he not worn studs, or kept even a flask in his pocket that he might barter with? Anything other than the token he had given to her with his pledge. Better he should give up his own ring than to take the one he had given her.

For a moment, at least, she had been his wife, just as she had in the ballroom when de Warde had frightened her and she'd looked to him for help. And he had been her husband, charged by God to love and protect her, and happy to do so.

The closed space of the cab was suddenly too warm, too stuffy and heavy with her perfume, but there was nothing cloying about the scent she wore. It was light, redolent of the first spring flowers, as though that hopeful season could be captured in a bottle. He would not be able to get enough of that scent, even if he pressed his cheek to her hair. Common sense told him that if he wanted his head to clear and his brow to dry, he should hang his head from the window and feel the fetid breeze of London, and let harsh reality draw him back.

Instead, he dropped the curtain on his window, making the space even closer and more shadowed. They had a long trip across the city to find his friend and the traffic would not move. They were creeping along, trapping him with a woman he could not have. Even covered properly to conceal her identity, he could imagine the body underneath, waiting for him. His fingers tingled, his mouth watered, all senses alive at the opportunity.

'Where are we going now?' she asked, her green eyes open, suspicious, her mouth curved softly down in disapproval.

'To find an actor friend of mine to help me in the next scene,' he said, cursing the fact that he must talk to anyone at all, other than Thea. Antonia could keep her tears and learn a lesson from her daughter. If this fresh-faced innocence could be brought under control, it was a weapon more powerful than her mother's excessive emotion.

'Pawnbrokers and actors,' she said with a

frown. 'I am totally out of my depth. Nothing at Miss Pennyworth's school prepared me for this.'

'I expect not,' he said, with a smile and slid across to her side as the carriage lurched to a stop again.

'Do you mean to tell me any of what we are doing? Or am I to be kept in the dark until after it happens?'

If he told her the whole truth of what was coming, she'd likely have put him out of the carriage and run straight back to her mother. Nor was he sure that she could keep the secret. With her lack of skill, de Warde might stare into those large, guileless eyes and see everything.

'You are still angry about the ring,' he said.

'I am not.' But just as he had feared, he could see the truth plain in her face.

'I am sorry. It could not be helped. And it is only a short time that you will be without it.'

'But what if your plan fails?'

'It will not fail,' he said, leaning close so that he might whisper. 'We will have it back before it is missed.' It was hardly necessary. Their driver was cursing loudly at the stalled traffic in front of them, oblivious to anything that might go on in the cab behind him. There was no reason to sit huddled like two doves on a branch, cooing into ear other's ears, but he quite liked being close to her. And he was sure that a fresh trinket would distract her. 'We will stop in Bond Street and get you another to take its place.'

'The ring itself is not important. It is the broken promise,' she insisted.

She was right. It had been unworthy of him. Kenton would have cut off his own arm before parting his wife from her wedding ring. But Jack Briggs had been thoughtless. 'I am sorry. Truly, I am.'

He leaned forwards and kissed her cheek to seal his words. But if one quick kiss was good, two would be better. A few kisses would do no harm, surely. He would not allow things to get out of hand.

His old self started in surprise at this sudden chivalrous desire not to take things too far and the fact that it had come from his more practical self, and not the normally self-righteous Kenton. Kenton seemed all in favour of the chance to make up for his mistake.

Jack waited for the rejection that should be coming, for surely Thea would have more sense and push him away.

'I suppose it is better that I allow this than to see you mooning over my mother, as you were this morning,' she said with a sigh. 'I thought, for a time, you had forgotten who you had pretended to wed.' Then she turned to the side to give him room on the seat next to her, tipped her bonnet to the side and raised a corner of her veil.

It was a trap of some kind, just as her last affection had been. And just as it had been the last time, he leapt into it, unable to stop himself. He slipped his arm around her shoulders and leaned closer. Without another thought, his eyes dropped down to her bosom, like a doomed soul towards hell. It was totally hidden beneath her cloak, yet he could not seem to help himself.

She noticed. 'Will you never stop staring at my body?'

'Never,' he said fervently, and kissed her lips through the veil of her bonnet. It was a strangely erotic obstacle. The taste of her was on his tongue, but he received only hints of it through the lace.

'I have no idea what you mean to accomplish by this,' she said. 'It is broad daylight. We are in a hired conveyance and I am covered from head to foot.'

'Where you hear a caution, I hear a challenge,' he said with a smile and pulled off his gloves. Then he ran a finger along the front of her cloak where she held it tightly together. 'You are sitting there like a wrapped sweet and telling me that it is not time for dessert. But I have never been good at waiting.' He plunged a hand beneath the cloak and wrapped it about her waist, pulling her body towards his. Then he kissed her again.

Perhaps it was the suddenness. Or perhaps she did not believe he could get up to much mischief in such surroundings. But she did not resist his touch and so he grew more daring, allowing both hands to travel freely over her body, touching breasts and belly through her gown, pressing down into her lap and imagining the soft place waiting for him there.

And as she did each time he kissed her, she

melted for him, throwing back her head and exposing her bare throat for attention. He obliged, tonguing into the hollow at the base of it, manoeuvring her breasts so that they crested over the neckline of her bodice, resting there like strawberries, waiting for his mouth. Then he buried his face in the opening at the front of the cloak, letting the cloth shield him as he tasted her. The wool muffled her sighs as she pressed herself into the carriage seat, arching her back, giving him space to cup her bottom with his hands, thrusting one into the pocket slit on the seam of her skirt.

He heard a little rip as he fumbled inside her gown and another as he fought with the petticoat. Then he was touching skin, following the crease of her leg to the centre of her and pushing deep inside her.

She froze in shock at the touch, then relaxed and arched again, her own hand stealing beneath the cloak to stroke his hair as he nibbled on her breasts, thinking of all the other bits of her he wished to find and suck.

And she was thinking of them as well, adjusting her hips so that he might go deeper and pressing her body against his thumb before giving a long silent shudder and collapsing back into the seat.

He withdrew then, leaving her breasts exposed inside the cloak, before pulling his gloves back on.

Her eyelids fluttered for a moment, as though she might swoon, and then she muttered, 'Wicked man.' But it was said with more amazement than annoyance. 'You took advantage of me.'

'Not nearly as much as I'd have liked to,' he said. 'You'd best keep your cloak closed tight. If I catch clear sight of those breasts, I'll have you flat on your back on the carriage seat and prove just how wicked I am.'

He had not time to do more, for they were coming very near to Covent Garden and the man he sought. So he took himself back to the other side of the carriage to be out of the way of temptation and admired the results of his efforts.

If possible, she was even more ripe and luscious when satisfied than she had been when cross with him. He could see her hands, moving under the cloak, trying to right the damage he had done to her dress, and noted each slight widening of her eyes as she touched her own sensitive flesh. 'I do not know what Polly will say about this gown, for I am sure you have quite ruined it.'

'As if a bit of torn muslin is your greatest worry,' he said with a grin. 'More like I have ruined you for other men.'

'Do not flatter yourself,' she said and turned away from him to look out the window.

I have ruined you...

The gall of the man. He had pawned her ring, then used his apology as an excuse to abuse her. Worst of all, he was thoroughly right to brag about it. As she tried to tuck her breasts back into her gown she could feel echoes of the discord he had created in the rest of her—her body was still damp from where his fingers had thrust.

If the feelings he'd engendered were a sample of what might occur if he bedded her, then she could understand her mother's recommendation to take advantage of the convenience.

It was wrong, of course. But so was lying and

stealing money, even if one was stealing it from a thief. This, at least, had been more pleasurable than talking to de Warde. And it was sanctioned by church, state and both families. If she had enquired of Miss Pennyworth what her responsibilities were when it came to her husband's needs and desires, she would have been informed that anything less than total and complete surrender was a failing.

Surrender. And there was another troublesome shudder, starting in the womb and spreading a luxurious glow from head to toe.

'I beg your pardon?' Jack gave her another self-satisfied grin.

'A chill. Nothing more.'

'Best keep your cloak fastened, then.'

As if she had any choice. Her dress was in no state to be seen.

The carriage had stopped in front of a tavern and he helped her to the street with a word of assurance. 'The place is frequented by actors. If we are to find the man I am looking for, it will be either here or in bed.'

'Drinking during the day?' she said in surprise.

'He works at night,' Jack reminded her. He opened the door and there was a swell of song that was bawdy, but surprisingly tuneful for what she'd have expected from an inebriated crowd. Even more shocking, the company was mixed, both men and women, although the females present were not so obviously improper as she might have suspected. They dressed no more indecently than other ladies. Nor did they cling to the men as though they needed them for support, instead drinking and singing just as their male fellows did.

'Actresses,' she said, eyes round.

'You say that as you might say whore,' he said with a bit of reproof. 'As if these ladies would waste their favours in that way. If they chose to sell themselves, they would do it to those who could afford them. If they share themselves here, it is from genuine affection and not with the intent of gaining some brief protection.'

At least he did not cite her mother's past as an example. Thea dreaded to think which category Antonia might fall into, or what unfortunate truths she might learn, should she enquire.

Jack was scanning the faces for one he might recognize. His eyes focused on a table near the back of the crowded room and he raised a hand in greeting. 'There he is. Just the man for the job I have in mind.' He was pulling her towards a dark corner which held an equally dark man who would have seemed quite forbidding had it not been for the brilliant smile he gave them as they approached. His features marked him as an Indian, or perhaps some sort of half-caste son.

'This is my friend, Danyl Fitzhugh.' Jack was smiling broadly at the swarthy man at his side.

'How do you do,' she said cautiously.

'Lady Kenton.' He stood and bowed low over her hand.

'You know.' She shot Jack a worried look.

'He knows everything. Or very nearly,' Jack said with a nod.

Fitzhugh laughed. 'And now you are thinking, the dark stranger will be our undoing.' Rather than be angry, he continued to smile, but dropped his tone to be discreet. 'You have nothing to fear, my lady. Jack and I are as near to brothers as it is possible to be.'

'We might even be brothers,' Jack insisted. 'Your father and my mother were quite close for a time.'

'And you can see the obvious family resemblance,' Danyl said with a cynical shrug. Even accounting for the difference in complexions, it was clear that they shared no common features between them. 'Jack has always been eager to know his father. Although why he should want mine, I have no idea. He brought my mother back to England with him, then abandoned us both. But that is my lot and it has not been unhappy. If Jack has found himself a rich wife and a plum spot, even for a short time, I do not begrudge him it.'

'And Danyl is the perfect man for the job,' Jack said, in the same reassuring tone he used for almost all of the rash statements he made to her. 'He will appear to be some friend I met on the exotic travels in the Orient.'

Danyl laughed again. 'You have never been farther east than Ipswich.'

'But Lord Kenton spent his life in the wilds of India,' Jack said with a reproving glare. 'And he met you there. You earned the fortune you possess in trade of just such items as Mr de Warde wishes to buy.'

'Bully for me!' Danyl said with enthusiasm. 'I suppose my father was a Brahmin and my mother a seer.'

'Your parents can be whomever you would like,' Jack said.

'How magnanimous of you,' Danyl said with another deep bow.

'Would that it were so easy,' Thea said with a sigh. 'My parents have always been just who *they* wished to be and have never given me a say in it.'

'I have not told you of my most recent discovery,' Jack said to his friend, leaning close over the table. 'You are sharing a table with the daughter of Antonia Knowles. Although why I did not see it from the first I have no idea.' Jack lifted her veil so that his friend might see her face. 'Just look at her. Have you ever seen a lovelier woman?'

Danyl's eyes widened in surprise. 'She is the very image of her mother. And it explains why I am unable to control my feelings for her.'

'That will be enough, Danyl,' Jack said with a warning. 'Lady Kenton is married, after all.'

'To you,' Danyl laughed. 'For now.'

The shameless flattery and banter between the two men paled in significance, next to the information that Fitzhugh had divulged so casually. 'You knew of my mother?'

'Who did not?' he said reverently.

Only she, apparently. 'Tell me about her.'

'I saw her as Cherry in *Beaux Stratagem*.' Danyl rolled his eyes heavenwards.

'You were barely a boy,' Jack said with a grin.

'But that day I wished I was a man. Saw her as Desdemona, too. And imagined myself rescuing her from the Moor.'

'She had range,' Jack agreed. 'There was not a role she could not conquer.'

'She played for kings,' Danyl agreed. 'And broke hearts all across Europe.' Then he looked at Thea, as though just remembering she was present. 'Then, one day she disappeared.'

'She met my father,' Thea said helplessly. And raised a daughter who did not believe a word of her stories.

Danyl smiled. 'A lucky man he must be, to have both a beautiful wife and a beautiful daughter. I am doubly honoured to meet you, Lady Kenton. And to be of service to your mother through you.'

'Thank you,' Thea responded, although it was more of a reflex than anything else. She had never thought of her father as a particularly lucky man, thinking her mother more of a burden than a gift. It was quite clear that she had understood nothing.

Jack smiled in encouragement. 'And remember, every lie Danyl tells is one that you do not have to.'

The other man took her hand and bowed across the table. 'You must allow me to assist you, my lady. I would not dream of anything less.' Then he looked at Jack. 'Now tell me more of your plans...'

Chapter Fifteen

Ignorance truly was bliss. Thea had not appreciated it when it had been in her possession. She had been assured that her education was comprehensive and left school sure that she was prepared for any situation she might encounter.

But Miss Pennyworth had been quite wrong about several things.

It had been a day of firsts for Thea. She had seen the inside of both a pawn shop and a tavern. She had been assured that every tale her mother had told her about the fabulous successes of her youth had been true. And she had seen her mother perform for Mr de Warde, turning the unlikely story that Jack had presented into something believable. Apparently, she owed apologies to Antonia for a lifetime of injustices. In twenty years, Thea had believed not a word out of her mouth.

In the carriage, Jack had educated her in quite another way. Then he had sat talking with his friend as though nothing had happened between them. Nor had he offered to continue the lessons on the return trip to Kenton House. He had said not a word about it as they'd had dinner, nor noticed when she had retired early, confused and exhausted. By that time he was deep in conversation with the earl, assuring him that they were nearing an end to the difficulties with de Warde.

Thea toyed with the ribbons on her nightdress, unable to be still. Was this plan really likely to be met with anything other than embarrassing failure? If word of it escaped, the *ton* would greet it as far more amusing than her mother's worst *faux pas*.

It would be impossible to recover from such a scandal. Jack would recover as easily as a Harlequin hit with a slapstick. And her mother was accustomed to handling such slips, recovering from them with a graceful smile and an infectious laugh.

Thea was not.

Her education had been in the manners necessary for the scrupulous avoidance of disgrace. But not a word had been said about the recovery from a mistake, for it had been assumed that such knowledge was unnecessary. If she had the chance, she must write Miss Pennyworth and tell her just how useless that had proved.

There was a knock upon the bedroom door that connected their rooms and she started. It could only be one person. How should she answer him? After a moment's pause, she decided to follow her heart. 'Come in.'

Jack stood in the door frame for a moment, as though waiting for applause. 'It is not locked? I'd have tried it earlier, had I known that.'

'Brigand,' she said. But her heart was not up to provoking him.

'That's my girl. I feared, after the loss of your ring, that you might be losing faith as well.'

'It is not just any jewel, you know. The discovery that it is missing will reveal just how low Spayne has sunk.'

He came forwards and took her bare left hand

in his, wrapping his fingers tightly around it. 'Do not worry. We will have it back in no time.'

'You are always so confident,' she said with a shaky laugh.

'Because I know how people think,' he replied, tapping his temple. 'In assuming they will follow their worst natures, I am seldom surprised. We must trust that de Warde's vaulting ambition will o'er leap itself.'

'Shakespeare again?'

'Of course. You may keep Miss Pennyworth. I have the Bard. Sheridan and Goldsmith are good for a laugh, but when one truly wants to know the hearts of men, one can do no better than Shakespeare.'

'I must trust you, then,' she said with a sigh. 'I had no idea that marrying would require I consort with actors and Lombard dealers and charlatans of all sorts.'

'*Consort* is a rather strong word,' he said. 'Although the urge to consort, when you look at me with those eyes, is impossible to resist.'

She shook her head, ignoring the little thrill

that the words raised in her. 'Do not talk nonsense.'

'I was merely wondering if you wished to continue what we began in the cab this afternoon.'

It was a brazen suggestion, one that required her to make the decision. She could not pretend, as she had earlier, that there was no way to control what was occurring. Tonight, she had but to send him away and she was sure he would bother her no more. 'If I say yes,' she said, looking gravely into his eyes, 'I do not know what is likely to happen, now or in the future.'

'None of us does, really,' he said. 'But I promise, you will enjoy what happens tonight.' He closed the door behind him and came across the room to stand in front of her, so close that she could almost touch him. 'I will be gentle. I will protect you from any dangers, just as any husband would. And afterwards I will guard your reputation with my life.' He was smiling at her and it was warm and fond and tender. His hands came to her shoulders and he pulled her into him, until his lips rested by her ear. '"Hear my soul speak: the very instant that I saw you, did my heart fly to your service."'

'Shakespeare again?'

He nodded, and she felt his cheek move against hers. 'But no less true, even if the words are not mine. When I am with you, I cannot help myself. I was yours from the first moment.' And then, as though revealing too much of himself, he tried to make light of the comment. 'It was the cut of your dress, I suspect. I'd have done anything for a chance to lay hands on those breasts.'

She sighed. 'And now you are trying to spoil it. What shall I do with you?'

She expected some sly comment in response, but instead he said, 'Forgive me. You are not the only one who was not prepared for the turn some things have taken lately.' He dipped his lips to the corner of her mouth and kissed her. Then he said in a quiet, amazed voice, '"When I saw you I fell in love, and you smiled because you knew."' He looked at her, his eyes blue and soft, and she believed the truth in them, down to her very soul.

'Hamlet.' She sighed.

He nodded. 'And you have a beautiful smile,'

he added, touching the corner of her lip with his fingertip.

'That did not end well for Ophelia, I think.'

'Because Hamlet was not truthful with her,' Jack said softly. 'He did love her. But he waited too long to share the fact.'

'How do you know that?'

'I have played him many times.'

Just as he was playing a part now. But she was tired and a little frightened and did not want to think about it. 'So, when you are Hamlet, does Ophelia ever learn the truth?'

'The next time, perhaps. I might make the ending happy, like Tate did for King Lear.' He looked solemnly into her eyes. 'Those who love deserve to be happy, despite what the playwrights may think.'

'Sacrilege,' she whispered with another smile.

'There is enough tragedy in the world, is there not? Far too many kindred spirits kept apart by birth and circumstance.' His lips were closer to hers now and she remembered the kisses they'd shared that afternoon, hot and passionate through the lace of her veil.

'Star-crossed lovers?' she coaxed.

'Exactly that. A couple who are totally wrong for each other, but meant to be together all the same.' There was an earnestness about him that made her want to believe, if only to have one more kiss. His lips brushed hers again.

She tasted his after-dinner port, licking the flavour away with the tip of her tongue. 'And what would you do to bring them together?'

'What else is there to do but this?' he whispered and kissed her back.

This was what she had hoped for, in the days before her marriage. And she had missed it more than she'd known. It had been a bitter disappointment to know that propriety would not allow it, but it might be even worse to enjoy it and then lose him for ever when he returned to his old life.

Either choice could end in a mistake, but she was tired of fearing what might happen, if it denied her what she could have right now. She freed her hand from his and wrapped her arms about his neck, going up on tiptoes to make it easier to reach his lips. He put an arm about her waist, pulling her up to stand on the tops of his stockinged feet, pressing the length of her body against his so she could offer herself to him.

He claimed to have wanted her from the first day. Perhaps it was true. Why else would he choose that particular quote to woo her now? For all his roguish talk, he was as gentle as he had promised, his kisses soft on hers, his tongue in her mouth, moving slowly so as not to frighten her.

But she wasn't frightened any more. She felt warmth flood into her body anywhere he touched her. Gradually, the kiss grew to something more than a kiss, hot and dark and wonderful, making her strong and weak at the same time. She could not seem to stand without his support, so she stepped away, leaning back, pulling him down with her to lie on the bed.

He hesitated only a moment, then followed eagerly, stretching out to cover her body as she relaxed back into the pillows. Eventually, he leaned back so he could reach the ties on the front of her nightdress and undo them one at a time. She felt the evening air on the skin above her breasts, the warmth of his fingers and the gentle tickle of the fabric being spread wide.

Why had she fought this? Hadn't she known, from the first night, the first kiss, that they were meant for each other? His hands, which had been cupping her face, slid to her shoulders, pushing at the neckline of her gown, and she wiggled against him, feeling it slip down her arms. He viewed the newly exposed skin and with a reverent sigh dropped his lips to it, brushing his open mouth against her shoulder, tracing designs with his tongue and following the path of love bites he had made that afternoon. His kisses made her restless, she hardly knew for what. She wanted this. Needed it more than she had expected. She was married. She deserved to be complete and have the love of a man.

Her mind offered vague warnings that none of this was real. He was no more her real husband than he was a real viscount. But it did not matter. He was Jack. And she liked to feel his lips on her breasts.

He pulled away and looked up at her, his hand under her, playing along her spine, up and down the thin fabric of her nightdress, then both fists gathered between her shoulders and she felt the cloth rip and the force of his kiss as he claimed her mouth again as she gasped in shock. He thrust his tongue into her mouth, circling hers, holding her lower lip between his teeth and sucking upon it, as he peeled away the scraps of her gown, tossing it aside and leaving her naked. Then he knelt, fully dressed, between her legs and pushed them wide apart, staring down at the juncture and then up at the rest of her body, stopping at her breasts.

She held her arms out to him in welcome, unable to pretend a modesty she did not feel.

And he fell forwards onto her, nearly crushing the breath from her body as he settled his face between her breasts, kissing his way up to the nipples, licking and sucking, taking them deep into his mouth and making her squirm beneath him. His hands gripped her hips, pressing them into the mattress, holding them firm for his inevitable entry and her throat tightened in a gasp at the thought.

He sensed the change and released her, slipping a finger between the folds of her body again and pressing until she released the held breath in another gasp, arched her back and cried out. She was falling to pieces again after one touch. If this was to be her undoing, she welcomed it, letting the feeling wash over her, taking her reason away.

When she opened her eyes, he was smiling at her, smug at her satisfaction. But the pause made her worry that the interlude was ending and, delightful as it had been, it could not be over so soon. She reached up and tugged at the end of his cravat, smiling as the knot unravelled and the strip of linen fell free, brushing against the tips of her breasts.

He watched it as she let it pool on her belly. Then he swept it away with one hand, undoing the buttons of his waistcoat with the other.

'I swear, Cyn, by marrying you I did the world a service and saved other men from this madness.' He struggled out of his coat and waistcoat, and pulled her tight against him again.

Perhaps she was mad as well. The feel of his linen shirt against her skin was exquisite, as was the solid feeling of the man beneath the cloth. Her hand strayed to explore the angles and planes of his upper body, then lower to grasp his hips as she tried to pull him down into her. She could feel the bulge at the front of him, pressing down, and wondered why she had never bothered to steal a peek at him to prepare herself for what was to come.

She had been too polite to notice such things before she met Jack, but now she was most assuredly interested.

He untangled her hand from him and kissed the knuckles. 'Soon enough, my dear. If that is what you want from me, you need not worry. But I am not ready yet.'

What more could he possibly do to prepare, other than removing his trousers? She had been under the impression that such things took little time at all for the men involved. He lowered his head again to the place that the linen had touched her and dipped his tongue into her navel, making her laugh.

Then he trapped her hips and slid lower, down her belly, until his face was buried between her legs and his tongue...

She clutched at his hair, trying to pull him off

of her, and then trying to draw him closer as he pulled on her with his teeth, just as he had done with her mouth while kissing her. Between them, his tongue was busy, driving her to distraction. His hands slid down the bare skin of her thighs, pushing them wide apart. She was breaking again, and again and again, sobbing out her passion, helpless in pleasure, barely aware of her surroundings. When he stopped to remove the rest of his clothing, the chill of the air on her skin as he left her brought fresh tremors of need. To warm herself she followed, rubbing her body against his, touching the perfect golden skin with her breasts, twining her arms about his athletic dancer's body. She ran her fingertips down the muscled arms, which had cradled her close, and rested her head against his strong shoulder so that she might kiss it.

'Cyn.' He was using the strange nickname he had chosen for her as a command to misbehave. *Sin.* But how could something that felt so good be a crime against God?

'Cyn,' he called to her again as he pushed into her. His beautiful voice was raw and uncontrolled, though the stroke was slow and careful. The actor was utterly gone, leaving nothing but the man. He wanted her. Needed her so much that he was willing to reveal his true self.

And she needed him as well. He was light and happiness, salvation and courage. And though she did not want him to be, he was her lover and had been from the first, winning her heart with a single smile in a darkened gazebo. She felt all control slipping, sank her fingers into his arms, her teeth into his shoulder, and pushed back to meet him, free. It was as if she was flying with him, riding the currents of the air like a hawk. Then, together, they fell in a burst of feeling, and her body shook where it held him, tight inside her.

They settled to peace in each other's arms. He was so quiet, she assumed he must have fallen asleep, but when she opened her eyes to look at him, he was admiring her, silent and smiling. He smoothed the hair away from her face and gave a shy shake of his head, as though he could not quite believe what had happened.

And then they began again.

Chapter Sixteen

Jack stared at the ceiling above his wife's bed, afraid to move. It was a shared bed, after all, and the least change would wake the woman sleeping in his arms. The warm weight of her was wonderful. Mouth open against his shoulder, breasts crushed to his side and the damp centre of her pressed close to his hip by the way her leg stretched over his.

He was used to feeling crowded after the act. He usually wanted to push the woman, whoever she was, away from him, roll to his side and sink into a satisfied sleep. He had slept with Cyn, of course. He'd slept well. But instead of moving away, he'd pulled her closer, settling her against his body with a sigh and a smile.

And now that he was waking, he had to admit

that he'd never in his life felt like this on a morning after. Of course, there had been damned few of those. Couplings tended to be hurried and done with, the girls as eager to be away as he was to have them gone. But on the times he'd seen dawn with a woman in his bed, he'd felt them to be awkward, uncomfortable and leading to quick partings and unmet gazes.

But this...

He glanced down at the head resting in the crook of his arm, at the coppery hair, the pale shoulder, felt the feathery touches of her breath against his skin and a desire to keep it just so for ever. The part of him that he thought of as Kenton was sighing in satisfaction, content and, dare he think it, deeply moved. The joining of the two of them had been more than a brief joy.

It had been pleasurable, more so than any coupling he could remember, but the experience had marked a change in his life and his spirit. There was a logical explanation, he was sure. It was probably due to the delayed wedding night and the anticipation built by it. It was the softness of the bed, the softness of the lady, the general opulence of his surroundings and the fact that, other than trying to get the better of de Warde, he had fewer worries than at any other time in his life. Of course this would be better, more memorable, more enjoyable.

And more profound, argued the imaginary Lord Kenton. Taking a wife was the first step in the founding of a dynasty. It meant the continuation of a line. It was also the beginning of a future with the woman he loved.

Jack sat bolt upright in bed, dumping the sleeping woman off his shoulder and startling her awake. 'What?' she said, rubbing at her eyes.

'Nothing. Nothing at all. I had a dream. Nothing more.'

'A pleasant dream?' she said with a smile. 'I would hate to think that last night was the stuff of nightmares for you.'

'It was nice,' he admitted cautiously. 'But the ending took a surprising turn. It woke me.'

She was toying with the hair on his chest now and it tickled. Kenton was easing him back down to the mattress, preparing to let the woman do what she would with him. Jack was fine with that. Or rather, he ought to be fine. Hadn't he wanted to lie with the wench from the first moment he saw her? And hadn't it been as good as he'd hoped? He'd had her three times last night. He should take advantage of the situation and have her again before she remembered how much she hated him.

Instead, he felt guilty.

He caught her hand, which had begun a journey toward his privates. 'If you keep on as you are going, you will wake me in other ways.'

'Would that be such a bad thing?' She was biting her lower lip in a way that made it almost impossible to refuse, looking up at him with naked emotion, her eyes wide green pools of expectation. Dear God, he knew that she was no actress, which meant the love he saw on her face was real. What was he to do with it? He did not want it. It was an unnecessary complication that would make it that much harder to get away when the time came to leave.

And if there was any such answering emotion on his face…

He wished he could look in a mirror to check.

He could not afford to fall in love, not with the end so near. What would it mean for either of them but frustration and disappointment? He buried his emotions to the best of his ability, thinking hard, cold thoughts, smothering affection beneath a false front. 'We have work to do, and cannot spend the day in bed. Tonight, perhaps, if you are still in the mood for a frolic, we will open another bottle and I will quote some more Shakespeare. That works every time with the ladies. And last night, it certainly worked on you.'

Her hand dropped away from his body, and he felt the absence like a sudden cold shock. 'Shakespeare does the trick, does it?' Her face, which had been soft, blurred by passion, seemed to sharpen into something hard and distant.

'Every time.' He forced a randy smile and felt his stomach tighten. 'Now that you have some experience, we need not waste time with romance. I can quote some passages that will put you in the mood right quick. Old Will is wicked when he has a mind to be.'

'Then I will have to guard against Shakespeare and against you. Last night was interesting. But

I see no need to repeat it, if it's left you thinking I am as easily swayed as a Covent Garden whore.' She turned from him and swung her legs towards the edge of the bed, presenting a nicely curved bottom as the sheet fell away.

To add emphasis to his dismissal, he swatted her on it and saw her flinch. It was a crass gesture, especially for a gently bred woman who had been a virgin until he'd taken her maidenhead. He wanted to reach out, pull her back to him and assure her that it had been a mistake. Instead he said, 'Oh, my dear, never think that you were easy to bed. It has taken me weeks to win you. But it was well worth the wait.'

'If you think you flatter me by saying that, you are sorely mistaken.' With each word, each breath, she was returning to the aloof beauty that he had seen since their wedding day.

And the portion of him that should be relieved to be free of her was growing smaller, replaced by the Jack who wanted to apologise to his dear, sweet wife for hurting her and Kenton, who was both disgusted and appalled at the behaviour of this interloper in his life and his bed. And all

Jack's carefully memorised speeches failed him, the words sticking in his dry mouth.

When she turned to face him, Thea's facade was carefully back in place, the only sort of acting that was allowed to virtuous young ladies, he assumed. She had been taught to hide her hurt and to cut the attacker dead with impeccable manners. She was staring at him like some curiosity, displayed under glass for the amusement of an audience. 'Well, don't lie there gaping at me. If we mean to succeed against de Warde, I assume we will have to get out of bed to do it.' She put a hand on her hip. 'I could stay here, I suppose. Throw my skirts over my head and trap him myself, just as I caught you. But I have made it clear often enough how distasteful that would be.' There was something about the way that she said it that implied lying down with de Warde was a slightly less unattractive prospect than another night with Jack.

He swung his legs off the opposite side of the bed, turning away from her as he should have done from the first, and yanked on the bell pull to call her maid. 'I think we can manage to spare you that. And if my company bothers you, I will keep my Shakespeare to myself as well.'

But he did not want to. He wanted to butter her with the words, to make her sigh over them, melting in his arms. She had been everything he'd wanted in life and everything he'd dreamed of when he'd first seen her. Now it seemed that their only night together would be a lone culmination, against which all future nights would be measured.

Until he could find someone better, of course. The lovely Cyn was not the only woman in the world. He had but to remind himself of the fact. Once he was away from here and back to being Jack Briggs, he would make a concerted effort to keep his bed full and his nights busy. He would forget her. There could be no good in remembering.

He returned to his room, where his valet was waiting with a robe and a basin, ready to see him washed, shaved and refreshed for the day ahead.

When the butler came to tell him that de Warde was below and had once again asked specifically for Lady Kenton, he was hardly surprised. It would be far more difficult to make the man forget his lust for Thea than it was to inflame him by denying access to her.

He went down to the morning room where the toad had been left to wait, preparing Kenton's set downs as he walked. What had he said to Thea the previous evening about protecting her? It had been the only true lie of the evening, for she would be forced into this man's company at least once more before his plan was at an end.

Let Kenton sorrow over it if he must. Jack Briggs reminded himself firmly that his first responsibility lay to the earl and that did not include keeping Thea Banester in a protective bubble, untouched and untroubled.

When he entered the room, de Warde looked up, clearly annoyed that he was not seeing the person he'd expected.

'Uncle de Warde,' Jack said, equally annoyed.

'Is your wife not at home?' de Warde asked, not bothering with a greeting.

'Not to you, she is not,' Jack replied, staring at

the man expectantly. 'I will relay any message for you.'

'I merely wished to discuss the scene I witnessed yesterday,' de Warde responded.

'Scene?' Jack said, arching his eyebrow. 'You intruded on personal family business, and now you wish to question her about it?'

'I am family as well,' de Warde reminded him.

'But hardly close family,' Jack said. 'I am unsure of the reasons for it, but my father refuses to speak to you at all. And I do not appreciate your excessive interest in my wife.'

'I am not interested in her, so much as the location of the statue that I sold to her father,' de Warde said. Watching him now, Jack was unsure how he had managed to trick Banester. The man was not a particularly skilled liar, his eye fairly twitching at each mention of Thea. But he wanted the idol, as well, even if he thought it a worthless piece of stone.

'If you wished to use it yourself, you never should have sold it to Banester,' Jack said. 'You could at least have taken the time to learn the way of it. The thing you had was quite useless. You extorted a great deal of money from my wife's family and it is only through good luck and my timely arrival that things have come right for them again.'

'You cannot honestly expect me to believe…' de Warde was laughing at him. It was hardly a surprise, for the thing he suggested was laughable to any sane man.

Jack gave a dismissive gesture of his hand. 'I do not expect you to believe anything, Uncle. As a matter of fact, I would much prefer you didn't. Thea is quicker to forgive than I am. Do not think that you can try the same with her, gaining the thing again only to sell it back to us.' He turned as if to go.

'Wait.' De Warde said it sharply and Jack brought himself up short, then turned slowly with a slight sigh, as though he were tired of being bothered.

'So it is true that Lady Banester is with child?'

Jack looked down his nose at his *faux* uncle. 'That is a secret I have no right to reveal. You have spoken to the woman yourself. If you do not wish to believe her, it is no business of mine.'

'Then is it true that you believe in the power of the statue...'

'Statues,' Jack corrected, as though the detail mattered.

'...and that you have convinced her that the child will be male?'

'I see no reason to share my beliefs on such a subject with you,' Jack said, turning again. 'They are no concern of yours.'

'Lady Banester seemed convinced that you would buy the things for yourself and use them to guarantee an heir.'

Jack turned back suddenly. 'Now I see why you are interested. Concerned about your own place in the succession, are you? Then let me assure you of one thing. You will never have my father's title. I am seeing to that myself and you will soon have two men standing between you and it. You had best learn to consider yourself fourth in line for the coronet and stop bothering me. I must speak to my wife's mother about being too free with information that I do not feel the need to share. But I have nothing more to say to you on the subject. Good day to you, sir.'

He exited the room with a slam of the door, startling the butler who waited nervously in the hall, then attempting to put the servant at ease again with a smile. 'Wait a few moments, Graves, and then show my uncle out.'

'If I may be so bold, my lord, as to offer advice?'

As if such a polite request was an act of bravery. 'Of course, Graves.'

'If the gentleman is bothering you, or Lady Kenton, there is no reason to allow him entrance to the house. If instructed, the staff will turn him away on his next visit.'

'Perhaps on the visit after next, Graves. But for a day, or maybe two, my uncle must be allowed access. The next time he comes, even if I am not present, bring him to the salon and notify Lady Kenton of his presence.'

'Very good, my lord.' Graves's expression said his opinion was quite the opposite of his words, but then he knew better than to express an opinion of his own to the master's face. Jack had no fear of opposition.

Chapter Seventeen

Thea wished that she could gather everyone who had ever advised her and demand that they sort out the muddle she had made of her life. Miss Pennyworth would have explained that it was her own fault for yielding, even for a moment, to a man who didn't deserve her time. Of course, standing firm would have lost what little good had come from this. The previous night had been a delight.

Spayne would likely have explained that brief pleasure was better than none. And her mother would have asked for details. The pair of them would likely have encouraged her to forgive Jack for being as he was and remind her that one must take the good with the bad.

Even if that was true, he'd had no reason to

lie to her. He had treated her like any common woman, who needed to be tricked into bed with shiny speeches. Could he not have just put it plainly, in terms of physical attraction and release? Was it necessary for him to make her believe so completely in the strength of his love?

She was angry at herself for being fooled. But more than that, she was angry at him for spoiling things, just as she had been ready to give in without question to hedonistic joy. She had thought that they would linger in bed for the morning, repeating what they had done. Perhaps he would whisper the details of his plans against de Warde, which she was sure would sound much more brilliant if explained while prone, naked and exhausted.

Instead she had sent him away and spent the day sulking in her rooms, writing letters and dreading the time when she would have to see him again and pretend that she was not hurt. Polly told her that there had been a visit from de Warde, and that Lord Kenton had sent him off with a flea in his ear. Thea had no idea whether that had been planned, or just a mad impulse on Jack's part.

And now they were at supper and he was looking at her over the table, saying nothing of importance about it and acting as if none of the morning's conversation had happened, as though they were somehow still lovers. 'You are most fetching tonight, my dear.'

'Please, spare me your compliments,' she responded, prodding at the sole on her plate.

'No false flattery, I assure you. Brown satin would be a drab on any other woman, but on you the colour comes alive.'

'Then perhaps I should change it,' she said.

He laughed. 'You mean to be contrary?'

'After last night, I would not believe you if you told me the sky was blue and the sun high at noon.'

He gave a surprised look. 'And I would have sworn that you quite enjoyed what we were doing.'

'The act itself was as pleasant as you promised,' she agreed. 'But I regret my choice of partners.'

For a moment, she thought she might have actually hurt him. The flinch he gave at the words seemed almost genuine. 'Better luck to you next time, then. Unless you would like to sport again tonight? I promise, you will find it just as nice as last night. I have other tricks to teach you before we are done with each other.'

And why must it be tricks? Why could he not have offered her anything real? Because he was an actor, of course. How foolish had she been to expect anything else? He had played the lover to get what he wanted. And now he could not be bothered. She glared at him and said nothing.

In response, he stood and walked around the table to her, tracing a fingertip along the bare skin of her shoulder, and her traitorous body seemed to actually consider the suggestion. She stiffened her spine and ignored the *frisson* of excitement raised by his touch. 'I think we are quite done with each other, thank you very much. My curiosity is satisfied.'

'And what of the matter of de Warde?' he asked.

'You can manage that by yourself, I am sure. You have said that you did not need me.'

'So I did,' he said thoughtfully. The finger

on her shoulder was still flicking idly back and forth, raising the hair on her arms. 'But as you can see, the excitement of the game is raising certain other needs. And it has been rather a long time for me. Until last night, I had been without satisfaction since before we met. It would be better if I were to expend this energy and tackle the man tomorrow while my head is clear.'

When she had wished for a less romantic approach, she had not thought it would sound so common, horrible and selfish. If possible, tonight's base truth was even worse than the previous night's flowery lying. She pulled her chair out and stood to escape his grasp. 'Are you seriously suggesting that I allow you another night in my bed?'

He gave her a wry smile. 'You have made it clear that you wish no part in the actual tricking of de Warde. But there is another supportive role you might play that would do me a world of good.' He compounded the vulgarity of it by reaching for her, drawing her into his arms for a kiss as rough and careless as any she might have expected from a man who thought only of his own pleasure.

And even worse, she was answering him with a kiss of her own, as though one day of intimacy had created a habit. She could be just as selfish as he, if she tried. To prove it, she forced her tongue into his mouth, urging him on, her leg rising to rest on his hip as though she expected him to bend her back on the table and have her here. She would prove to him that she could be as wicked and as careless as he. Tonight, when they were finished, she would be the one to leave.

And that was not what she wanted at all.

She fumbled behind her, until her hand found a heavy silver fish slice and grabbed it, poking the flat blade into his ribs and pushing him away from her. 'Leave me be, Jack Briggs. Or I shall…' She was unsure what, for the weapon she'd chosen was hardly sharp enough to do him any damage.

He looked down and laughed. 'Is that how they taught you to threaten a man in Miss Pennyworth's school? If you mean to do me an injury, a real knife might work better.'

'I will show you injury, you lecher.' And she swung the thing as hard as she could at the side of his head.

He caught her wrist before she could make contact and backed away in surprise. 'You truly are angry with me, aren't you?'

'Merely coming to my senses, which were lost briefly yesterday.' She brandished the serving piece at him, backing towards the table.

'I have a good mind to do just as you ask and leave you alone for the evening,' he said. 'I could take my diversion elsewhere.'

'I suggest you do that. Find a whore who can appreciate Shakespeare and perhaps you will not even have to pay for it.'

'Very well, then.' He had the nerve to look indignant and reached back to the table to drain his wine glass. 'I'm off. There was no part of my agreement with Spayne that said I had to stand for your abuse. I will return in the morning in a better mood. We will see how long it takes you to regret this behaviour.' And he was out of the room and down the hall, shouting at servants and grumbling all the way to the carriage, making such a commotion that she would be surprised if half of London did not know that Kenton and his lady had had their first row.

She decided, almost immediately the door was shut, that he had been right. While she was not sure that it was safe to take him into her own bed, she did not want him leaving the house to consort with other women. What did this say about her feelings for him, to be simultaneously jealous and repulsed by the man? And how many of Miss Pennyworth's rules had she broken in the last hour? She'd refused her husband, argued loudly enough for the servants to hear and taken notice of the fact that he might wish to satisfy his needs with another.

She had also threatened him with a serving piece. There was not even a rule to cover that. It simply was not done. Even her mother, at her most outlandish, had never done anything so foolish. All the efforts to mask the taint in her blood had been for naught. When sufficiently aroused she was as volatile, as common and as prone to inappropriate actions as Antonia ever had been.

There was a quiet clearing of the throat behind her, as if the butler feared the reaction he might get should he interrupt her thoughts. 'My lady?'

She turned to him. 'Graves?'

'I know the time is late. But you have a guest. Mr de Warde. And he has requested...'

'To meet with me alone,' Thea said with a sigh. Why tonight, of all nights, must the man come to bother her? 'Show him to the drawing room. I will speak to him there.' She took a moment to straighten her skirt and smooth her hair, making sure that no trace of the recent tussle with Jack was visible. Then she walked down the hall to meet her guest.

She allowed the footman to announce her and stood saying nothing and forcing de Warde to rise and come to her. She did not bother with a smile, for really, what was the point of pretending? It did not matter if her mood furthered Jack's plan or not, she could not stand to pretend a moment longer. 'Mr de Warde?'

'Lady Kenton.' He offered a slight bow.

She ignored it. 'What is the meaning of your

visit this evening? If you wish to see Spayne, he has gone back to Essex.'

'And your husband is out for the evening,' de Warde supplied. 'I have just seen him at Boodle's. He is well on the way to being foxed and cursing all of womankind.'

Damn Jack for leaving in such a pet that the world must know of his absence. His fine talk of keeping her safe had proved to be just as false as his lovemaking. 'All the more reason that you should not be here,' she replied.

'On the contrary, it is the very reason I have come. We have a matter to discuss, Lady Kenton, and I will not leave until I am satisfied.'

'Very well, then. What is it you wished to know?'

'I have had quite enough of this nonsense that your husband is attempting. He is up to no good, I am sure. But I cannot make it out.'

'I have no idea what you mean.' It did not sound particularly convincing, but then she was in no mood to play-act. And the story she would have to tell of Hindu deities and magical pregnancy was too ludicrous even to attempt.

'I am sure you do. The statue that I sold your father is in a shop somewhere, along with its mate. I wish to have them back, quickly, cheaply, and before your husband can attempt to sell them to me.'

'He would do no such thing.' She tried for a staunch denial and defence of her beloved Kenton. But she might as well have yelled 'Right in one!' for all the effect it had on de Warde.

'Really, Lady Kenton? Is that the best you could do?' He shook his head. 'After all the fine apologies from you, and your mother, I thought we might be friends again.'

'I am willing to forgive the trick you played on my father, because of his recent good fortune.' She choked out the sentence, making one last effort to stick to the plan. 'But I will not stand for you pawing at me, drooling over my hand or making any further attempt to see me alone. I was never interested in your suggestions. My opinion of them has only diminished, now that I have married.'

'Very well, then.' He held his hands palms up before him in a gesture of surrender. 'I apologise if my interest has been misconstrued. I will trouble you no further. Nor will I offer you this.' He waved a piece of paper briefly before her eyes before beginning to tuck it back into his pocket.

It looked suspiciously like a bank draft. 'Wait.' She could not help herself. 'What is it that you have there?'

'The money that I took from your father. I meant to give it back to you as a wedding gift, but your husband would not allow me to speak with you...'

Could it really be that simple? Had the answer been before her all this time? And had it been obscured by a play-actor too clever for his own good? 'Why would you give me such a thing?'

'Because I would rather your family had it than Kenton's,' he said. And that, at least, had a ring of honesty to it. He held it out to her so that she could read her father's name, twenty thousand pounds and his own signature smoothly across the bottom. 'As I said before, Kenton is up to no good. I will take back the statue for the amount I was paid. But I need you to bring it to me.'

'I do not have it,' she said, 'or I'd give it to you tonight. I am sick to death of hearing about it.'

'Your mother said it was sold to an antiquities dealer.'

'A pawn shop,' she said, not bothering to maintain the pretence.

'Do you have the address?'

'It is somewhere in Whitechapel,' she said. 'The door was green.'

'You have been there?' His eyes widened in surprise.

'Only briefly.'

'Then take me there, immediately.'

'Me?' She was squeaking like a schoolgirl. She could not seem to help it. And she had been doing so well in asserting herself. She still could not act, of course. But the truth had served well enough for most of this conversation.

He gave her a smug smile. 'Do not tell me you are afraid to be seen in my company. We are family now, as your husband keeps reminding me.'

'You know that is not what you are thinking at all,' Thea snapped, unable to contain her disgust.

'If you will soon be breeding, as your husband

claims, than you have nothing to fear from me. I will admit defeat. If Kenton is any kind of a man, he will not need Indian magic to do the job. But I am tired of games and will not allow myself to be swindled.' He set the bank draft down on the table. 'Take me to the source of these supposed idols. Do it now, and not at your husband's convenience. The draft will stay here, as proof of my word.'

'I cannot guarantee that the statues are there, or even that the shop is open,' she said, eyeing the draft on the table.

'Take me to the shop and I ask no more of you. But do not try to fool me or lead me on a wild goose chase through London. I will know if you lie, for you are really quite hopeless at it.'

She could have her father's money. And if the shop was closed, she might not even damage Jack's plan to help Spayne. He might still succeed, if she could find him and warn him of this recent development.

And if she could not? Then it would serve him right for leaving her alone and sharing so little of the truth with her. 'Very well, then. If you will give me the draft, I shall call for a carriage and show you the way.'

'We shall take mine,' he said. 'It stands ready outside.'

'But the draft stays here.'

He gave a small nod.

'I will be but a moment to get my wrap.' She stepped into the hall and signalled furiously for a footman, handing him the draft. 'Send this to my father immediately. And send someone else to find Kenton. He may be at Boodle's or perhaps not. Tell him I have gone to Whitechapel with his uncle.' And let Jack make of that what he could.

The man gave a single nod before de Warde was upon them again, gesturing impatiently to the door where his carriage waited. 'My lady?'

As she passed him, she tried to keep her head held high as though the trip did not frighten her. But even she could see in the mirror of the entry hall that she looked near to panic and quite guilty. She glared back at her reflection. There was no way that Jack's scheme could have succeeded. She was doing no harm by giving up and would possibly even be saving him some embarrassment. Tomorrow, she could borrow some small portion of the money back from Father and reclaim her ring. It was all for the best.

For his part, de Warde looked triumphant, sure that he was near to a revelation, as he most likely was. 'Whitechapel,' he commanded and the carriage started forwards.

'I really cannot tell you more than that,' she warned. 'I was not paying attention.'

'We will go round every street and down every alley until you see the place with the green door,' he responded. 'I will see the truth in your eyes and that will be that. But I will not let you down from the cab until this matter is settled, even if we drive through the night and into the morning.'

'Very well, then,' she said with a sigh and watched out the window for the tarnished gold balls on the sign.

When they arrived, the windows were dim, as though the shop might be closed, but de Warde sprang down from the carriage. At his touch, the door swung open easily to the same brassy jangling of bells.

Thea had not anticipated this. It seemed that, like it or not, de Warde would get what he wished; either the idols, or proof that Kenton meant to cheat him. Then it occurred to her that Joseph knew nothing of Kenton.

He did, however, know an actor named Jack Briggs.

She hopped out of the carriage and followed de Warde into the shop, hoping that, for once in her life, she might find some of her mother's talent, for she very much needed it, if she was to keep her husband's secret.

But as she crossed the threshold, Danyl appeared from a back room. Either the servants had got word to Jack, or the scene was already prepared. Thea gave a silent prayer of thanks that she need be nothing more than an observer from this point forwards.

Danyl was eyeing de Warde with suspicion. 'I am not open for business, *sahib*. Come back tomorrow.' His accent was thicker than she remembered, as though he was play-acting the Indian. Instead of a normal coat and neckcloth, he wore a heavy brocaded robe and his thick dark hair was hidden under a turban.

But de Warde seemed to see nothing amiss. 'Your door was open. Because you were expecting someone, perhaps?'

Danyl stared at him, giving nothing away.

'Then I think you must be waiting for me. I am a friend of Lord Kenton. I have his wife here with me.'

'Why he does not come?' Danyl allowed himself to look ever so slightly surprised.

'If what I seek is here, then there is no reason to involve him. Whatever amount he would take from the bargain, I would give his share to you, if the business can be settled quickly.'

Danyl watched him in silence for a time, as though trying to gauge the value of the offer. 'If I anger him, I will lose business. He is a viscount. And who are you?'

'Never mind who I am,' de Warde snapped. 'I will pay whatever you ask. Now give me the damn statues.'

Danyl was staring at de Warde again, as though trying to set his price, and the tension drew even tighter. 'We shall see, shall we not? I have the statues you seek. It is rare to find the pair of them, as you must know.'

'Very well, then. Let me see them.' De Warde looked around the shop as though wondering why they were not on display.

'I have them here.' Danyl walked to a locked cabinet at the back of the room and loosened his collar to remove a key that rested on a chain around his throat. With great ceremony, he unlocked it, throwing the door wide and removing a carved wooden box. He set it down on the counter and removed a second key from his pocket, working the little lock and opening the lid.

Everyone in the room leaned forwards, and Thea felt the silence of anticipation and the bated breath of three people as the statues came into view.

Then de Warde laughed. She could not blame him, for even in the dim light and incense-scented air there was no mystery about the little figures before them. They were exotic, of course—how could a multi-armed, blue-skinned man and his consort not be? But they were in no way mystical. It was obvious that they were cheaply made and badly painted, set with gaudy paste jewels and daubed with gold paint.

They looked like what they were: a trick for the gullible.

Without warning, de Warde's hand shot out and cuffed the actor on the ear, sending the box crashing to the floor, the statues shattering. 'You pathetic huckster. Do you really expect me to believe that Kenton is tricked by this? I do not know the man well, but I take him for better than an idiot.' He turned to Thea.

She took an involuntary step back, bumping into the display case behind her. 'What was it, my dear? Did you think I would part with another penny for a pair of useless statues?'

'That is not what I thought at all,' she argued, staring at the rubble on the floor between them. Far too many hands reached up from the fragments, their fingers pointing at her in accusation.

He laughed again. 'You could at least have taken the time to find a better bait for me. I might have actually bought the things as a curiosity had they any real value. And you, sir, whoever you are…' de Warde turned back to Danyl, who was rubbing his ear and cringing like a coward. Despite Jack's faith in him, it appeared that one slap was all it took to render him useless. 'I assume Kenton put you up to this game, whatever it might be. If he holds something over you, you have nothing to fear. If it is only money you need, I will pay you to tell me what you know.'

Danyl maintained his silence, which now seemed more petulant than inscrutable.

'If you think to keep his secrets, know that I am powerful enough to have you up on charges for trying to trick me. I shall not stop persecuting you until you are hanged, or run from business. Now tell me what you know.' De Warde's voice shifted from coaxing to demand.

Danyl's eyes went round and white in his dark face. 'I know nothing, *sahib*. I swear it. Only that Sahib Kenton wished me to sell you these statues for a prodigious sum and I was to give him the money afterwards.'

'And what did you gain by it?'

'Nothing, *sahib*. I swear it.'

'I do not believe you.'

'A watch fob. That is all.' Danyl was proving to be as bad a liar as Thea and the constant questioning was making him perspire.

But de Warde did not seem to notice. His gaze was fixed on the open drawer of the cupboard behind the counter and the velvet tray that contained the shop's more valuable jewelry. There, at the front, next to the assortment of worthless statues, was the ring she had pawned to Joseph: the pride of the Spayne emeralds. In comparison to the dull clay gods on the floor it seemed to glitter all the more brightly.

There was a chance, she supposed, that if she stayed very still, and prayed very, very hard, de Warde would not see it. But from the slow smile that spread across his face, she could see that, as usual, her prayers were to go unanswered.

'I see nothing here to interest me.' He was turning away and hope flared anew, then he turned back and pointed at the ring. 'Except for that, of course. My, but it is a very handsome piece.'

'Not for sale,' Danyl said bluntly. 'I hold it for the true owner.'

'I expect you do. Now give it to me.'

'Give it?' Danyl's greed seemed to rally, growing stronger than his fear. 'There are some things that I fear more than your idle threats—losing that ring is one of them. If you want it, you will have to take it from me.' He parted the front of the brocade robe and revealed a long curved knife tucked into his belt. He fingered the jewelled handle lazily, drawing himself to his full height and looking more like the intimidating man she had met a few days before.

For a moment, de Warde weighed the possibility of success, should the day come to violence. Then he said, 'I wish to buy it.'

'I cannot sell it to you.' There was a trace of a whine in Danyl's voice, as though he did not know how to proceed, now that the play was not going according to the script.

'If you do not, I will have you up on charges of theft.'

'And if you do, the owner will charge you with the same,' Thea pointed out, unable to stop herself.

De Warde shot a triumphant glance in her direction. 'Nonsense. I shall see that it is returned to him in the most public way I can. Or he can retrieve it from me privately, for a cost that is far more than what I spend for it.'

Danyl hesitated, as though unsure which way lay the greater risk.

'It is worth thirty pounds to you, surely,' de Warde prompted.

Danyl sensed his way out and laughed derisively. 'It is worth more than that, I am sure. The stones, should I pry them out, would be worth several hundred.'

'Two hundred, then,' de Warde offered.

'And then there is the gold.' The Indian picked it up in his hand as though weighing it. 'It is quite heavy.'

'Five hundred, then, and no more arguing.' De Warde reached a hand towards it and Danyl withdrew.

'And then, of course, there is the sentimental value.'

'A thousand pounds,' Thea cried, unable to stop herself. Then, as if to cover her tracks, she added, 'I am sure it would be worth that, at least, to the owner. It is very lovely.'

'You should know. You had one very like it, didn't you?'

'Have,' she said firmly. 'It is being cleaned. Sized. Sized and cleaned.'

'And that is a family heirloom.' De Warde smiled. 'I suspect Spayne would give anything to have it back.'

'Spayne, you say?' Danyl seemed surprised, as though this was the first time he'd realised he was playing with those famous emeralds.

'Fifteen hundred,' Thea said, hoping the distraction would be enough.

'Pay no attention to her,' de Warde announced. 'She has no money of her own to offer. I suspect her husband will pay dearly, though, to keep his father from seeing what he has done with his inheritance.'

'Perhaps I should call on Spayne with it,' Danyl said with a greedy smile. 'If it is true, as you say, that he will give anything.'

'You would not get past the front door. Even if you did, he would have you arrested for possessing it to save his son's reputation,' de Warde said with an oily smile. 'Spayne is…a friend of mine. I will take it to him.'

'But you are no friend of mine,' Danyl pointed out. 'How do I know that this ring will arrive safely to the man I have never seen for myself? If it is his, better that I should return it to him. The reward will be great.'

'And my reward will be greater. Ten thousand pounds.'

'Spayne is an earl,' said Danyl triumphantly, as though this would finally settle the matter. 'And they are all rich.'

'Not all,' said de Warde. 'Some are not as rich as they used to be. And if the loss of the ring is revealed, Kenton will be worth nothing at all. His friends will turn from him, his bank will refuse him. His father will shut the door against him.'

'No!' Thea made a desperate grab for the tray, but Danyl pulled it clear of her hand. She thought of the draft that a footman was delivering to her father at this moment. She could have it again, before the banks opened. 'Twenty thousand.'

The Indian seemed to waver.

'I have the money, Danyl,' she said in an urgent

whisper. 'You can have it all. But do not betray Jack. I beg you.'

It must have affected him. When he spoke next, his accent slipped a little. But his words were to de Warde. 'You want the ruin of Kenton? And you want to do it by my hand. You would also make me betray a man I consider a friend and do something quite illegal in the bargain. The weight on my conscience would be heavy after such an act.'

'And that weight would be lifted with enough gold,' de Warde assured him. 'Fifty thousand pounds.'

'Do you even have that much? And if you do, how can you part with it?'

'I will have far more if one man puts a bullet in his brain from the shame of this. But, yes, I have fifty. I have twice that in the bank right now.'

Danyl folded his arms. 'Then sign it over to me. Do it now and the job is done.'

De Warde hesitated.

'You villain,' Thea hissed to Danyl, between her teeth. 'I knew you were not to be trusted.'

'Thank you for your confidence, Lady Kenton,' he replied, voice dripping irony. 'It is no less than I expected.'

De Warde laughed again. 'No need to be so emotional, Cynthia. I will take the thing now, if for no other reason than that you do not want me to.' He wrote a draft from the bank book he removed from his satchel, signing with a flourish. Then he passed the paper to Danyl, who in turn placed the ring on his palm.

Thea grabbed for the bit of jewellery, and Danyl seized her arm and pulled her away before she could reach it. De Warde was laughing at her, taunting her with it. She felt the unladylike rage returning, made even worse by her powerlessness, but there was one thing she could do. Without regard to all she had been taught, she spat in Henry de Warde's face.

He looked almost as shocked as if she had hit him, before reaching in his pocket for a handkerchief to wipe away the spittle. 'If it is so important to retrieve this bauble, you may come to my rooms tonight. We spoke once of a way to make your family fortunes right again. My offer at that time still stands. It is now doubly important that you consider it.'

'And as I have told you before, I would sooner die.' She struggled in Danyl's grasp, ready to fly at the man, to tear him tooth and nail if necessary, to regain her ring. 'I am faithful to my husband and happy to be so, for he is worth ten of you. It has nothing to do with his father's title. It is because he is a man. And you will never be more than a worm.'

De Warde drew back from her with a hiss, then laughed when he realised that she could not reach him. 'We will see if you feel the same in a week, when your world has come apart. The law might protect his father, but it will not save Kenton from charges of theft, or from debtor's prison if he cannot pay to keep me quiet. I will see to it that you are all ruined, every last one of you. But I will not be denied. Now, if you will excuse me, my dear, I must find someone to show my acquisition.' As he exited the shop, he was whistling a tune not unlike the one Jack favoured, as though he had not a care in the world.

Chapter Eighteen

For a moment, the brassy jangle of the bell echoed in the room. When it stilled, she could hear de Warde's carriage leaving her behind. She did not particularly wish to face Danyl. But even that would be better than travelling back with de Warde, listening to his gloating and rude suggestions.

Then she heard the sound of hollow clapping coming from the back room of the shop and Jack stepped out from behind the curtain that separated the back room from the shop. 'Well done, my dear. Well done indeed.'

'You were here? You heard?' She fought free of Danyl and grabbed at her husband's arm, tugging him towards the door. 'We must follow him. He took the ring. He saw it when the tray was removed from the safe. So he bartered with Danyl, who did not know the meaning of it and took his money. He has betrayed you.'

'We have the money and that is the important thing,' Jack said with a smile. 'And you notice, Danyl made him pay dearly for it, since he knew what we needed.'

'De Warde paid many times what it was worth,' she agreed, 'but that is not the point. Now he has the ring. He will use it to disgrace you, and Spayne.'

'If that were the ring, of course,' Jack said with a smile.

'Of course it is. You took it from my finger.'

He was smiling and saying nothing. Realisation dawned slowly. 'You gave me a paste ring?'

'Of course not, darling. I merely put a paste ring in the lock box when I opened the shop tonight. It would not make sense for Joseph to leave his only security here with us as we worked. I am sure the real ring is safe in his pocket, even as we speak. I will get it from him when I pay him what is owed.'

'But that means…you knew all along.' Then a

thought struck her. 'De Warde thought himself quite clever, arriving when you were away from the house and convincing me to show him the location.'

Jack looked at her with sympathy. 'I had to do something to bring the two of you together, and to get a natural performance from you that would convince him to come here. It is good that you are a lady, my sweet, for truly you are an abominable actress.'

'I take that as a compliment,' she shot back at him. 'And tonight, when you provoked me to argue...'

'I could not very well say, "I am leaving you alone so that Henry de Warde can come and harass you." Or, even worse, "I do not trust you to keep what you know a secret." How would that have sounded?'

'How it sounds is unimportant,' she said. 'It was truly horrible of you. You put me at risk when you swore you would not.'

'In no way,' he assured her. 'I followed him back to the house from Boodle's and waited outside until you had gone and I could question the servants. When I was sure that you went willingly away with him, I came here to wait for you and hid in the back of the shop to watch the fun. What did he say, precisely, to convince you to bring him here? Or was it my bad behaviour that made you to betray me?'

'He gave me the twenty thousand pounds that he had taken from my father. The draft is already on its way to my old home.'

Jack looked at her with amazement. 'Well done. I was ready to be hurt at your faithlessness. But for that much money, I'd have turned coat on myself.' He laid a hand on his heart as though overcome with emotion. 'And I must say that your behaviour, when you were sure he had beaten you, was most dramatic and very flattering. I am worth ten of him, am I?'

'You are not worth the brass of a coat button, although you share much in common with it. Crass, base, low ruffian.' She pulled her hands from his coat sleeve, remembering that a woman with such a disgust of a man should not be hanging on him as though she could not bear to let him go. 'I hate you.'

'You do not,' he said with a laugh. 'You are furious with me and I probably deserve it. But you feel something quite different from hate, my dear, or you would not be as angry as you are.'

'You used me.'

'As I have from the first,' he agreed. 'I do not know why it is a surprise to you now.'

'And you allowed that man to make another awful suggestion.'

'And he will never do it again.' His arms wrapped tight around her, pulling her close, rocking her gently in his arms. 'I will send Danyl to the apartment above and get your ring back from Joseph. And first thing tomorrow, we shall go and cash the draft Uncle Henry has given him, just as your father will cash the one you procured. De Warde will have little left but the emerald ring that he will be waving in the faces of the *ton*, convinced that he is humiliating his brother. And when examined, it will turn out to be paste. If he is wrong in that, can we trust anything he might say?'

Thea readied herself to bat the soothing arms that held her. Then she thought of de Warde and the tales he would tell tomorrow. 'He might even claim that my mother is with child and that Kenton believes a magical idol will give him a son.'

Jack nodded. 'That is quite nonsensical, is it not? I suspect that certain people he might accuse of unspeakable crimes would have reason to counter-sue because of his obvious madness. Really, who would trust a man who would slander his own brother? I doubt anyone shall listen to a word from him after this.' Then he gave her a sidelong look, as though seeking approval. 'It is not the best plan, of course. Far less thorough than coshing the man and dumping the body in the Thames. But Spayne said no violence. And I did promise.'

'You did it.'

'Did I not say that I would?' Once again, his expression was young and unguarded, and perhaps a little worried at her response. It made his knavery at supper seem like nothing more than a harmless prank.

'I did not think you would succeed.' Her lack of faith in him made her feel guilty as well. She was sure that Miss Pennyworth would have scolded her for it. Was it not the duty of a wife to trust her husband in all things?

It was good that Jack knew nothing of that, for her lack of confidence only made him laugh. 'If this had failed, then I would have found another way. You were a lady in distress, my sweet. And as a gentleman, I could not have allowed such suffering to continue. Was that not why you married me?'

She wanted to argue that this was not why she had married him at all. She had expected Kenton to solve everything with a few words and a stern look, or perhaps by offering a large bank draft.

And instead?

Jack had done exactly what she had wished, but he had not done it in the way expected. 'Yes,' she said, exhausted, 'this was why I married you. And perhaps for one other reason.'

He put an arm around her, pulling her close and kissing her on the top of the head. And while Miss Pennyworth might argue that such public displays were not proper, her venerable teacher could take her rules and go to the devil.

It appeared that Jack would be there ahead of

her. He leaned away and stared down at her, all trace of innocence gone from his expression. 'Let us go home and I will show you again why I married you.'

He was hinting at bed play, in public, where anyone might hear. And, even worse, she was enjoying it. It made them no better than her parents. Perhaps that was not such a bad thing after all. She ran a finger along the lapel of his coat. 'A man has needs, after all. And if I do not wish to be bothered with them during meals, I suppose I must submit to them now.'

His eyes flared once, and then a slow smile spread across his face. His fingers wrapped around hers. He barely noticed when Danyl passed him the ring and bid them goodnight. Then he slipped the jewel on her finger and they walked in silence towards the Kenton coach. As soon as the door was shut, he pulled her into his arms.

Chapter Nineteen

If a honeymoon was meant to last a month, then Jack could no longer deny that it was time to go. He had retired to Spayne Court with Cyn as soon as the drafts had been cashed. And for nearly five weeks they had behaved just as one might expect a newly married couple to behave: retiring early and rising late, sharing smiles and talking little.

For his own part, he'd avoided any mention of Shakespeare, remembering the trouble it had caused the last time. It was better to say nothing at all than to spout words of love, only to sully them with panicked denials the next morning.

And Cyn did not seem to need them. In the weeks since he'd first loved her, she had thrown aside Miss Pennyworth's instructions and become as fiery and passionate as her red hair. She seemed to enjoy their time together for what it was, a pleasant interlude that could end at any time.

If this made her seem distant, and not quite the devoted Thea he might wish for, he could hardly complain of it. What did he have to offer her, really? He was not Lord Kenton. He had only been pretending.

Of course, it had felt quite real to him for quite some time, but in the end it was nothing more than an illusion.

And if, last night, when she had rolled to face him, after a particularly strenuous bout of lovemaking, and announced that she would 'certainly miss him when he was gone...' he'd had no right to be hurt by that. Hadn't he told her often enough that just such a thing would happen? His response to her, 'that he had been thinking it was about time for his departure...' had nothing to do with a fear that she might be growing tired of him.

It was simply that he was very close to losing himself in this part. If he did not go soon, he would forget how to make a graceful exit. So he had announced to Thea and Spayne over that morning's breakfast that it was 'about time to go for a sail', and enquired about the boats available on the coast.

There had been an awkward pause, as the others in the room digested the information. Then the earl had announced that he knew of just the place, but that he must beware of the treacherous conditions at this time of year.

Thea had said nothing at all.

On his way to the door, Jack considered for a moment, bypassing the library altogether. The earl must know what he had meant. The plan had been clear from the first. All monetary settlements had been made. Was a further interview required? Surely a great man would have had enough of speaking to a lesser one. It might save him the bother of pretending courtesy.

But avoiding a farewell was cowardice, pure and simple. The man had been a father and mentor to him for over a year and deserved more respect than that.

There was no such thing as cowardice, he reminded himself. Only self-preservation. Bravery was a gentlemen's virtue and more likely to be punished than rewarded. In Jack Briggs's experience, heroes often got exactly what they deserved.

But it was not as if the earl waited on the other side of the door with a drawn pistol ready to finish him. There was no need to slink out the door unheralded. If the peer did not wish to speak to him again, Jack would know it soon enough.

The idea that a curt dismissal might hurt him entered his mind. He laughed it away. If he was bothered, then it was proof that he'd got above his station and deserved the set down. A year as a viscount had made him soft. And the actor, Jack Briggs, could not afford such tender feelings. The world was a harsh place and had been so for as long as he could remember. Best face the music and get it over with, one way or the other, so that he could take to the road.

He knocked on the door and heard the jovial 'Enter!' just as he always did. When the earl looked up from his work, he smiled. 'Jack.' As usual, he seemed truly pleased by the interruption. Was it that way with all company? Or had Jack the right to view this as friendship reserved for him? For it had seemed, from the first, that Spayne liked him.

At first he'd viewed it with suspicion, but as time had passed, he'd grown to accept it. Now he must forget it. Should he ever see the man in public again, in an audience, or on the street, there could not be even a flicker of recognition between them.

But that was tomorrow, not today. 'My lord.' Jack stood in the doorway and offered a proper bow, but the peer had left his seat and come round to the front of the desk to clasp his hand.

'You are leaving us so soon?'

'It is hardly soon, my lord. I have been in company here for thirteen months.'

'But the matter of de Warde and the money is only just settled. And settled handily, I must say.' Spayne smiled at him. 'It has come to my attention that my brother has been waving a paste ring about London and spouting all sorts of nonsense about fertility idols and secret ceremonies. The *ton* cannot decide whether he has come unhinged or is simply a terrible liar. In either case, I doubt they will trust any word from his mouth for a very long time.'

'There can be no threat of revelation from a blackmailer whom no one believes,' Jack agreed.

'I could not have hoped for a better result when I took you on.' The earl was beaming at him with something very like fatherly pride.

'I am glad that I have pleased you.' And it did give him a warm feeling, when he thought about it.

'You have pleased me in more than that. All tasks that I put to you were handled beyond my expectation. The efforts you have made on behalf of the tenants were much needed. In the absence of a real heir, I let things go for too long.'

His flush of pride was an involuntary response, but Jack could hardly allow himself to be so transparent in his feelings, if he meant to return to the stage. 'I saw a need and filled it. It was no less than any man might have done.'

'On the contrary. Can you say that my true heir, de Warde, would have taken the time?'

'I suppose not.'

'You have a sympathy for others that is absent

from him. It will fall to him in the end, I suppose. But you have put him in his place for a while. Perhaps it has done him some good.'

'One can hope,' Jack said, wondering if he was allowed an opinion. But it was troublesome to think that his careful work of recent months might fall apart if de Warde had the chance to recoup and regroup.

'The addition of Thea to my little family is also welcome,' Spayne added with a smile. 'She is a sweet girl, is she not?'

'Indeed.' Why must they discuss her now? That would be another hard and necessary parting. He did not wish to be reminded of it.

'I don't suppose you are leaving her with child,' Spayne hazarded. 'A grandson really would be most handy when dealing with my brother.'

Which made Jack feel like his poor duped wife. Did he need to explain the truth and the law to the man? Spayne was acting as though his bastard spawn deserved a title, when it had all been a horrible, complicated jape. It had been a game that Jack had been happy to play, since it was at the expense of the nobility. He should laugh in the earl's face at the idea and call him a fool for hoping.

Instead, he said, quite simply, 'No, my lord. I do not believe there will be issue.' There might be, of course. He had been cautious all his life with the lovers he'd taken, fearing the appearance of a by-blow. Jack Briggs did not need a wife. And the world did not need another hungry mouth to feed, another boy or girl with no future.

But he had not withdrawn from Cyn's body or her bed. It had been too sweet to stay there. It gave him a strange, warm thought to know that his offspring, if there was such, would be well loved and cared for.

Then he realised that the earl was staring at him, expecting some sort of response. 'It is possible, I suppose, that there might be a child.'

Spayne nodded with approval.

'But she has given me no reason to expect one.'

Spayne sighed. 'A pity. I suppose it means that she will not be staying for long. I am sure such a lovely and pleasant girl will have many suitors in her unfortunate widowhood.'

And why remind him of it? The idea of her

with another left a bitter taste in Jack's mouth. 'I am happy that I have made you happy,' he said rather lamely, because someone in this ought to be happy. Jack could not help but feel that he was not as happy as he should be.

'Of course, if you wanted to stay on for a bit, I would not fault you,' the earl added in an offhand manner. 'You have accomplished much. Taking leisure as Lord Kenton would not be frowned upon. Another month, perhaps.'

Was the randy old goat actually suggesting that Jack continue to enjoy the favours of his illusionary wife until Spayne got his grandchild? At one time, Jack might have been foursquare behind that thought. But now it just seemed wrong.

'That would hardly be fair to Cyn,' he said, trying to keep the reproof from his voice. 'Now that I have nothing to offer her, it would be little better than suggesting that she take a lover. Should she wish to do that, I think she could manage better than some itinerant player.'

The earl sighed. 'I suppose you are right. Better to make a clean break now than overstay your welcome. You were always one to love and leave, were you not?'

He could not argue that it was not truth, but he'd seldom given it that much thought. And he'd hardly have called any of the previous couplings love.

But this time…

'You hired me to play a part,' he said simply. 'When the play is over, it is time to leave the stage.' He reached down and pulled the ring from his finger that Spayne had given him to prove his identity as Kenton. It was a mate to Thea's more ladylike band, set with a huge cabochon emerald. He offered it back to the earl, and to remind himself that the job was truly done.

The earl waved it away. 'Keep it, my boy. There is no one else to wear it. And you have certainly earned it.'

'It is entailed,' Jack had reminded him, surprised at how automatically the words had come.

'And no longer a part of the property. Lord Kenton is to be lost at sea, remember? The ring will be with him when he dies.' Stayne looked down at the jewel on Jack's palm without expression or passion. 'When you sell it, I would appreciate your prying out the stone and hammering the gold until it is unrecognisable. It would not do for you to be caught with the thing as it is.'

'I suppose,' Jack said, trying and failing to view the jewel with as little emotion as Spayne had mustered.

'It is nothing more than gold and stone, after all,' Spayne reminded it him. 'If people see it as more than that, they have fallen victim to a clever illusion, but now we must see nothing but the truth. We must learn to make the best of that.' The earl looked strangely sad at the prospect.

'It does no one any good to become enamoured of the parts one plays,' Jack agreed. 'They are phantoms. Not meant to last.'

'Of course not,' the earl added, but he did not seem fully convinced. And why was he not? Shouldn't it be he who was reminding Jack that the arrangement was never meant to be a permanent one? Holding out hope for anything more was a sort of cruelty he had not expected to find in the normally genial man.

Then the old man gave a sigh and clapped him

firmly on the shoulder, his left hand lingering, a heavy staying weight. The right reached out to clasp the hand that Jack offered him. 'Farewell, Jack Briggs. Travel safe. Live well. Be happy.'

'And you, my lord.' There was something else he was supposed to say, but damn him, for the first time in a long time, he was at a loss. Finally, he said, 'Thank you.' But that was not right, nor was it sufficient. 'It was an honour, my lord.'

'For me as well.' The hands released him and the man turned away quickly, as though he'd had enough of the distraction. 'Go now. It is a long drive to Southend and you are losing the light.' Then Spayne returned to his desk and the awkward interview was at an end.

Thea paced in the hall nervously, knowing that Jack was in the library, making his final farewells to the earl. If ever she would say something to him, now must be the time. There would be no other opportunity.

He opened the door and she saw him a moment before he could notice her. Worried, puzzled, hesitant. His face and posture were without their usual confidence. Nor did they have the arrogance she had seen when he'd been Jack Briggs for the pawnbroker.

This new man was yet another person. An odd blending of the two he had been, as though he could not quite manage to settle on a way to represent the change in his character.

He had doubts. It gave her hope. Perhaps the right word or action might be the tipping point that made him decide to stay. All she had to do was to tell him the truth.

And then he turned, saw her and all the character rushed back into his face. He was jaunty, insouciant, blustering and insincere.

And she could not help herself. She frowned in disapproval.

He smiled back. 'And that is how I'll remember you, darling. Sulking and irritable.' He put his hand to his heart. 'And heartbreakingly beautiful.'

'As if you had a heart to break,' she answered, although it felt like hers was well on the way to tearing in half.

'Ah, the times we had.' He sighed. 'Now give me your lips. I must be going.'

'If that is what it will take to make you leave.' She would not cry, she reminded herself. If she did, he would taste the salt on her lips. Instead, she gave herself over to the kiss, pouring all her feelings into it. She could feel the crisp hairs at the back of his neck bristling under her fingers, the ache in her breasts as he pulled her body against his. His mouth moved on hers possessively, reminding her that they knew her body and would know it again, should he decide to stay. It was the sweetest possible lie, and, for a moment, she gave herself up to the idea that he loved her, that this was a new beginning and not simply the end.

She gave back eagerly, soft and compliant, knees weak, making it clear that, with the slightest push, she would be on the floor, her skirts around her waist and her legs spread wide for him. They were at war and submission was her greatest weapon.

Then he broke from her, giving an admonishing wag of his finger. 'If you keep at me like that, I will never leave.' He touched her chin with a finger. 'And we both know the trouble I will cause if I stay. I am not the husband for you, my dear. I would embarrass you, just as your mother does.'

'You are not the husband for me because you are not real,' she reminded him. But he seemed real enough when she touched him.

He laughed. 'Neither are you. You tailor your moods, your likes and your dislikes to the current fashions and the people around you, just as you have been taught to do.'

'Perhaps you would prefer that I do not blurt my secrets and opinions out for all to hear.' She narrowed her eyes and glared at him. 'There is such a thing as too much honesty, Jack Briggs. And, sometimes, there is not nearly enough.'

'Point taken,' he said, glaring back at her. 'Since we will never agree on a happy medium, it is better that we part.'

'We would be quite hopeless for more reasons than that,' she said. 'You would likely expect me to follow you about the country, waiting in the wings as you play-act, applauding your every falsehood. I think we can both agree that is no life for a gently bred woman.'

But perhaps, if you loved me, you might have suggested it.

He kissed her again, on the forehead, but his lips were cold and the contact brief. 'In time, you will meet the man who deserves you. I hope you are happy with him.'

It sounded like a sincere blessing. But there was something in it as well that sounded like a curse. In return she said, 'And you should go back to the sort of women you favour. It is hardly my place to wish you joy of them.'

'I shall,' he assured her. 'Very much so. They are simpler than you. But just as easily forgotten when I am through with them.' He offered her as courtly a bow as any he had made on stage before placing his hat upon his head and pulling on his gloves. 'I bid you adieu. I'd say that parting was such sweet sorrow, but I know how you hate it when I lie.' And with that, he turned and was gone.

Chapter Twenty

Jack whistled as he walked down the path to the beach and as he got into the little sail boat. He continued until he was well out from shore. It was an annoyingly cheerful song for such a grim day. The slate-coloured clouds threatened a storm and warned that it was no day for an extended outing.

But then it was not to be a grim day at all for Lord Kenton. He was young and in love. The world must think him happy. And Jack Briggs should be happy as well, for it was the first time in over a year that he'd had his freedom and a chance at his old life back.

Yet it was a struggle to keep up the role. He could be in bed with Cyn right now. The minx had done her best to keep him there a little while longer. She had not resorted to embarrassing and sloppy sentiment. Instead, she had used her body. It was much harder to part from eyes and thighs and lips and breasts all eager for his kisses.

The man who would have her was lucky indeed. Jack stopped whistling and cursed that man, whoever he might be, to all the hells he deserved for the heaven that he was about to receive. His Cyn would likely pick some proper gentleman, just as she had been trained to. The fellow would be as dumb as a fencepost and probably faithless. But he would have money and a title, which was all she had wanted from the first.

It was no concern of his. She would be a widow and free to do as she liked.

And she had given him a full demonstration of just what she liked. She had been the enthusiastic lover that he'd wished and hoped for on that first day when she'd waylaid him. It was highly unlikely that she would wait past the minimum time of mourning before finding another to warm her bed. Declarations of a life of abstinence had been conspicuously absent from their parting.

As had words of love. On his part as well. He

hadn't bothered, for she'd have seen it for the lie it was. Jack Briggs did not love anyone.

No one save himself, of course.

Which was why it went against his nature to aim the little boat back towards shore and straight for the nearest rock. It was a mad risk, but he could think of no better way to provide an explanation for his disappearance that would provide sufficient evidence of death, but no body. So he tied the rudder and threw himself over the side into the icy water.

Dying was both harder and easier than he'd thought. The chill hit him like a slap, ringing on his skin, shocking his mind into paralysis. Then he was sinking, dragged beneath the surface, his boots a lead weight at the end of his legs, his fine clothes growing heavy in the water. His head cleared, reminding him of the need to fight for shore. And another voice came, calm, clear, and louder than the urge for self-preservation.

Why bother?

His shocked limbs did not move as his brain processed the idea. It would be easier to do nothing. Spayne wanted a death. A body to go along with the wrecked boat would be the final thing that would convince all. A last gesture to complete the finest performance of his career, and a fitting curtain call. Never mind what Jack felt for himself. The parts of him that were Kenton were profoundly depressed that it had come to this. Returning to his old life meant an end to warmth and peace and comfort. An end to the intriguing challenges of the estate and the knowledge that he must grow to become Spayne.

And an end to his life with Cyn. He'd had a wife. He could have had a family. Most of all, he'd had the love of both a father and a spouse. They had not said so, exactly, but now that it was gone he was as sure that there was no point in living without it.

A wave crested over his head and he looked up at the fading light, clinging to the gulp of air that he'd instinctively taken before he hit the water.

Then he shook himself free of Kenton and kicked to the surface. He managed the swim to the rock, which left him cold and shaking, almost too weak to pull himself out of the water. But he was still alive, and owed no thanks to love for that. It was his own self-interest that ruled him, that could keep his heart beating with or without a wife and family.

The decision was made, but the fates were still against him. The damned boat could not manage its part, hanging up against the stones largely unharmed. In the end, he had to swim back to it, haul himself over the side and hack at the hull with a hatchet until the thing went down, but it did give him a nice piece of clearly marked wreckage to wedge between the rocks along with a torn bit of his shirt. Not as convincing as a corpse, perhaps, but a much saner choice than noble suicide. When they searched for him, there would be no doubt what had happened.

And so he was finally free. He made his way to shore to the clothes he had hidden there, dried, dressed, then built a small fire and warmed himself as he burned every last trace of Lord Kenton.

All save one. The ring his father… No. The ring Spayne had given him was still on his hand. He stared at it for a moment, remembering what the earl had suggested. Then he pulled it off, set it on the ground and reached for a rock to smash it.

His hand froze in mid-air as he stared down at the emerald. Sell it? How could he? For months it had been as much a part of his hand as one of his fingers.

That was Kenton, the character, speaking to him again, whispering righteous nonsense in his ear. Of course Jack would sell it. The thing was worth at least thirty pounds, even melted down and passed to the meanest fence.

But it was worth far more than that, if he counted its true value. He balanced it in his hand for a moment, feeling the weight. It was heavy with tradition, just as Cyn's ring had been, and made from another stone of the set that the king had given the first Earl of Spayne.

He wet his lips and said aloud, to add a matching weight to his argument, 'I do not want to go back to the gallows over a simple misunderstanding.' If an actor was caught with this ring, people would suspect theft, and possibly murder. The real Kenton would not have given it up without a fight. Even now, he had to struggle not to return it to his finger, where it belonged. He raised the rock again.

Yet he could not manage the blow that would crush it. To Jack Briggs, it should be nothing more than ready money, but it was all that was left of Kenton. And despite his dramatic protestations in the water, the man was not ready to die.

Jack sighed. He did not really have to make the decision now. Perhaps at some future date, when his skills faltered and he could no longer hold the speeches in his head, not even fit to do a convincing King Lear. He must simply keep it safe and out of sight. He slipped the ring into an inner pocket beside the fat purse that Spayne had given him. Though it was rather shabby by Kenton's standards, the plain coat he wore now was better than anything Jack Briggs had owned. The bespoke fit made it clear to all that he was a gentleman, down on his luck, but still able to pay for a night's lodging. He would have no trouble with innkeepers dressed as he was. He would have no trouble with anything for quite some time.

Why did this not make him happy? He was rich, single and free. He was very much alive, which was more than he'd expected as he marched up the steps towards the noose a year ago.

He fingered the circle of gold in his pocket and noticed the light aimlessness of his right hand. Thirteen months should not be long enough for a simple piece of jewellery to become a part of one. But this one had got heavier as he'd come to carry some of the burden that had come with it. When he'd been faced with the pressing demands of Lord Kenton's actual responsibilities, he'd gone back to Spayne and demanded help.

The man had shrugged and said, 'Do the best you can. Anything is better than nothing. And that is what they are used to from me.'

Managing had not been nearly as hard as he'd thought and more interesting than he'd ever have suspected in his old life. Much of the politics was play-acting, and he had always been good at that. The management of tenants and rent was common sense. And being married...

It was all gone, he told himself again. He'd given it up, just as he'd always planned to.

He walked down the road to the nearest inn, wishing for the horse he'd left safely back by the docks. But he thanked God and Spayne for Kenton's boots, which fit well and meant that the walking would not bother him.

* * *

By the time he reached the alehouse, he was well and truly parched, and in need of more than one drink.

His purse would be lighter by the end of the evening, he was sure. He'd be blind drunk and have a woman in his bed. Perhaps two. As many as it took to put the recent past behind him and get back to being who he was.

It appeared he was in luck. His first pint was delivered by a buxom ginger-haired girl named Rose who was as interested in him, and his money, as he could wish her to be.

'What's yer name then, sir?'

'John Briggs.' He had very nearly said Kenton before stopping himself. This was the moment of decision. He gave a half-hearted flourish of his hand. 'Itinerant thespian, at your service, madam.' There were many inns that would not have him at all after that admission. But he'd best get re-accustomed to the sudden frostiness which came with the knowledge of his profession.

The girl gave him a blank look. 'You speak well for a foreigner.'

'An actor, my dear,' he said patiently. 'A playwright. A singer of songs. Teller of tales. Weaver of dreams.' He reached out and pulled the gold coin he had palmed, from behind her ear. 'I belong to the trunk that you have been holding in the best room above. And I paid in advance.' Let her make what she would of that.

She eyed the coin in his hand, as though surprised to see it there, and wondering how he'd come by it. Then she decided it did not matter and gave him a look that was properly impressed. 'An actor. I expect you are full of pretty words for a girl like me.' She batted her lashes and waited to be dazzled.

Shakespeare.

Now he struggled to think of a single quote that did not make him think of the woman he was trying to forget. 'I did not say I was a good actor, did I?'

Since he was being of no use, she took control of the situation and the chair opposite him, leaning forwards so that he could have an ample view down her bodice. 'Who needs talk when you have money. Are you in need of company?'

Hadn't he thought just the same, only a few moments ago? But now, when the opportunity presented itself to rectify it, he said, 'I prefer my solitude. I am quite tired, you see.' Where were his manners, flirting with the girl and then rejecting her a moment later? And where was his skill? His protestations of fatigue were in no way convincing.

She glared at him for wasting her time, so he pushed the coin across the table and in front of her. 'See to it that my meal is sent to my room. And that is all I will need from you tonight,' he added, as he imagined the girl forcing her way in after the plate.

She did a creditable attempt at a flounce as she left his table, but it was lost on him for he was already heading for the stairs. While the old Jack would not have refused such an offer, Kenton was not willing to let go of his conscience just yet. Tomorrow, perhaps. The girl would be just as willing as long as he had another coin. For tonight, he could open his trunk to assure himself that nothing had been taken from it in his prolonged absence and re-acquaint himself with his old life.

The large brass-bound crate that waited in the bedroom at the top of the stairs was the sum total of his possessions. Or at least, it had been until Spayne had caught up to him. Jack had nearly lost it that day, thinking it sold by the innkeeper, but the earl had rescued it as well as him, and shipped it on when they'd settled on this as the place of his eventual death and rebirth. Jack fished in his pocket for the key, with the chain that had been attached to hang the thing safely about his neck when he was on stage and could not guard the contents. As an afterthought, he strung the Kenton ring beside it and dropped it back inside his shirt to rest over his heart.

It was strange to feel the weight there. Kenton had no need for such securities. For these long months, the key had rested in a bureau drawer, very nearly forgotten. Someone here had watched over the luggage, keeping it dry and oiling the lock. The mechanism turned smoothly, and he popped the latch and lifted the lid to reveal his treasures.

The pots of stage paint and rouge had gone stale or dried up from lack of use. They would have to be replaced, of course. A series of beards and wigs that he had once thought quite realistic would need to go as well. Now they appeared mo-theaten and he could not imagine bringing them close to his face without a shudder of disgust.

Wrapped in a piece of worn flannel, he found the crown that he had worn for any number of performances: Henrys four through eight, both Richards, John, and other kings as well, indis-criminate of era or nationality. It was gilded and set with glass jewels, and had been the envy of his fellows. But now he saw it for what it was, a dull thing, clearly false, too light compared to the coronet which Spayne had allowed him to wear one night in jest.

'See how it feels, my boy.' The earl's voice had been almost seductive and Jack had allowed him-self to succumb. 'Kenton would know of this. He would expect it. If you wish to be him, even for a while, you must walk as if it is always on your head.'

Jack tossed the false crown aside with a curse, trying to shake the memory of the very real weight of the coronet and the sense of pride and confidence it had brought. That had been just as much an illusion as the dross in front of him. He was not Kenton. He never had been.

He took up one of the costumes instead, the rich robe that went along with the crown. Not so rich, of course, now that he'd seen real court robes. The velvet on this was threadbare, the ermine little more than white rabbit, trimmed with splotches of paint. The antique coat beneath it, which he'd worn in *She Would if She Could*, had been a true gentleman's coat, when it had been new. As a costume, it was quite better than anything else he could afford. But the gold lace was tarnished and missing in patches on the great bucket cuffs. He slipped into it, for it had always made him feel better, young and dashing, full of wit like the comedies of Goldsmith and Sheridan that it suited.

Today, it bound and pinched. It was too narrow in the shoulders and too short in the sleeves. It had been fine thirteen months ago, but now, it seemed to be made for a smaller man, a lesser man, an actor who could twist himself into the shape needed to fit it and pretend that it had been made for him.

He yanked it off and tossed it back into the trunk, slamming the lid. When last he'd seen it, he had been quite proud of this accumulation. He was sure it looked the same as the day when he'd put it aside.

But he was equally sure that he never wanted to see the trunk or its contents again. He might as well have stored the lot at the bottom of the ocean, for all it mattered. It was ruined and useless, to the last button and thread. His old things did not fit him. It was as if, far later in life than was natural, he'd grown the last few inches to make a proper man, and this new self could find no peace in playing a king when there was work to do, or apeing Romeo, only to go to bed alone.

He reached up and yanked the chain from his neck, freeing the key and fitting it back in the lock to save the innkeeper the trouble of breaking it when it was sold.

The ring he slipped back on his finger. Then he went down the stairs and to the stable to arrange for a horse.

Chapter Twenty-One

They were burying an empty coffin.

The mourners knew it, of course. The fishermen had discovered the broken boat, washed up on shore, with a scrap of linen the only evidence that her sometime husband had been aboard. But with the outpouring of sympathy she'd received, some sort of public memorial service had seemed necessary.

The church was near to full, friends and acquaintances dabbing delicately at their eyes and remarking at the suddenness of her widowhood, the tragedy of it, and the level head and likability of Kenton. He would be missed by all and Thea was to be a symbol of pity and sympathy.

Spayne was there as well, giving up his seclusion for a trip to the metropolis, white faced, tight lipped and clearly suffering the loss.

The only one absent was Henry de Warde, who had sent a tersely worded note, but showed no sign of returning to town, even to gloat, while the memory of his embarrassment was still fresh.

Her mother was draped head to toe in black and weeping so hard that Thea feared the woman would throw herself into the open grave. Could she not manage to maintain decorum? 'Come away, Mother,' Thea had said, sincerely worried. 'You needn't weep so.'

'But I cannot seem to help myself,' her mother said. 'I have had such news, my dear. And I cannot decide whether to weep from joy or sadness.' To Thea's surprise, she wiped away real tears. 'I did not want to share it with you today, for it might make your expressions of grief even more difficult.'

Her mother was concerned for her ability to play the part, even now. And the fact that, after trying so hard for so long, Thea was on some level a disappointment, added yet another sting to the wound on her heart. 'I will manage,' she said, feeling the tears gathering behind her eyes, even if there was no real reason for them. 'What is your news?'

'We have had a letter from Grandfather. After all this time, he has relented. And it was all because of you, my darling. He heard of your marriage to Kenton and was so impressed by the worth of the match and the tragedy of its sudden end, that he has acknowledged the union of your parents and freed your father's portion of the money. Do not think, should you choose to marry again, that you need to concern yourself with our welfare.'

'I have no intention of marrying again,' Thea said flatly. It was, perhaps, the last full truth she could ever speak.

'Come now, darling,' her mother said with a worried frown. 'You are young yet. It is too soon to think of shutting yourself away.'

Perhaps not the last truth. 'Jack is lost to me,' she added. 'And I miss him terribly.' While her mother wept, her own eyes were still unfortunately dry. She should be able to produce at least one tear from them. What was it Jack had said about acting? Think of something sad. The prospect of never seeing him again was quite sad enough to act convincingly, she was sure. She felt the stuffiness of the head and the prickling of the lashes that indicated a proper widow's grief. It was a pity that he could not be here to admire her newfound skill.

'Yes, my dear.' Her mother stroked her hands, then thought the better of it and gathered her close in for a hug. 'You will go on without him. Wait and see. You mustn't be angry with him for leaving you, for he has finally made you a success.'

'Now that I do not need Grandfather's help, he wishes to know me?' Her own efforts had been for nothing after all.

'You married well, bagged a title and now you are a rich widow.'

'I did none of those things.' She had trapped herself in a lie so perfect that no amount of protesting would make people believe the truth.

'It is the appearance that matters, not the truth.'

'You are very wise,' Thea said, surprised that

she had not noticed it before. 'Grandfather was wrong to not have acknowledged you from the first. From what Jack told me, you could have had more money than Grandfather might offer had you kept to the stage.'

'But then I would not have had your father,' her mother said. 'The choice was quite simple, really.'

She gave her mother a worried look. 'I was wrong to disapprove. I have not treated you as I should, Mother. You have been good to me. And I have been nothing but false.'

Her mother gathered her close and kissed her upon both cheeks. At one time Thea might have scolded her about the continual display of excess emotion where anyone might see, but today it felt good to know that she was loved. 'You have been my daughter. And I am proud of you.'

'But I should have been proud of you as well. People are such hypocrites.' She stared out at the crowded pews. 'They claim to be better than others, but they do it with a smile on their face and a lie on their lips.' Her mother had left her old life behind and chosen to live amongst people who would never accept her. She claimed the choice had been easy.

But it was one that Jack had refused to make.

Thea wiped away her first tear.

'Truth is like staring into the sun, my dear,' her mother said. 'Just as blinding as a lie might be, but far more damaging. It changes you.'

Thea wiped at her eyes with the back of her hand. Her widow's weeds were not red, as she had threatened. They were subdued, tasteful and dark as jet, just as Jack had predicted. And the black-edged handkerchief that she held to her face was becoming quite damp.

They should be tears of relief. The charade was finally over. She had justice for her parents and could go on about her life just as planned, alone.

Without warning, a sob erupted from her and she crammed her knuckles into her mouth, trying to stop another. Damn the man. He had made her care for him. Then he had left before she'd admitted the truth.

And the worst of it was she could not be absolutely sure that he hadn't died when the boat had sunk. Suppose he'd drowned when his shirt caught on the rough boards of the hull, and the battering of the waves and the heaviness of his lifeless corpse had dragged him away from the boat? She would never know. Even if he was alive and healthy, there was no way to reach him. He would stay far, far away from her, never writing, never visiting, giving no sign. She might spend the rest of her life haunting the theatres of England, looking for some out-of-the-way performance where a handsome blond man with a majestic profile declaimed Hamlet or wept over the body of his Juliet.

It was not fair. Not at all. How could he be allowed to go back to his old life after changing everything about hers? How could she marry again, knowing that it was Jack she loved, Jack she'd wed and Jack she wanted? How could he leave her alone like this?

And now she was weeping like a widow. All the world would see her for what she was, a woman who had been young and happy and in love, and who had lost it all. But not in the blink of an eye with one hapless wave. From almost the first moment of her marriage, her love had been dying and she had ignored it. She had told herself that it would not matter. She had let him die when she could have stopped it.

She could feel Spayne's hand, heavy on her shoulder, as he took her mother's place and drew her away from the other mourners so that she might compose herself.

She leaned upon him, letting him be strong for her and taking comfort in knowing that he was the better for what they had done. 'I cannot believe he's really gone,' she admitted.

'Yes,' the earl whispered back. 'It was a surprise to me as well. I had hoped, once he'd got used to the life I offered, that he would carry it through.'

'It was your decision to keep him or send him away,' she reminded him. 'It was not as if he was actually your son.'

There was a long, awkward pause from Spayne.

'He was not your son,' Thea insisted, glancing around to be sure they were alone. 'Your heir died in Italy years ago.'

And still Spayne was silent. At last, he said, 'Long ago, over thirty years, when I was barely engaged to my Catherine, and sewing wild oats, there was a certain golden-haired beauty who acted the breeches parts in Shakespeare as well as any boy.'

'You are not implying...' Cynthia said with a raised eyebrow.

'Certain promises might have been made,' the earl said with a vague wave of the hand. 'I knew a Fleet marriage was as no marriage at all. But if the vows were said in earnest?' He looked embarrassed. 'I was given to understand that there were consequences to our time together. And I paid her to be gone. By then, I had a wife and was starting a family of my own. The woman might have been lying, of course. She did not ask for as much as she could have. And the child might not have been mine. She was not ungenerous with her favours.' He shrugged again. 'But after that, if I chose to follow the career of a certain young actor with more than unusual interest, I could hardly be blamed. And he did grow to look rather like me.'

'If you had told him...' Then perhaps he would

have stayed. It was as grossly unfair and mis-guided as anything the earl had come up with.

He surprised her by drawing himself up stern and powerful. 'I found the man on the gallows, my dear. It may not seem so, but even I take more care with my title than to give it to a common criminal. He might not have been the man I wanted and needed him to be. For all I knew, he was not even my natural son. I'd put nothing into his education or welfare for half a lifetime. He could just as easily have grown into the sort of rogue who deserved a quick end at the end of a long rope. Better that he think it all a ruse and easy to part from, than a truth that could be worked to his advantage.'

The earl looked sadly back at the casket. 'He fulfilled all of my hopes. He was Kenton and my true son in all ways that mattered. But in the end, he left because he did not wish to stay. No amount of hoping will bring him back.'

'But I do want him back,' she said, embarrassed at the tears, the wateriness of her voice and the display of emotion that would have horrified the instructors at Miss Pennyworth's school. 'I love him.'

'Did you tell him so?'

That was the most damning question the earl could have asked, for it proved that she was as much at fault as anyone for Kenton's departure. She had not tried hard enough. She had not given him a reason to remain.

'No,' she said with a sob. 'For all my talk, I was not honest in the one moment of my life that demanded full truth. I should have begged him to stay. And I let him go.'

She turned back to the church and took her place beside the coffin, leaning against it, pressing her face to the wood, letting the tears flow freely.

'It is most flattering to see such a generous display of affection.' She looked up at the familiar voice to see her wayward husband framed in the doorway at the end of the aisle, looking not the least bit the worse for wear.

Her mother gave an undignified shriek and fainted dead away. Although from where Thea stood, it appeared that Antonia made an effort to catch herself and break the fall on her way to the floor.

And Thea could not help herself. She threw the handkerchief aside and lunged at him, pelting down the church and throwing herself into his arms. 'How dare you! You beast. You horrible, horrible man. How can you come here now? Can you not see how we have suffered, surely you must have known.' She beat senselessly upon his chest, hoping that he felt some of her fear, her anguish, her worry.

He must have done, for the laugh he gave in response was a trifle weak and not the least bit affected. 'I know, dearest. I know.' Then he whispered, 'Given the opportunity, you must know that I could not resist the dramatic entrance.' His arms held her tenderly, even as she hit at him, waiting for the anger to work its way out of her.

Eventually, it did. Her blows slowed and then stopped, and she sobbed weakly for a time before settling in his arms, letting him support her as he explained to the mourners about the wreck of the boat, dragging himself to shore far from where he'd set off, the fever which had confined him, insensible, to his bed for a week. And the surprise at reading of his funeral in *The Times*.

The audience responded with appropriate oohs and ahhs, Jack punctuated the story with murmured endearments and little kisses to the top of her head, pushing her veiled bonnet out of the way and generally treating her as a man might when he'd very nearly lost his life and returned to find his wife weeping over his casket.

Then he pressed his mouth close to her ear and whispered, 'God knows what Spayne will think of my resurrection, but I could not leave without you. If he will not acknowledge me, then we will take the boat out together, next time.'

She laughed through her tears. 'How dramatic of you, my dear.'

'Me?' He pressed his hand to his breast and gave her a wide-eyed, innocent look. 'I am the heir to a peer. If that is not serious business, I do not know what might be.'

She slapped his arm. 'Do not toy with me, Jack. Why have you really returned?'

'Because I cannot live without you.' He kissed her. 'S'truth. I cannot die without you, either. If

Romeo and Juliet does not end happily, I can't be bothered with it.'

'You know what this means.'

'Not a clue,' he admitted and kissed her again.

'No more Jack Briggs. No more play-acting.'

'Nothing but play-acting. All the world's a stage, m'dear. And some of us are more players than others.' He grinned at her. 'As for Jack Briggs? I knew him well. But his departure is no great loss to the world. Kenton is the better man. And a happier one.'

'Because he is rich,' she said suspiciously.

'Because he is well married,' Jack insisted.

'And the loss of your freedom?'

'At least I shall not be lonely,' he said with a satisfied sigh.

'The responsibilities of a viscount, and some day those of an earl? What will you make of those?'

'Probably I shall make a great hash of them. But having met the nobility and looked in its collective eye, I doubt I shall do any worse than they do. And I mean to begin by taking an extended vacation to Scotland with my wife. A second honeymoon, perhaps.'

'We have barely finished our first one,' she reminded him. 'And I cannot imagine why you would choose Scotland, in any case.'

'The marriage laws are less taxing on the other side of the border,' he reminded her. 'And if a certain actor named Jack Briggs should choose to marry the exceptionally well-bred girl who has stolen his heart, no one would question them.'

'Jack Briggs has a desire for a legal wedding,' she said, trying to hide her smile.

'Indeed,' he said. 'I understand he is very much in love.'

'His wife loves him as well,' Thea said with a sigh.

'He is the most fortunate of men,' Jack said, smiling, and pulled her close and gave her a kiss that was far too passionate for a funeral.

Epilogue

As the months passed, Lord and Lady Kenton were very much in demand by the *ton*, both as guests and hosts. Lady Kenton combined all the charm and vivacity of her mother with the wealth of her husband the viscount. Her entertainments were extravagant without being tasteless, and always ahead of the current fashion. Since his return from India, her husband had settled easily into his role as heir to the Earl of Spayne, managing the estates and smoothing the feathers of the many families that Spayne had snubbed with his reclusion.

It was obvious that the pair were enamoured with each other by the way Lady Kenton would swat her husband playfully with a closed fan and murmur, 'You odious man,' breaking into even his most entertaining stories and pulling him away to the floor whenever the musicians played a waltz. When they danced, the couple was so arresting that those who had not seen them before sometimes stopped and stared in amazement. They moved together as though they were a single body, seldom speaking, but so close that, should they choose, their words could be exchanged in passionate whispers.

Opinions were divided as to whether their behaviour was actually shocking or merely seemed so. There hung around them a palpable cloud of passion, like a musk or incense, that made matrons smile knowingly, innocent maids blush and young men stumble over their own feet in their eagerness to partner with the ginger-haired beauty.

She accepted each offer graciously, turning away those who were too late with such gentle apologies that they were quite smitten, but she would allow no one but her husband to share the waltzes.

There was no dancing at all on the evening that set half the tongues in London to wagging. That night, they attended a salon were Lord Byron was reading from his latest poem. The hostess had warned the company that the man was rather scandalous. But his presence would make for a memorable evening, as long as he could be kept from excessive drink and Caro Lamb did not arrive to spoil things.

And so it proved, for at his introduction to Viscount Kenton, the poet quite embarrassed himself by being over-familiar. He stared and asked, 'You, sir. Do I know you?'

The normally good-humoured Kenton seemed to flinch at the rudeness of it. Then he turned and faced the playwright, looking down his famously aristocratic profile. 'I'd hardly call it an acquaintance, Byron. All of London knows you. And much of it knows me.'

'That is not what I mean,' the poet said, snapping his long white fingers. 'Have we met at some other time? In the theatre, perhaps?'

'I do not frequent plays,' Kenton replied.

'Are you sure?' Byron examined him more closely. 'For I could swear that you'd sought a part in a planned production of *Manfred*.'

Kenton reached for the quizzing glass that hung from a ribbon beside his fob and examined the man closely. 'What the devil are you talking about?'

'My allegory, *Manfred*. The performance never occurred. The story was too expansive to be contained by a mere stage.'

'Bloated, you mean?' Kenton pressed.

'Grand in scope,' Byron said haughtily. 'It is set in the Alps. No painted scenery can do it justice.'

'Very interesting, to some, I'm sure,' Kenton said dismissively. 'But I fail to see what this has to do with me.'

'I could swear that you, sir, before you became the toast of London society, were an actor called Jack Briggs.'

All the room hung in awkward silence, waiting to see what would happen next.

Then, from across the room, came a laugh so full of mirth that it that bordered on the unladylike. 'Kenton, an actor?' Lady Kenton appeared at his side with a graceful sway of her hips, twining her arm in his. 'Oh, do tell, my lord. I must hear of this exciting previous life of Kenton's. Was he a good actor?' She leaned close, as though to whisper a confidence. 'When he thinks to woo me with poetry, he cannot seem to keep two lines of it straight in his head.'

'You do me an injustice, darling,' he said. 'I am distracted by your beauty. And I have no trouble, as long as I keep the book to hand.'

'But perhaps I should like to meet this actor Briggs,' she said with a smile. 'He could pretend to be you and woo me properly. I would quite fancy a man who could quote Shakespeare.'

This brought a deep and horsey guffaw from the Regent himself. 'Lud, Lady Kenton, but you are diverting. Kenton an actor? What will Spayne say to that?'

'I expect he shall ship me back to India,' Kenton answered with a chuckle. 'Or Italy, perhaps. I hear that is an excellent choice for scapegrace sons with an air for the dramatic.'

The room erupted in laughter, but the happy couple at the centre of it hardly seemed to notice. Their eyes were only for each other and they smiled as if the world was no more important than a shared joke.

The most celebrated poet of the age left unnoticed in a fluttering of poorly tied neckcloth.

* * * * *

AUTHOR NOTE

Writing a story featuring an actor is so much fun, and it gives me a chance to share with you some theatre history research that did not make it into the book.

The stage in Jack's day was raked, with the front being lower than the back. Going upstage was actually like walking uphill. Scenery included a painted backdrop and flat wooden wing-pieces painted to match. These gave the audience an illusion of depth, and left actors with places to enter and exit on both sides of the stage. At the front of the stage footlights, or floats, rested in a trough of water to prevent accidental fires should a candle tip over, and they could be lowered below the stage when not in use.

The theatre's chandeliers had to be raised and lowered as well—but never during the performance. Once the candles were lit the house lights were always up, which made it easy for the audience to watch each other as they watched the play. As they are now, the cheap seats were in the upper balcony or gallery. If the audience there was unhappy, they booed by hitting their boots on a loose 'kicking board' in front of their seat.

And, as there are now, there were theatrical superstitions. Green has always been an unlucky colour for a costume. Not only is it unfavourable to most complexions, it was supposedly the colour Molière was wearing when he died on stage in 1673.

Happy reading. And 'break a leg'!

Cynthia stared back at him, large green eyes narrowed in scepticism. 'If I give up the gun, what will I have to protect me from your advances?'

Absolutely nothing. She blinked at him, as though she had heard his thoughts, and her mouth puckered, ready to be kissed.

'Is it really necessary to keep me at a distance? You must understand that if I remain as you wish your honour will be compromised. When we are discovered, as we well might be, I shall be forced to marry you.'

She nodded vigorously. 'That was precisely what I hoped,' she said.

That was most unexpected. But it certainly saved him time in wooing. 'Your methods for seeking my offer are rather unorthodox,' he said. 'I will not hold them against you, should we marry. I am not opposed to the institution itself, and I am willing to entertain the proposition that there be a union between us. But I will not allow the woman I marry to bring a pistol into the bedroom.'

'Perfectly understandable,' she agreed. But she showed no sign of relinquishing her weapon.